Gold from Heaven

Also by Peter Rand

The Private Rich
The Time of the Emergency
Firestorm

Gold from Heaven

PETER RAND

crown publishers, inc. new york

Copyright © 1988 by Peter Rand

Published by Crown Publishers, Inc., 225 Park Avenue South, New York, New York 10003 and represented in Canada by the Canadian MANDA Group.

CROWN is a trademark of Crown Publishers, Inc.

Manufactured in the United States of America

Library of Congress Cataloging-in-Publication Data

Rand, Peter
    Gold from heaven.

    I. Title.
PS3568.A48G6   1988   813'.54   87-27262
ISBN 0-517-56880-2

Designed by Lesley Blakeney

10   9   8   7   6   5   4   3   2   1

First Edition

For Jamie and Bliss

"Because it's always fun to be rich."
Gretchen Albrecht

THE SUN

T here was no Henry Albrecht. I only came to know this some years later. He had met his death at the hands of Ivan, in a violent manner, on the grounds at Cavemoor, the year that Wilhelm showed up at boarding school for the first time as a student. This is what I was later told. Very few people were aware of what had happened to Henry Albrecht, and for many years his murder never came to light. Monsignor Cathcart knew about it. Ann Albrecht, Ivan's twin sister, who was his staunch ally and friend, also knew, as did her mother and Teddy Beresford. Monsignor Cathcart actually saw it happen. Ivan, evidently, had come up behind his father and sliced his head off with a Russian saber, which he had whetted to a razor sharpness over many patient months upstairs in the playroom on the third floor. He took the modified stance of a batter to swing it once. The lopped head flew up into the air and then tumbled forward onto Henry Albrecht's lap and onto the paving stones, where it bounced down the steps and onto the Cavemoor lawn while the headless Henry Albrecht kept trying to rise out of his chair even as a gusher of bright blood spouted from the severed neck. Ivan said he'd done it because he hated Henry Albrecht. Gretchen Albrecht called up Teddy Beresford at once to get him to come and help her dispose of the parts, which he did, one presumes, against his better judgment because so much was at stake for him. He was a man of action, Teddy Beresford, a former military man who had attended Sandhurst and served with the Supreme Allied Command during the war in Asia. He did not on this occasion hesitate to act on the orders of Gretchen Albrecht, whom he served in the House of Albrecht, which was a law unto itself. They worked with the help of old Lorenzo, the Italian majordomo. Together, the three adults managed to get the obese, headless trunk of Henry Albrecht into a wheelbarrow so that they could run him out across the vast back lawn at Cavemoor to the far end and into the thick wood beyond, where there was situated some fair distance into it, concealed by an almost impenetrable thickness of second growth, a timber-and-stucco pavilion, now abandoned, that matched the outward appearance of Cavemoor itself and wherein was to be found a disused indoor swimming pool and two chambers used for changing rooms. Teddy Beresford had to hack a pathway through the woods to reach the now abandoned poolhouse. There they wrapped the body in a tarpaulin, trussed it with a rope, stored it in one of the dressing rooms along with the severed head, and retired to the house as evening fell to consider what they should do next.

On the occasion of his discovery that Henry Albrecht was indeed no longer among the living, Wilhelm had been called to Cavemoor as a guest of Ann Albrecht, to keep her company on an afternoon in September, less than a week after the murder had taken place. Nothing about the house in any way reflected the passing of her master. The Albrecht standard, a silk banner of gold and pink, flew at full mast above the front entrance to the house. The afternoon sunlight penetrated the interior gloom of the house and gleamed on silver cigarette boxes and the silver frames and gilt mirrors of the great drawing room. Ann never said a word about her father's death to Wilhelm or imparted even a suggestion to him that something was awry, the cause of which, her brother Ivan, had been removed at once to a school in Switzerland.

Ann was capricious. She was slightly older than Wilhelm. She had been entertaining a flirtation bordering on the overtly sexual with this charming, altogether appealing son of her father's British subordinate. She no doubt intended to bring Wilhelm into the picture, to implicate him, if only to relieve her own sense of isolation. This is a matter, however, purely of my own speculation, based on her subsequent behavior toward Wilhelm over the years. She did not want to lose him. She wanted to keep him with her in that private, rather twilit Albrecht dominion within which she was now forever compelled to dwell. She drew him into the woods on what he understood would be a tryst. He had every reason to think so. She was now, he believed, leading him to their appointment at the swimming pavilion, their trysting place in the woods, as indeed she must have thought of it herself. They took a path deep into the woods now overgrown with ivy. Sure enough, when they drew close, a timber-and-white-plaster structure, two stories high, surmounted by a high gabled roof, revealed itself through the trees quite suddenly.

Wilhelm had never seen this miniature Cavemoor. It matched the great house in appearance, even to the leaded diamond-shaped window panes that were visible through the brambles that had grown up from the ivied forest floor as high as the second story. One of the double doors, which had for many years been boarded up, was now open onto the verandah.

Wilhelm, as he stood with Ann at the end of the path where brush had been cleared away to make a passage up the verandah steps, could hear voices echo within. People must be swimming, he supposed. Instead of departing as they might have done, Ann had another idea and motioned Wilhelm back into the woods whence they had come. She was really in some ways a tomboy, up for adventure at all times. She appealed to his wilder impulses always. They managed to work their way around to the back of the pavilion. But for two mullioned windows, it was sheer wall. Here too the forest pressed against the back wall of the swimming house. Fir trees and oak. The window space was just wide enough for them to climb into one of the changing rooms, which they did by getting access to it from a tree trunk. First Ann climbed in, then Wilhelm. Ann helped Wilhelm lower himself onto the rotting ledge of a changing bench. It stank in here. Some trapped animal must have rotted in here, Wilhelm thought at the time. The stench in this airless, dark closet seemed to clog his nostrils, cling to his clothes, his flesh, even in the narrow passageway beyond, where they moved hastily to escape the foul odor. They went no farther. The voices they had heard outside were now close by. His father and her mother and the old Italian majordomo had come back to dispose of the body and were performing this beastly chore in the tiled pool enclosure, which was lit by clerestory windows that ran along one wall of the two-story high chamber just below the eaves.

Teddy Beresford in a white cloth face mask such as you see worn by surgeons and orderlies in an operating theater was pushing Henry Albrecht's body with his hands to the edge of the pool. A dark red-gold lock of hair fell across his brow. His bright blue eyes blazed with stress, and his brow glistened with sweat. Gretchen Albrecht paced along the opposite side of the pool so that at the angle from which he observed them from the shadows of this inner hallway Wilhelm could clearly see Ann's mother, her mogul eyes above her white mask wide with impatience while Teddy Beresford did the deed on her behalf of rolling Henry Albrecht's naked, corpulent body into the green-black waters of the half-filled, algae-coated pool. The old Italian, down by the shallow end, they could not see, but they could hear his pathetic whimper even so.

"Can't you just roll it in with your foot?" Ann's mother said.

Even then, Wilhelm could not quite believe what he was seeing. He stood on tiptoes, the better to look, and what he saw left him in no doubt that Henry Albrecht was indeed the one who had been beheaded, for Wilhelm could clearly see the head of Henry Albrecht floating in the half-empty pool down at the deep end. His gray hair, which he had always worn long to conceal the roll of fat at the nape of his neck, and combed straight back over his scalp, floated about him, fanned out on the surface of the water. Teddy Beresford, wearing an ascot of navy-blue silk and Peal loafers, pushed the torso with his white-gloved hands over the edge of the pool, where it landed on the surface of the water with a dull splash. Old Lorenzo had been allotted the task of pouring a gallon of acid into the water from a metal bucket. He scooted along the poolside in his white servant's jacket sloshing the lemon-lime corrosive onto the water, which hissed on contact and sent up a thick white fog as the chemical solution went to work.

"This won't take awfully long," said Teddy Beresford in a voice muffled by the white cloth mask, as he stood with his arms akimbo and watched the action of the chemical upon the remains of Henry Albrecht. The old Italian had gone around to the far side of the pool. He too wore a white cloth mask over his mouth. His eyes above his mask appeared to reflect sorrow more than horror. He'd seen many things in his long life. The three were silent for a time. It was like a magic trick. Once the heavy white vapors that clung to the surface of the pool had finally dispersed into wisps and then evaporated altogether and the water had ceased to seethe, no sign remained whatever of Henry Albrecht's earthly remains on the gently rocking water. Wilhelm never told anybody what he'd seen until some years later when he confided the experience to me. It would have been utterly tactless to have mentioned such an embarrassing matter to his father, for whom he had the greatest respect. He was not too keen, however, after that, to visit Cavemoor. Ann had told him what Ivan had done as they returned together through the woods in the lovely late summer evening, having huddled together in the shadows to await the departure of their elders, which seemed to take an agonizingly long time, for even as their voices dwindled along the newly hewn path, Lorenzo suddenly reappeared to retrieve Henry Albrecht's bloody garments, which in his nervous state he'd forgotten to throw in the pool. Within ten days or so Wilhelm went away to school, as did Ann, so that the occasions when he might have been called upon to visit Cavemoor were few and far between. He remained, always, a friend of Ann's, but it must be said that the madness she had brought him in on, the discovery that he was the unwilling sharer of the Cavemoor secret, while it married him to her in a dark, unspoken intimacy from which there was no escape, also made Wilhelm wary of her enthusiasm, even as he was vulnerable to her special appeal. He felt smothered by her claims on him and early on resolved to keep away from her, even though he loved her very much.

Now that I am a member of the Albrecht family by marriage, people often ask me how in the world I ever came to be so intimately involved with them, and I have to give full credit to Teddy Beresford. I was Teddy Beresford's acquisition. That was the term he always preferred to use. "You've really been an excellent acquisition," he used to like to say to me, and it was true, for although I was a good friend of Wilhelm's at school, and we've maintained a cordial relationship over the years, Teddy Beresford became my sponsor. He appropriated Wilhelm's friends when it suited him, and Wilhelm never stood in his father's way. He respected Teddy Beresford's patriarchal omnipotence. His father took over my scholarship at prep school, and later on he paid my college tuition, all with the understanding that I would spend part of my school vacations with his family and eventually become his ADC at the House of Albrecht.

Teddy Beresford was a junior partner and vice-president in charge of corporate development at the House of Albrecht. He was by professional training a mining engineer who had served as a financial adviser to Sir Rupert Skene, the South African baronet who owned gold mines. Henry Albrecht had hired him away from Skene and brought him to this country to help him revive his failing family company, which manufactured mining equipment. Teddy Beresford had succeeded so brilliantly that before long the House of Albrecht was not only showing a wide margin of profit, but had branched out into other industrial fields. He had also helped the Albrechts acquire the Skene mining interests. When these went into receivership he used his connections and arranged the necessary financing for the Albrechts. This turned out to be a financial bonanza of astronomical proportions. Thanks to Teddy Beresford, Henry Albrecht overnight was transformed from a mere multimillionaire into one of the richest men in the world.

I had never heard of the Albrechts until I visited their apartment in the Waldorf Towers with Wilhelm. The night we went there—it was during Thanksgiving break of the year he and I became friends—his father was presiding over a dinner party. Teddy Beresford was slouched in his chair down at the head of the table. He was a big, broad-shouldered man. He wore the same self-gratified smirk on his cherubic, Saxon face I had seen in photographs of the young Winston Churchill. It was a lively expression of aggressive scorn. Wilhelm's mother was the only woman present. She sat at her end of the table in her wheelchair, dressed in a full-length Dior gown, every inch the stricken prima ballerina, somewhat severe, her jeg-black hair pulled into a chignon, but exquisite even so, with a smile of inquiry for her dinner partner that was at once gallant and amused. Dinner was over. The table glittered with wineglasses and brandy snifters. A blue haze of cigar smoke hung in the air above the table. The talk and laughter of all those businessmen in tuxedos was curiously muted, as though the acoustics of the room were affected by the sumptuous, thick, satin floor-length curtains that had been drawn against the Manhattan night, so that the room was like an inner sanctum lined in bronze. The muffled, carpeted atmosphere pervaded the other rooms and gave them an odor of preserved ancien régime, of musty imperial swag. This was the boudoir of the House of Albrecht. It was my introduction to Gretchen Albrecht, who dominated the premises even though she wasn't actually there. The lighting was soft. Lots of feminine bric-a-brac, Limoges boxes and little Meissen figurines, cluttered the side tables, which were dressed in floor-length pieces of silk. The French art that hung on the walls was of a kind that might have delighted the eye of Marie Antoinette. Especially memorable was a Fragonard landscape in a gold-leaf-encrusted frame, illuminated by the discreet glow of a frame lamp, that depicted a pastoral scene of women and children in silk breeches and hooped skirts at play under a canopy of great poplar trees as thunderheads darkly mount the sky over the valley that supplies the background of the painting.

The Beresfords were servants of a corporate personality that I now realize was almost indistinguishable from that of Gretchen Albrecht. Although she ruled her employees absolutely, Gretchen Albrecht treated them extremely well when it came to all the creature comforts. Teddy Beresford received a huge salary, one that enabled him to live grandly in a fieldstone manor house, called Harrow Hill, where he maintained himself and his family in baronial circumstances with a beautiful view of the surrounding countryside less than an hour's drive from New York. The Beresfords, for example, always had corporate limousines at their beck and call. In New York I went everywhere with the Beresfords in long, black Cadillac limousines. An Albrecht limousine arrived every morning at Harrow Hill to fetch Teddy Beresford, and every evening an Albrecht limousine returned him safely to his front door, even though Beresford owned four very serviceable automobiles, including a Silver Cloud.

They lived, the Beresfords, in a highly polished environment at all times. This had something to do not only with Teddy's Albrecht wealth, but with his regimental background as well. Certainly the Beresford household recapitulated the gleam and order of a well-run regimental HQ. Beresford's butler, Reggie, had been his batman in the army. Reggie maintained Harrow Hill immaculately, and I must say it was at all times an agreeable house to visit. On its eminence it received a great deal of daylight, so that even on bleak winter days it was airy and bright, and there was a morning room at the end of the front hall, overlooking the valley, where Wilhelm's mother could sit in her wheelchair during those long days when she pined for the sunshine and warmth of the Transvaal. The floors were buffed to a shine, carpeted with rugs that Teddy Beresford had acquired in India during the war. The furniture consisted for the most part of good, eighteenth-century English antiques interspersed with comfortable chintz-covered armchairs and sofas that I later realized were like the furniture in an officer's mess. The brass was always polished. Silver cigarette boxes and ashtrays inscribed with the dates and places of polo matches in which Teddy Beresford had played on the winning team brightly ornamented the side tables in the den. The walls were decorated with reminders of Teddy Beresford's service in the Brigade of Gurkhas. The entire wall above the stairway to the second story from the main hall was used to display Teddy Beresford's collection of kukris, those curved daggers that are the traditional weapon of the Gurkha warrior. A ceremonial kukri, silver-handled, which had once been used to slaughter buffalo during the Hindu New Year festival of Deshira, occupied the place of honor over the fireplace in the drawing room. Framed aquatints of East India Company skirmishes on the northern frontier of India covered one wall of the den. An oil portrait of a Gurkha rifleman hung above the sideboard in the dining room, where the place mats on the long oval dining room table celebrated in illustration acts of conspicuous bravery by Gurkhas in various nineteenth- and twentieth-century military campaigns.

It isn't hard to understand why, given these surroundings, Wilhelm chose the British army as a career, even though he had never indicated a preference for soldiering in those early days of our friendship. For Wilhelm did not appear to have any ambition, and it was one of his many endearing qualities. I, who was so zealously ambitious in my own particular way, could only marvel at Wilhelm's effortless success in the classroom, on the playing field, on the dance floor. His performance was always remarkable for the blithe indifference of its excellence, as though Wilhelm were at all times half-asleep. He had been schooled to perfection under the supervision of his father, but he was neither covetous nor ambitious. He really liked to play cards and listen to music, activities that we both enjoyed, and this is how we whiled away our vacations together out at Harrow Hill, which Teddy Beresford had wired throughout for stereophonic sound, so that no matter what room you happened to find yourself in, you could turn a knob and out would flow the orchestral music of Mantovani or André Kostelanetz. This I believe was an innovation, by the way, of Wilhelmina's; I don't believe they have constant Muzak running day and night through British officers' quarters. Wilhelmina yearned for music, and I must confess that despite my own high cultural standards, I felt liberated beyond my wildest hopes in this environment. The music contributed a constant effervescence, like continuously available champagne. It was the sort of music that went against all my cultural prejudices, for I was the child of parents who had been strictly trained as serious amateur musicians in a classical repertoire; yet this schmaltz, as my mother would have called it (Father didn't have the heart, alas, to raise his voice in protest), made me forget at last about those two people and the world from which I came. Wilhelm in any case would have found any such cultural snobbery difficult to understand, since he was without any hard prejudice.

Wilhelm, unlike our rich but inhibited classmates, was not at all self-conscious about his wealth and never made any attempt to conceal it, either. Not for Wilhelm the Brooks Brothers look, the button-down shirt, the Weejun loafers that formed the basis of the New England prep school uniform. Wilhelm wore monogrammed silk shirts made for him in Hong Kong. He wore cuff links. He favored British footwear, which he purchased on Jermyn Street. I was first of all drawn to him because of his mischievous charm, but above and beyond that he enjoyed a hedonistic outlook I admired and wanted to possess for myself. I wanted to share his life, I was prepared to do anything to be Wilhelm's friend, and I think Teddy Beresford must have realized this the first time he met me, when he came to visit Wilhelm at school, and the Beresfords invited me out to lunch. I came to share Wilhelm's romantic view of life. In his company it was not hard to think of myself as a golden youth. Life was there to serve us. We went everywhere together as companions-in-privilege: to New York, where we dined at elegant restaurants and went to nightclubs and bought cocktails using false identification cards I'd obtained through my cousin Bernie in Piscataway; to the country, where we went for long walks around Harrow Hill, played tennis, and, in the warmer weather, went horseback riding. Eventually, the summer of the year we graduated, I stayed with the Beresfords in Cannes, in a large villa up in the hills above the French Riviera that Wilhelm's father had taken for the season.

It was a life at variance with the one I had grown up to be familiar with, and it made me unsuited, finally, for anything less sumptuous, or so I came to believe. That it was richer goes without saying. It was glamorous, also: the kind of life I had secretly yearned for myself in the back of my parents' cleaning establishment, where I was supposed to be employed folding shirts every day after school but managed to bone up on the lives of movie stars in *Photoplay*, which was one of the best movie magazines, and devoured novels about anything to do with cafe society and the sophisticated world of the very rich. I was familiar with *The New Yorker* stories of Sally Benson when I was in sixth grade, although I was not permitted to write a book report on that particular author. I greedily consumed the gossip columns of Walter Winchell and Louella Parsons and the great Cholly Knickerbocker so that I could stay abreast of the serial adventures of Baby

Pignatari and Barbara Hutton, whose husbands I could name from memory. I knew them all at a glance when I saw them on the pages of _Life_ magazine. Wilhelm, of all the boys at the boarding school for the well born I was fortunate enough to attend on a scholarship, was closest to this world of my fantasies. He was my entrée to the life of unlimited wealth.

I never met the Albrechts when I stayed at Harrow Hill. Yet they were present, somehow. They were in the air. Or I should say Gretchen Albrecht was in the air, teasingly, it would seem, to remind Beresford of his immediate allegiance. Once, we returned from an afternoon walk on the grounds of the Beresford estate to find the front hall filled with flowers that Gretchen Albrecht had arranged to have delivered from wherever she was. I was not sure where that might be. She may have been across the valley at Cavemoor. She may have been somewhere else. For a while she was present, spiritually, at the Beresfords', in the bright effusiveness, the extravagant largesse, of the floral bouquets of chrysanthemums and peonies and gladioli, and in the messages that accompanied the flowers and the big tin of caviar she had sent over. Had she just returned from a journey, or was she about to leave on one? Whatever the occasion, she was thanking the Beresfords for some kindness or service they had performed. "Oodles of kissies too too good of you both I love the presies too love you both Gr.," she had written. Teddy Beresford turned brick red when he read this note, whether out of embarrassment or chagrin I cannot say. He hated to be patronized. He disliked, in the end, to be under the command of someone else, unless that person happened to be Lord Mountbatten of Burma. Yet I think it would also be true to say that he would have preferred if at all possible to perform the role of Supreme Allied Commander himself.

Quite unexpectedly one night while I was visiting the

Beresfords at Harrow Hill for the first time, Teddy Beresford took me over to Cavemoor for dinner. We drove over alone in his Silver Cloud, without Wilhelm, who had elected to stay behind with his mother. Thus I was able to borrow Wilhelm's dinner jacket for the evening, which was a lucky break for me, because I did not own one myself and would have been underdressed for the occasion otherwise. Teddy Beresford gave no reason for why he'd decided to take me along. He spoke not at all until we had reached the Cavemoor gatehouse. Then he said:

"I think you'll be amused by the vicomtesse."

"Who," I ventured to ask, "is the vicomtesse?"

"She is the wife of the vicomte de Roissy," Teddy Beresford replied. "He stables the Albrecht ponies at his château outside Paris." He erupted with mirth. "Though not actually inside the château, where they might die of pneumonia." He stared straight before him down the long driveway that led between two long carpets of lawn to the front door of Cavemoor. "Her magic is *intarissable*," he said. "Her papa was a Greek banker. Her mother came from one of those upstart French families that flourished during the Second Empire, but she's altogether Greek. She's a Circe."

The vicomtesse was our hostess for the evening. She was a tall, bony, olive-skinned woman who might have been called striking, for although she was not exactly beautiful, she was animated and theatrical and used her husky voice as an instrument of enchantment. She presided over the dinner party with all the authority you might expect a woman to wield whose husband owned a château, and she needed it; even so, her magic couldn't quite fill the hollowness that Gretchen Albrecht would have banished with her ferocious energy and her laughter. The rooms were so large and the ceilings so high that the corners were lost in shadow. The windows were draped with heavy dark blue velvet curtains, and the ornately carved darkwood furniture in the great drawing room where we sat before dinner was upholstered in the same material, only it was red and gold and green. Once again, as in the Waldorf Towers apartment, the round end tables were covered in floor-length skirts and jammed with signed photographs in silver frames of the great and near great and the merely infamous. The duchess of Windsor smiled forth from one such frame, Nubar Gulbenkian from another, and I recognized a Cecil Beaton photograph of Coco Chanel. Naturally I knew who all these people were and immediately felt right at home.

The vicomtesse was draped in a blue velvet gown that clung to her legs when she walked and showed them in outline. Her long bony fingers flashed with rubies and diamonds in antique settings, fine silver rings and thick gold ones.

"I see you've taken the trouble to put on a little *papillon*," she said to me almost at once with an enchanting smile and gave my bow tie a slight adjustment. After that she made me her *chevalier d'honneur*, as she put it, and seated me next to her at dinner, where she baffled me with her fragrance of l'Heure Bleue and exalted me well above my customary station with her intimate opinions about Francoise Sagan, whom she thought was really quite an amusing writer, and General de Gaulle, whom she said had ruined his eyesight by trying to look at the tip of his nose, without success, because he was already cross-eyed, and too cross, she added; and she enlightened me about other, more obscure French subjects with which I had not yet acquainted myself. You could also say, I think, that this was my formal introduction to the House of Albrecht. The other guests were all somehow employed by the Albrechts: the Mexican architect who had designed El Parador, the Albrecht hideaway on the Gulf, was there that night, along with Adrian Gilbert, the Albrecht purchasing agent, and Mrs. Stoddard, the decorator, and her husband, the colonel, and Monsignor Cathcart. The Beresfords had been altogether discreet on the subject of the Albrechts, and most of what I knew about them I had gleaned from snatches of overheard but diffident conversation at Harrow Hill. I was unaware of who any of these people were, and I had not even been informed of the existence of Ann and Ivan Albrecht until I sat beside the vicomtesse at dinner. She was shocked to discover that I had never met Ivan.

"But I mean you really have to know Ivan to understand how really brilliant he is," the vicomtesse leaned her head close to mine to say, "because you can't tell exactly at once that he's an idiot savant, not normal, not like the other children, but I mean truly extraordinary in his own way and of course his *maman* refused to send him to school which I think was the great mistake because it turned him into a sort of *enfant sauvage*. He used to take private lessons with Monsieur Hearn upstairs, which I don't think was good for him, I don't know what he learned but I don't think he did anything except the chess. Now he plays chess in a Swiss dungeon," she added with a wicked grin, "where they locked him up for the *crime passionel* of wanting to kiss his *maman* good night." She snorted. "At least in his little *castillo* in Locarno he'll make a few *copains*," she said.

On the drive home, Teddy Beresford was quite curious to know what the vicomtesse had told me over dinner and grunted while I recounted our conversation. Luckily, he did not inquire about the conversation I had after dinner with Monsignor Cathcart, over coffee and brandy while the other guests played bridge. He it was who further enlightened me on the subject of the Albrechts. Ivan, he told me, was a dreadful problem child, and Ann, his twin sister, was hardly an improvement. They were both hellions, and in his opinion it was a very good thing they had been locked up in different Swiss schools, for it was all that Gretchen could do, he said, to manage the problems of her husband without having to mediate between her unruly children and the servants they molested all the time. Monsignor Cathcart was Gretchen Albrecht's confessor. Henry Albrecht, he told me, was out of it. The complexities of international finance were beyond him. He had been trained strictly to be a factory manager. Gretchen, on the other hand, had been married to an elderly Belgian businessman, the father of her twins. She was bright and had taken an interest in his business and had never lost an opportunity at dinner parties in Brussels to bone up on the latest developments in international finance. Gretchen, not Henry, had foreseen the opportunity to expand vastly the House of Albrecht. She it was who had hired Teddy Beresford, the prelate told me. Henry presided over board meetings and kept his executive suite on Wall Street, but he had begun to develop his interests in other areas because Gretchen and Teddy Beresford had forced him to one side. He now lived in isolation in the English countryside. Gretchen traveled abroad constantly so that she could oversee the international side of the business and at the same time visit Henry at Great Wyke House. This explained her absence that night, in fact, he told me.

Monsignor Cathcart explained something else that I had been wondering about. He told me that Wilhelmina Beresford had always disliked the rapport between her husband and Gretchen Albrecht. He told me how dreadfully confined she felt at Harrow Hill. He told me how an automobile accident, Teddy at the wheel, had destroyed her career as a dancer when she was at her zenith. He told me what a lothario Wilhelm's father really was. He told me that Teddy had always been half in love with Gretchen Albrecht and half in love with Henry's power. He told me that Teddy's breakfast tête-à-têtes with Gretchen Albrecht to discuss company strategy had gradually come to an end. He told me that it was quite likely that Teddy Beresford's usefulness at the House of Albrecht may indeed have come to an end. He could not say so for certain, but he thought perhaps it had. He thought it might be best for everyone concerned if this were so. He told me, confidentially, that between Wilhelmina and Gretchen Albrecht, Teddy Beresford stood little chance of staying on much longer in the House of Albrecht. "The only question now," he'd said with a fond, rueful expression on his sallow face, "is how, and when."

Ann Albrecht returned from school in Switzerland with Ivan when we were seniors. I don't know what on earth they hoped to do with Ivan, but clearly he could not remain indefinitely in that Swiss dungeon. He'd learned cabinet-making at his Swiss school, and perhaps they thought that he would devote himself to woodworking once they came back to live at Cavemoor. He was immensely gifted with those elegant long pale hands; he was not only a well-tutored crafts-man, he was loving and painstaking with his work, and he'd become skilled at making copies of antique pieces. Ivan was one of Ann's escorts at the coming-out party that Gretchen gave for her daughter at Cavemoor that June, the month we graduated. I had the opportunity to observe him then looking ill at ease among the other young swains, our contemporaries in the social swim who were far more comfortable in those waters than Ivan. He had grown to a freakish height, and you caught sight of him in the thronging rooms, suddenly, with a start, because he loomed above all the other guests with the expression on his face of a child who has lost his mother. His tuxedo was tailored for someone at least an inch shorter than he was. He'd applied some Wild Root Cream Oil to his thin black hair to plaster it down, and this had the unfortunate effect of allowing his white scalp to reveal itself in patches. He looked as though he'd just gotten out of a fish tank. Also I remember his shoes. He wore long unpolished black shoes of the kind you sometimes see discarded on the streets of New York for no conceivable reason without their laces. They drew attention to the size of Ivan's feet on the single occasion when he was led out onto the dance floor by Ann. Her experiment was mercifully interrupted by Teddy Beresford. It was the first fox trot of the evening. Few others had ventured out onto the ballroom parquet, and they were the center of attention out there. Ivan did not actually know how to dance, and Teddy Beresford, who saw at once what a disaster it was to put Ivan on display like that, cut in on the dancers, although I rather doubt that he was acting on behalf of Ivan.

Teddy Beresford was Ann's great champion. He would have liked to see Ann and Wilhelm become engaged, if only to realize his own ambition of establishing a dynastic claim to the House of Albrecht, and to further this end he had presented Ann with a necklace to celebrate her debut, which the jeweler Harry Winston had fashioned from diamonds that had at one time glittered on a stomacher worn by Catherine the Great of Russia. Now they glittered on Ann Albrecht's neck and enhanced her youthful beauty with just the right accent of glamour, as Teddy Beresford had known they would. They made her stand out among the other debutantes that season. Her looks and her style attracted the attention of the press, which was ever on the lookout for a new star of the social circuit. Ann Albrecht had exactly the right looks for that role, for she had become what is known as a striking blonde, with a white, even smile and something else, a fragility. She was a haunting beauty, to use another cliché the press dished up to describe her. She was, as of her Cavemoor debut, the most sought-after debutante of her time, and from that night onward her face appeared frequently on the society pages. Ann was besieged by suitors, myself among them. She received gifts of jewelry in the mail from unknown admirers asking for her hand in marriage. She was photographed at show jumping events, leaping fences on her horse; she was snapped at the Metropolitan Opera on opening night and at the White Russian Ball at the Pierre; she appeared in photographs taken at the Cresta Run in St. Moritz, and looking tanned and adoring by the side of some equally tanned and glamorous young socialite at the Everglades Club in Palm Beach, or in Saratoga during the season there. Nothing was ever said about Ivan, however. No mention was ever made about her twin brother, Ivan, in the society columns. He was cropped from the picture. He was hardly known to exist. He appeared as a shadow in Ann's life, occasionally, at Cavemoor, or at Black Pond House, the Albrechts' summer place on Fishers Island. He hovered near her—always, however, unseen.

In spite of all the attention she received from other men, Wilhelm remained the object of Ann Albrecht's ardor. He was her other escort on the night of her coming-out party, and he rose to the occasion with gallantry, even though it went against his unspoken pledge never to cross the frontier of Cavemoor again. Ann wanted to ensnare him, and she made of this a sport and an adventure that I, for one, found myself drawn in on without exactly realizing what was happening. She wanted to finish the job she'd failed to complete at Cavemoor during their early adolescent romance. She wanted to seduce him. On the night of her party at Cavemoor she invited him to stay for breakfast and persuaded him in the hour before dawn to join her for a skinny dip in the new swimming pool because she thought that by so doing she could have him at last. She had no intention of marrying Wilhelm, of this I was always convinced. She wanted to enslave him. I'm sure of it, now, because Ann tells me everything, and she has confessed as much. However, Wilhelm never batted an eyelash, as my mother used to say. Down at the pool, he swam laps while Ann sat by the deep end, slumped forward on the palm of her hand, waiting crossly for him to finish. He swam seventy-five laps, she told me later. Then, naked, he made cannonball runs off the diving board over and over again, exploding on the surface of the water two or three feet from where she sat, until he had expended his sexual tension in exercise, as we had learned to do at boarding school, and was all set to doze off on the poolhouse couch, in the arms of Ann, like a blissful child.

Two years passed before Ann had another chance to try to bag him, this time on Fishers Island. I suspect this was a trickier episode for Wilhelm because he'd gone up there aboard an Albrecht plane on an errand for his father, who was now in exile, for he'd been fired by Gretchen soon after the coming-out party at Cavemoor. Wilhelm had been invited by Ann to stay at Black Pond House, so for several days they slept under the same roof. Wilhelm, however, possessed the curious ability to make himself physically unappetizing at will. He became sort of dry and puffy. That was how Ann put it when she described to me what it was like to try to kiss him under those circumstances. She said he reminded her of a porcupine fish. His apparent lack of desire for her was an unpleasant embarrassment to them both, and it may have been caused in part by the presence of Ivan, who was lurking around up there. Ann thought it had something also to do with the distance that now existed between them. Wilhelm was now at Sandhurst. His father no longer worked for the House of Albrecht, he'd returned to South Africa, and Wilhelm no longer had so much in common with the Albrecht children. He'd got away. He was stiffly British now, more reserved.

I saw him then, for we were renting a bungalow at that time across the sound from Fishers Island at Niantic, and the Albrechts sent for me to come and visit while Wilhelm was there. I had never visited Fishers Island, which is a low-key preserve of the very rich located off the coast of Connecticut opposite New London. Several classmates of ours had houses there, but it was never a place you visited without an invitation. Its exclusivity was daunting, reserved as the place was for rich people of mostly Anglo-Saxon provenance, which presumably did not exclude Catholics, if, like the Albrechts, they were rich enough to own a piece of it. The island was all privately owned real estate, with the exception of the beaches, which were all but inaccessible to the public, and the estates were what you might call beach—opulent, down rutted sandy driveways, hidden from the two-lane blacktop main road, camouflaged by luxuriant beach vegetation, well-aged oaks, and bayberry. It was a beautifully landscaped summer paradise that appeared wild and unkempt from the road, although up at the northern end where the main road broke out of the overarching great shade trees it burst upon a rolling expanse of brilliant green golf course. The sleek beach club was situated up at this end with its vista of open ocean.

Black Pond House was located somewhere around the middle of the island. It was discreetly tucked away on a tidal lagoon on the side of the island that faced the Connecticut shore. It was a newly built, rambling structure covered with dark gold weathered shingles. A cedarwood deck ran the full length of the house on the lagoon side, onto which sliding glass doors opened from various rooms, but the house was constructed so that the bedroom decks were private, and on hot summer days the high-ceilinged rooms had the great virtue of remaining cool because they were shaded by the overhanging roof.

My brief afternoon visit to Black Pond House itself I recall as distinctly unpleasant. I had been imported at the request of Wilhelm. The Albrechts had sent their caretaker over to fetch me in a speedboat, but they were indifferent to me once I'd arrived. Ivan was there with his fourteen-year-old sweetheart, Amber Drayton. Lansing Noble, Ivan's boyhood playmate, was present also, and Ann. They all gave the impression that they had recently gotten up, although it was two o'clock in the afternoon. They were sitting indoors on cool leather chairs playing poker. I would have to say that they were rudely indifferent to my presence, which Wilhelm admitted to me later was to him extremely embarrassing. Ann, in particular, ignored me. Ivan was his supremely remote self. Amber and Lansing were taken up with the business of playing cards.

Wilhelm and I went off in one of the Albrecht cars to

Chocomount Beach for a swim. We spent the next couple of hours lying in the sun and walking on the beach, talking. He related all that had happened to him since we had last seen each other. He hoped to be selected as an officer by the Brigade of Gurkhas and appointed to his father's regiment, so that he could serve in the Far East. He was enagaged to a girl from Belfast named Doreen, who worked as a receptionist in the London branch of his father's merchant bank. He'd come over to settle some of his father's affairs, which Teddy Beresford, for tax reasons, could not return to the United States to look after himself. His Albrecht money had been frozen in a New York bank pending the outcome of a huge lawsuit that Gretchen Albrecht had slapped him with to seize part of his fortune, which she claimed he had illegally appropriated while he was employed by the House of Albrecht.

"How about Ann?" I asked Wilhelm as we sat in the sand together, propped up on our elbows, looking out to sea on a perfectly blue August afternoon.

"The beautiful Ann," said Wilhelm. "Why don't you marry her?"

"Oh, my God," I replied. I was so flabbergasted by this notion that I burst out laughing. "You have to be kidding. She won't even say hello to me."

"I'm afraid that's my fault," Wilhelm said. "You see, I rather took them by surprise. They weren't exactly prepared for my visit, I fear, though God knows why not. Still, I daresay they regard it as an intrusion. That's why Ann seems so unfriendly. I'm very sorry. Why don't you call her sometime in New York? Invite her out to dinner and the theater? I can see by the way you're blushing that you still have rather a crush on the girl."

"She's too rich for me," I said. This was how I felt then,

for much as I may have dreamed about getting in with people of such extreme wealth, they still intimidated me. The Albrechts were too hard. They were made of platinum. It required, I thought, a tougher metal than I was made of to consort with people that rich. I was surprised that Wilhelm Beresford agreed. After all, he knew how to play bridge, and he could waltz like an Austrian prince. Furthermore, he was not without a considerable fortune of his own. Yet he concurred. He'd been very attracted to Ann once upon a time, he reminded me. He was still, as he put it with his usual reticence, extremely fond of her. "More than just fond of her," he said. "I find her terribly moving. Still, I refuse to get caught up in all of that. It's bound to make a man feel madly confused and quite useless. It's too bad, isn't it? The whole thing could have been such fun."

We had a good laugh in the sun over that, and we felt, together, that the ominous dark cloud of great wealth had passed over us both only long enough to trouble our hearts briefly before it moved on. We both pitied Ann at that moment, because with all her beauty and all her money she was doomed to live, we thought, without the freedom of pure laughter and joy that right then at that time on those golden sands we were enjoying so much. We were still friends, and that was a good thing. We shared a way of seeing the world that was at once romantic and innocent. Wilhelm was going to be a soldier, and I? I wasn't sure, but it would have to be in some way or another artistic, and I was leaning, even then, toward photography as a profession, because it so admirably combined the possibilities of social advancement and making money.

Ann eventually married Lansing Noble. He was enormously rich by anybody's standards. He was also very good looking. Lansing's looks matched Ann's: he was blond, a Nordic Apollo with green-blue eyes and a dimpled smile who owned a well-muscled body that could have served as a model for Praxiteles. He was the heir to a utilities fortune. He had fashioned himself after the nineteenth-century gentleman explorer who traveled to out-of-the-way places on elaborately arranged expeditions. I had met Lansing Noble that one time at Black Pond House and judged him then to be a cold sort of person, and I think it may be said in all fairness that he and Ann did not marry out of a feeling for one another of great warmth. They were considered, however, to be a perfect match, economically and socially. They made excellent copy for _Town & Country_ and _Vogue_. They continued to visit Fishers Island in the summertime. Lansing Noble was someone you could expect to see anywhere in the world: on Piccadilly, in the Via Veneto, in the White Highlands of Kenya, or in the wilds of New Guinea. He continued, after his marriage to Ann Albrecht, to spend about half the year traveling, on his own, to far-flung places, cutting the figure of a latterday Phineas Fogg on the pages of travel magazines, for which he wrote the occasional essay to let everyone know where he had been and what he was doing.

Ann also traveled. They saw each other intermittently on their travels. They would meet up in London to go off together for a weekend in Sussex, where some Greek shipping magnate they knew owned a country house. Or they would meet in Vienna and travel to Salzburg to attend a house party at the _schloss_ of the Austrian count who looked after the Albrecht forests in the Tyrol. They had no children. Ivan was their child. They were married at his insistence, Ann told me later, because he needed to have Lansing on the board of the family holding company, from which he had been removed by his mother. Upon his marriage to Ann Albrecht, Lansing automatically had acquired a family vote, which he'd agreed to use as a surrogate for Ivan. Ann and Lansing were on call to Ivan, who had gone to live with Amber Drayton on the island of Corfu, in a house that Ann and Lansing had purchased for them, above a remote cove on the northern end of the island where they also kept a yacht. Lansing and Ann were bound together by their affection for Ivan; otherwise they were vaguely annoyed with one another, as spoiled people very often are, without being absolutely incompatible.

She had not forgotten Wilhelm Beresford. He was part of her plan. She knew what she was doing. Wilhelm had gone to live in Paris after his marriage. Ann found out where he was, and when the time was ripe to do so she went to see him there. Ivan, her brother, her twin, remained aloof, as always, but he was never far away. He preferred to stay behind the scenes. Ann was the one who wanted to draw Wilhelm into their conspiracy. She wanted him back as the playmate of her youth, as an aide-de-camp. Wilhelm by now had finished his course of training at the Royal Military Academy at Sandhurst. He had received his commission. He had married Doreen, the former beauty queen his father had introduced him to one summer at Ascot; they had eloped. It was a very unusual circumstance for a young married man to receive permission to serve with the Gurkhas in Nepal, however, and Wilhelm had been attached to the British embassy in Paris as a subaltern while his application for special consideration was being processed. Ann called him at the embassy from her mother's suite at the Ritz, and Wilhelm found that even after two years of married life she still appealed to his sense of adventure. She asked him to dine with her, alone, at Maxim's. Ever chivalrous, he consented to do this. His acceptance, however, was not submitted without a slight thrill, a sense of danger. She wore the famous diamond necklace his father had given her on the occasion of her debut, which had been designed, it seemed, to resemble, in the abstract, a pair of doves kissing in flight. Ann had ordered a table in the back room, where they could dine intimately, with a sense of privacy.

"What's become of Ivan Ivanovich?" Wilhelm asked her.

"He's an arms dealer," she replied with a grin, so that he couldn't be sure whether what she told him was true or just some kind of private joke. "We finally got him set up in business on Corfu, but it's strictly *entre nous*, because he's in hiding with Amber, and as far as we know they're still looking for them."

"Who do you mean, 'they'?" Wilhelm wanted to know.

"Interpol, I guess. Her parents. My mother. I don't know. They eloped. He operates out of a great big boat Lansing bought for him in Trieste. Clients do business with him on the boat. Lansing spends a certain amount of time with him and Amber."

"I gather you don't spend all that much time with Lansing."

"Not a hell of a lot," she said with a shy grin. "We get together every six weeks, unless he's off exploring some jungle. He's a travel adventurer, so he keeps going off into the unknown. God knows what he does once he gets there. I _never_ ask."

Ann's beauty was if anything more stunning now because she had a touch of color in her cheeks that Wilhelm did not recall ever having seen before, brought out perhaps by the wine they were drinking. Perhaps it was the wine. It was a trademark of Ann's not to wear cosmetics. She always gave forth the scent of a perfume, which she sprayed in the air all around her before embarking on any social engagement. The base was a commingling of hyacinth with attar of roses. With her looks, Ann could afford an indifference to fashion. She rarely added more than a touch of lipstick to her natural coloring, and she always wore her shoulder-length platinum-blond hair in a loose wave that fell along one side of her face and which she held back with the tips of her fingers so that it wouldn't get in the way while she ate. Although the business of clothes bored her, Ann always made it to the seasonal showings at the Paris fashion houses and allowed herself to be fitted by the great couturiers. She relied on their judgment, and they never failed to dress her effectively. On this night she wore a strapless silver gown of form-fitting silk, cut just low enough to arouse Wilhelm's warm speculation before his attention was drawn to the necklace, which always excited him, and then to the color in her cheeks and the sparkle of her light blue eyes, as they dined.

After dinner, ever chivalrous, Wilhelm walked Ann back to the Place Vendôme. She allowed him to accompany her into the foyer of the hotel, where she invited him to join her for a nightcap upstairs in the Albrecht suite. Gallantly, he accepted her invitation. In the entrance vestibule of the suite, while he was helping her out of the absurdly long black mink coat she'd worn, Ann turned and kissed him lightly on the lips. Wilhelm was caught off guard. She hadn't given him any time to turn into a porcupine fish. In the living room, by the subdued glow of the table lamps that had been left lit by the chambermaid, Ann slipped off her evening gown, not wanting to go on into the bedroom, in case Wilhelm changed his crazy little mind, as she put it. She helped him to get his trousers off while he sat on the couch, and then, wearing only Cate the Great's diamonds, she straddled him playfully and fitted herself onto his erection. He was surprised by the celerity of her action. He could only thrust himself with some effort as she covered his face with kisses and licked the inside of his ear, as she had always dreamed of doing but never had. His exploding laugh had often made her wonder how he sounded when he came, but he was a soundless, Rolls-Royce lover. That's how she described him. His face got pink, and he wore the same petulant expression of intense concentration he might have displayed while taking an exam in algebra. When he found the right answer his face relaxed into profound relief, and he smiled, slightly, eyelids fluttering, and released his tension in great bucking movements. Then, at that instant, he became unexpectedly aggressive, for as Ann lay astride him, flat on top of him, Wilhelm, not yet having greatly exerted himself, rose up violently and thrust deep within her so forcibly that she began to scream like someone at a horse race as he got her onto the floor and pumped way up into her an ejaculation that drew itself forth from the soles of his feet. She would never let him go again.

So you see Wilhelm was drawn into this thing very swiftly without really having planned for it. He was smitten. Once he'd slept with Ann he couldn't stay away. He went back the next day to lunch with her at the Ritz and then met her again for drinks at the Cafe de la Paix, which led to another visit to the Albrecht suite. I was there at lunch. He was surprised to discover, at lunch, that I was somehow around and about, but he was also very equable. I must explain that I had not turned up just by accident in the dining room of the Ritz Hotel the day after their affair began. I had been out of touch with Wilhelm for quite a while, but at the time I was supposed to be working as a free-lance photographer for various society sheets and had occasion to see a good deal of Ann. I was free to travel, and in due course I became almost indispensable to Ann, rather against her will, I might add. There I was, for instance, in Paris, when her love affair with Wilhelm exploded into blossom, and she invited me to join them as a chaperon. I was a convenient cover, and I think Wilhelm appreciated this fact, because he seemed very glad to see me again, and we three had a jolly lunch talking about all sorts of people we knew in common. Ann was radiant.

Wilhelm had told Doreen he'd been assigned to the duchess of Gloucester, whom he said was in Paris on an unofficial visit to do some shopping. It happened to be one of his duties as a subaltern that he was asked to escort the wives of visiting members of the royal family around Paris, so this alibi fitted in smoothly with Wilhelm's work. He didn't know what to do. Ann had caught him. On the weekend, while Ann was out at the château visiting the vicomtesse, Wilhelm was in a state of agony. He almost couldn't stand it. He tried to telephone her out at Roissy without success. He then tried to reach her through me.

"Tell her I must see her on Monday at the latest," he insisted to me over the telephone from St. Cloud, where he was calling from a pay phone at the corner bistro. "Tell her in the meantime to let me know through the embassy when she gets back. I must see her," he said.

On Monday he waited all day for her to call him at work, and by Tuesday, when she went around in person to see him at the embassy, he was ready to explode with anxiety. He went with her at once back to the suite so that they could make love. He couldn't wait. He had been thinking all weekend along fairly drastic lines, for although he loved his wife, in the brief absence of Ann life with Doreen seemed to stretch before him interminably. He did not think he could bear to leave the children, yet he had to be with Ann. He thought perhaps he'd have to leave the British army, resign his commission, go to work for Ann, do something mad like that, just to be near her. Then when they had made love once again he came somewhat to his senses. He laughed. Nothing desperate needed to be done, he realized. My own suggestion to Wilhelm was that he simply try to take it on a day-to-day basis. This was an attitude I had evolved out of our youthful hedonism. I tried to armor myself against scruple, although, being as anxious as the next young man, I found it hard to do this without a twinge of guilt now and again. You have to work at it. You have to adapt yourself to the moment. I passed this on to Wilhelm.

"Whenever you want to go off with Ann for a few days," I suggested, "why don't you tell Doreen that you've been called away on some kind of military intelligence mission."

"What a sly, social-climbing ruffian you are," Wilhelm said, not without a twinkle in his merry blue eyes.

I had my uses. I got to Paris not infrequently, I told him, on free-lance assignments. I was free to come and go, I told him. I would gladly supply the occasional alibi. I could see that Wilhelm didn't always like having me in the next room while he and Ann were making love, but Ann told him not to worry. "He's always trying to get me into the sack," she told him one day when we were all having a _fête champêtre_ in the Bois de Boulogne. "This way it's much easier because he can't try to pretend that I'm available." Wilhelm didn't complain. He could only dumbly follow along as Ann led the way. She always behaved just as though Wilhelm was aware of everything that we were up to, as though he'd already joined the conspiracy and was a full-fledged active member of her core group of plotters, as, in a sense, I already was.

Ann pursued the love affair. At first it seemed to me that Wilhelm was reluctant to meet with her after their first Paris idyll. It was my impression that Wilhelm's good intention was to resume his placid married life with no further interruptions of this sort because sexual adventure, while all very well and good as far as it went, was not that high on his list of things to do in life. Passion was not an issue when it came to the organization of Wilhelm Beresford's priorities. He tried never to permit the wild element in his nature to influence his life in the course that he had charted. Adventure could only be a by-product of his otherwise smoothly controlled upward career. This is not to say that Wilhelm Beresford did not allow himself the greatest possible enjoyment of Ann's uncamouflaged affections. He was highly amused by her audacity and in thrall to the suspense of conducting an affair, but he was far too intelligent to think that they would ever marry, and in his present bourgeois view of life, the object of any romantic attachment ought to be family life.

He was the adored one, and it was not hard to see why, for although he was not handsome in the classic sense, as was Lansing Noble with his Apollonian physique and his faint, narcissistic fleer, Wilhelm exerted an appeal of his own. He was pumpkin-faced with a toothy grin and rubbery nose and eyes that made him appear to be drowsy and even dim-witted in repose. His face was the model for a Shropshire lad or a Huck Finn. He could have gone barefoot with the bottoms of his trousers rolled up and wearing a straw farm boy's hat down a country lane with a haversack slung over his shoulder, and all the milkmaids would have dropped their pails at the sight of such unconscious pleasure passing their way. Ann loved to make him laugh. He gave himself over to it so utterly. He was overwhelmed by his own laughter.

After two weeks Ann went home. I think Wilhelm breathed a great sigh of relief. He was a romantic soul, but he did not want to destroy his marriage to the beautiful Doreen. He loved his babies. He had no appetite for the kind of risk that would threaten a merry Christmas. He had never been unfaithful to Doreen, and even as he met in the Albrecht suite with Ann he did not think of his love affair with her as exactly an adulterous one. They knew each other too well, he thought, for any such designation. He thought, This is really something that ought to have happened four or five years ago, so it's really unfinished business. He was rectifying his failure to consummate their passion on Fishers Island, and so, he told me in Paris, it was as though their idyll were taking place in a parenthesis.

"It's a parenthetical relationship and somewhat removed from the situation of my present life," he told me.

Except that Ann had managed to connect him to her electric current and kept sending him little messages at the British embassy with photographs of herself she had clipped from various periodicals that showed her wearing Cate the Great's diamonds. She used me as a courier. In the spring she got me

to contact Wilhelm for her while I was in Paris to tell him
that she was going mad, had to see him, couldn't stand it. I
met with Wilhelm at the embassy and told him I was doing a
fashion spread in Marrakesh. I talked him into meeting us for
a few days at the Mamounia at the end of April. I set that up.
The lovers met there for a long weekend, and we had an
enchanting time, all three of us together once again. This
time I think Wilhelm was distinctly relieved to have me
along. We went to the Jmaa El Fna in the late afternoon to
watch the performers, and we wandered through the medina
together, where Ann persuaded Wilhelm to buy a silver caftan for Doreen. We drank cocktails and dined outside under
the stars. One day we hired a car and driver to take us over
the High Atlas to visit the Sousse valley. In Taroudant we
smoked kef and sat in the mellow evening in the garden of
our hotel among the oleanders, and together forgot about our
cares and fears, and at night the lovers held hands while we
walked through the village streets, and it was possible to
imagine that neither of them had any other attachment in the
world.

In the autumn Ann wanted me to set up something else
with Wilhelm, who was reluctant at that point to do it.

"I say, this is a rather open-ended parenthesis," he said to
me while he was considering Ann's latest proposition.

Yet he was excited: dry throat; white, dry lips. We met at
the Cafe Flore on the Boulevard St. Germain. Wilhelm had
been anticipating a tranquil domesticity out in St. Cloud and
planned soon to take up his service in Nepal with his regiment in the Brigade of Gurkhas. That was why, perhaps, he
was willing to meet Ann for one last assignation. It was like a
narcotic: the high was thrilling, and he thought he could take
it or leave it.

We flew down to Corfu. It was just a quick weekend trip. That's how we'd both put it to Wilhelm. We flew down on board a twin-engine jet that Ann had chartered in London. It was late October, very blue by day and briskly cold at night. The house on Corfu was a pink summer villa situated above a secluded bay within a grove of pine trees and black cypresses. From the terrace we looked down at an abandoned island chapel or one rarely used for worship, built by some shipwrecked sailor upon his safe return home. It looked cold, white, and desolate out there in the afternoon shadow. The house had been closed up. The terrace was littered with pine needles and branches that had blown down

from the surrounding trees during a recent storm. The villa
with its dark rooms and bare, marble floors was hard to keep
warm, although someone, Lansing Noble perhaps, had imported the kind of gas heater that in Italy is called a _bombola_
because it looks like a man-sized bomb on casters. In the
evening we sat in the living room off the terrace that over-
looked the bay and drank ouzo and ate pâté de foie gras in
the company of our _bombola_. Ivan and Amber, Ann told us,
had made one of their rare trips to Athens. We were alone.

The next day we rowed out to Ivan's boat, the _Zephyr Echo_,
which lay at anchor out beyond the mouth of the bay in the
Adriatic. It came as a shock to see it as we rounded the point.
It did not look like a boat that had been built to sail on any
such waters as these. It was a three-masted cargo ship with a
black hull that sat on the water like an iron cradle. It could
only have been towed to such a desolate spot, because no
engine could have hauled that tub through the water. It presented an unpleasant challenge. Wilhelm released a low
whistle at the sight of it. My instinct, I must say, was to
admire it at a distance and then row in the opposite direction.

It waited out there, ominously still, with no friendly port-
holes or anything like that, no one on deck to greet us
through a bullhorn. Ann, up at the bow, directed Wilhelm to
row us right alongside the _Zephyr Echo_ to the hemp rope
ladder that hung down the starboard side. The oars sounded
spooky as they cut through the placid wine-dark water. It was
somehow as though we were being observed from the ship,
and I wondered whether Ivan and Amber had really gone to
Athens at all. When we were right out in its shadow, the
Zephyr Echo loomed above us. The hull rang dully when our
rowboat bumped it as Wilhelm secured our little craft to the
rope that hung from the ladder. Ann climbed up the ladder

first, then Wilhelm, then I climbed up and over onto the wide deck, which was the length of a football field and a third again as broad at its widest point. Great canvas storm awnings had been lowered amidships port and starboard to protect the decks from the elements out on the open sea. It also gave Ivan a measure of privacy.

The first thing that Ann did was to lead us to a hatch door on the deck, which with some effort she pulled open to reveal a yawning, dark emptiness. Wilhelm and I took turns peering down into a cavernous drop of about thirty feet; at the bottom of the boat I could discern only what appeared to be oil drums and the quicksilver flash of water that had accumulated down there.

"He's going to store the guns down there," Ann told us. We stood over the open hatchway for some time in silence, like spectators at the Grand Canyon. Then we wandered about the boat.

As we explored the officer's cabin space on the afterdeck of Ivan's pirate ship, I could almost have sworn that he was somewhere near at hand, having fun at our expense, although I couldn't have said where he was hiding because I did not know as yet about the secret office behind the dining salon, where Ann's twin brother and his inamorata took turns spying on us through a peephole, suppressing their childish mirth as they did so. For I am a spy myself, and it takes one to smell one out. Besides, they almost gave themselves away more than once with the occasional unexplained creak of a floor-board, which, however, was easily mistaken for the sound a vessel makes when it drifts at its mooring. It was Ivan's cus-tomary role to keep out of sight, and he was a past master at the art of concealment. Ann had always been the one to keep him in the shadows, it seems, except for the time she'd dragged him out onto the dance floor, where he briefly humiliated himself in full view of their social peers, most of whom had not even known of his existence until that night. He was an embarrassment. He didn't fit in, and this was partly the result of having been educated at home, which, as the vicomtesse had pointed out to me that night at Cavemoor, had deprived Ivan of a normal childhood. He was starved of playmates. He was starved of laughter and love. His mother worshiped him with an unhealthy rapture, but she was prevented by her husband from showing it, so it was bestowed in secret, as a shameful rush of passion, on the rare occasions when she was around long enough to be alone with Ivan, and then she snatched it back, went away, left him once again cold and solitary. He was always in prison.

He'd hovered in the shadows of Ann's play world when they were children. He'd been in the habit of observing Ann and Wilhelm at play. He was rarely to be seen, at any rate by Wilhelm, who never knew that he was there, hidden, watching all along. Ann taught Wilhelm how to kiss, upstairs, on the second floor at Cavemoor, while Ivan watched them from a closet. He liked to watch them as they kissed with their parted lips and explored with their hands the mysteries that until then they had withheld from one another. As a child Ann was not altogether uninhibited; she'd received a Catholic education, and her passion was checked by misgivings of a superstitious nature, which Ivan with his scorn for what he called old wives' tales helped her to surmount, and she let him play the "power behind the scenes" role. Now he was the chief motivating force behind Operation _Zephyr Echo_. He was the genius behind Ann and Lansing Noble. They never would have been emboldened to undertake their scheme without Ivan's shadowy exhortations, his passionate whispering, his demands. He was recessed, dark, arrogant. He had that pale moon face, framed by black locks, with its sullen, sensual mouth that could radiate sudden bliss when it lit up his face. He had his mother's sloe eyes, but he resembled in the white purity of his looks his sister, Ann, with her demeanor in repose of faint desolation that vanished into festive brilliance when she grinned. They were not identical in appearance, but they were twins in spirit; they both called out for love across an abyss of wealth.

Ann told us that Ivan had acquired the *Zephyr Echo* in Trieste with the financial assistance of Lansing Noble while she was in dry dock undergoing extensive repairs. In her day she had been unsurpassed in luxury by any other waterborne residence except possibly those of a very few of the fabled "Golden Greeks." She had served most recently as the floating munitions warehouse of the now deceased Norse arms dealer Har Osvaldsen. Her skipper, a pirate by the name of Masterson, who'd been in the employ of Osvaldsen at the time of the arms dealer's unexpected death outside Dubrovnik, had sold the Bayeux tapestries and the Flemish masters that had once ennobled the stateroom walls. Never mind. She still bore vestiges of her rich and recent past. Her fittings were all made of hand-worked brass. Ivan had personally restored the original oak and walnut paneling in these salons. The lounges and the dining salon and the captain's quarters were all located on the afterdeck, under the race poop. These were good-sized cabins, high enough to stand up in comfortably, which was why, Ann told us, the boat had appealed to Ivan. He was still in the process of transforming the captain's mess into a showcase for the antique furniture he liked to make. The original teak floors had been sanded down, and the mahogany dining room table was covered with a drop sheet that was littered with Ivan's carpentry tools. He was restoring, also, the filigreed woodwork along the moldings, which bore the carved names of the original ship's owners.

The gold-plated fixtures in the bathroom Ann showed us had been ripped out, but we could imagine by the lavishness of the black marble basin and the free-standing bathtub how they must have enriched the experience of bathing. Ivan was planning to replace the fixtures with new gold-plated faucets and spigots, Ann told us.

"That's what he's doing right now, in Athens," she added. "Shopping for spigots."

The cookhouse was located on the forward deck, next to the bunkroom where the deckhands were quartered, although, as Ann pointed out, there weren't any deckhands. Yet.

"It takes at least thirty hands to man a ship this size, with those great big sails," Ann explained. "So they don't do a whole heck of a lot of traveling around. This thing has a putt putt, but it's not supposed to go over twenty knots. It's their home, really. More than anything. And their place of business. They never go up to the house. They use it to put up arms merchants when they come down here. It's really a convenience. It's where we're going to barrack the men. Isn't that what you say?" She grinned. "We're going to barrack the men there, and then we'll use them on board. We'll teach them how to man the sails. We'll fly them to places we've targeted," she said. "Once we get the operation under way."

She said this cavalierly, as we were preparing to disembark. Neither Wilhelm nor I said anything. One by one, we climbed back down the rope ladder to the rowboat. It was a relief to set out back to shore, to get away from that ghostly vessel. It was lovely to round the rocky promontory and see the cold white monastery on the dark water of the bay and the pink villa, framed by black cypresses, on its pine-clad hill.

S I X

W hat operation?" Wilhelm finally asked Ann when we were back at the villa in front of the *bombola* again with our glasses of ouzo.

"I'm so glad you finally asked," Ann replied.

What she proposed to do, she told Wilhelm, was to organize a revolution within the family company. She told Wilhelm she wanted him to help her do this. She was already gathering to her side loyalists within the House of Albrecht among the blue-collar workers and clerical staff. She wanted to start an insurrection among the employees. Her plan was to take several Albrecht factories by force and, if this didn't work, to lead a companywide strike, with the possible use of further violence to achieve her ends, so that she and Ivan could take control of the company. Wilhelm was impressed by the sheer scope of Ann's daring proposal. He continued, also, to be moved by her. He was vulnerable to her beauty and to her unhappiness. He loved her, but he was reluctant to put himself on the line. His father had greatly assisted the Albrechts to become very swiftly among the most powerful people in the world, and he had been summarily fired by Gretchen Albrecht when she could no longer see any advantage to keeping him at her side. Wilhelm did not want to duplicate with Ann the relationship that existed between his father and Gretchen Albrecht, and I, for one, could perfectly well see his point, although I kept this observation to myself. Furthermore, Wilhelm had no desire to enter the business world. He wanted to get away from all that. He intended to pursue his career as an officer in the Brigade of Gurkhas. He told Ann as we sat close together before the blue flames of the open gas fire that he had no intention of seeking a future in finance or industry.

"That's not what I'm asking you to do," she told him.

"Well, then, what on earth do you want?" Wilhelm wondered out loud.

"I want you to help us take over the House of Albrecht by force," she said. "You're the only person in the world I can count on to help me do it. I can't trust anyone else. Not the same way."

It is true that Wilhelm was a person of uncommon loyalty.

"How preposterous," he said. "I can't believe you think you can get away with anything like that." The very idea, unimaginable though it was, immediately excited him. She called him to adventure at once. "How on earth do you think you can possibly take over an enormous company by force?

Do you know how many factories and subsidiaries there are in the House of Albrecht? Three hundred easily, and more, if you count that new mining house they've just acquired, the Compagnie Belgique et des Etrangères. Or was it the other way round? Nowadays it's rather hard to tell who buys whom, isn't it? Anyway it can't be done. It's a worldwide empire. It's spread all across the bloody globe."

Ann grinned whitely, hands in the pockets of her red velvet slacks. She always did something to add a dash of glamour to her otherwise unadorned beauty. Tonight she wore scarlet slacks, a pair of gold sequined slippers, a white cashmere V-neck sweater, and a St. Christopher medal that Wilhelm had given her when he was thirteen, which hung from a thin platinum chain. She said:

"I'm sure it can be done, Wilhelm. I haven't figured out the logistics, but that's your department."

"I can't afford to do anything of the sort," he said.

"You don't have to pout about it, pussycat, I'm only asking. You are a military man, are you not?" Ann said.

"Whose idea is this?"

"Not too many people know all the details," she said. She nodded in my direction. "He knows about it. Ivan is in on it, of course, but only in a general way. It was my idea all along to ask you. I've just been waiting for the right time."

Wilhelm looked somewhat stricken. Ann always went too far. I could see that he was crestfallen. He'd let himself get too involved with Ann. She confirmed his suspicion that fundamentally you couldn't trust the rich because all they do is use people for their own selfish ends.

"First of all I'd have to quit the regiment, get out of the army altogether to do it," he told her in the somewhat labored, patient tone of voice he used to explain things. "Then we would have to organize an army, gather arms and ammunition, and on a far larger scale than anything you appear to have assembled thus far. Frankly I still don't quite see what it would accomplish. We'd be outnumbered and outmaneuvered even with our secret army. This does sound like one of Ivan's more madcap schemes, I must say, although it has the virtue of being less single-handed," Wilhelm said pointedly. It was the only reference I had ever heard him make in the presence of Ann to the murder of her father. She ignored it.

"Ivan dreams," Ann admitted. "He'd like to do something to get back at the duchess. You know what she did? She cut him off without a nickel when he ran away with Amber. He doesn't have a red cent to his name. He's off the board. Lansing supports him. Of course he'd like to get back at her, but he can't even rob a house without getting caught. That's why I need your help. Just to get a jump on crazy Ivan."

"Supposing we should succeed. What then?" Wilhelm wanted to know.

"We're going to destroy Gretchen's power base. Force her out. We can't do it by vote because she's had Ivan declared mentally unfit, and she's had him legally removed from the Sylvania board."

Wilhelm understood the intricacies of all this as well as anybody who was intimately connected with the House of Albrecht because his father had created the system. No two companies are ever exactly alike in the way they are constituted; this particular holding company Teddy Beresford had set up so that the Albrecht family could maintain control over the conglomerate once it had gone public. Gretchen and Henry Albrecht had each possessed a single vote. They had held, in addition, one proxy vote for each of the twins, whom Henry Albrecht had adopted. On his death, Gretchen had secretly assumed the Albrecht chair and thus held an extra vote. Even with Lansing Noble's vote in hand, Ann and Ivan still lacked the necessary power to oust Gretchen Albrecht as chairman.

"Once we've forced her resignation we can reorganize," Ann said. "So that even if she hangs on to her Albrecht stock, we can keep her from getting back on the board."

"You'd have a bloody mess on your hands," Wilhelm said. "Who'd run the company? You need managers. You need a chief executive. Someone like Teddy. He'd adore to be asked, of course. You could ask him. He might help you. I could never do it. It's completely beyond the range of my capabilities," he said. "But then I gather you just want me to help you organize your strategy, or some such thing."

"I want you to recruit the men and train them and go with them to the points we've targeted to strike."

"What points?" Wilhelm asked her.

"Our factory in Turin is *numero uno*. We'll take it over. Then the one outside Munich."

"You won't be able to hold them with a mere handful of men," Wilhelm said.

Ann looked annoyed.

"Maybe we won't. We can cripple them, though. Anyway, you're the tactician, and I'm sure when the time comes that you'll know exactly how to play it."

She was determined to bring Wilhelm into the picture. Later, when we got back to Paris, Ann confessed to me that Ivan and Amber had been aboard the *Zephyr Echo* all along the day of our visit. She had taken us out there, she said, to show Wilhelm Ivan's setup, but she knew that Wilhelm would be put off if he had to spend any time in the company of the killer Ivan, and she'd warned Ivan to make himself scarce. Yet they needed Wilhelm to achieve success. Ann knew this. It was her contribution to Operation _Zephyr Echo_. Ivan was willing to let her bring him into the operation, he was game, because he only wanted his fair share of Albrecht money. He didn't care who ran things. Ann, however, wanted Wilhelm Beresford. She wanted to own him, to keep him, to love him, to order him around, to be advised by him, and to have him always there. She'd let him keep his wife, provided she could have him nearby always to do as she desired. She did not want him to be free of her, however, to come and go as he pleased, and she was coldly indifferent to his happiness outside the realm of her own desire. In that respect she was every inch the heiress, who, as a type, I have had occasion to observe, must own exclusively all that lies within her realm. Wilhelm's continued existence outside that realm was of importance to her only insofar as it held out the hope that once again he could be induced to come inside it and then be held captive there, for without him it was her conceit that she was incomplete. And why? Because although her husbands might come and go, only Wilhelm, her darling Wilhelm, could provide the warmth and happiness she needed to really shine.

Wilhelm decided to get out of it. He told me in Paris. He said:

"Tell Ann I won't do it. I can't see her again. The whole thing is off. I'm getting out of this bloody affair. I'd no idea she was all along planning to rope me into some conspiracy. It's madness," he said. "I'd be court-martialed for even considering it."

He knew this much: the Albrechts were always willing to sacrifice their own people. Gretchen was the worst, in that respect, but Ann appeared to be just as cold-blooded in her own way. They were brutal. So it was with great relief, I believe, that Wilhelm bade farewell at last to his love affair with Ann. He thought that in Nepal he'd be able to shake the addiction and finally elude Ann altogether. The intrigue he loved. Her sexual abandon also appealed to him. It was all the same dream of extravagance summoned up by the fire of the diamonds. He thought, however, that in the fastness of a remote military post he could barricade himself against Ann and the dream, the brilliant, underlying passion for adventure that she alone knew how to arouse. He was appalled to discover the depths to which he'd been lured by Ann's siren song. He'd joined the British army to achieve a high order of discipline and security. Now he'd found himself dragooned into betrayal and subterfuge. He awoke with a shock. When at last he heard that he had been assigned to the Gurkha cantonment in Nepal, he felt that he'd been saved from certain doom at zero hour.

Ann Albrecht was not going to let Wilhelm get very far away for very long. I knew she'd got him, had him, and wouldn't let him go. He couldn't escape her because she knew where to find him, how to exercise her power over him, even though he tried to get away. She found him in South Africa. He'd gone with Doreen and the children to stay at Windveld. He was en route to Nepal, where he would take up his duties as a captain at the recruiting depot in Dhahran. Ann and Lansing Noble had just flown in on Boxing Day, the day after Christmas, aboard *Nightrider II*, with Gretchen, for the big Arabian Nights party that the Albrechts threw every New Year's Eve at Craig Court, their mansion on the edge of the Transvaal. There was little time for Ann to lose, as she must have known, although how she could have guessed that Wilhelm was leaving for Hong Kong the next day is a mystery even to me, and I was, I must confess, the most reliable central listening post in the Albrecht network. Perhaps it was just good timing. Perhaps it was sixth sense. We'd flown down together. Ann did not call ahead to say that she was on her way over to Windveld because that would have given Wilhelm the opportunity to escape. Instead, she told the syce to saddle up her gelding and rode cross-country by herself, from Craig Court to Windveld.

I was not invited to accompany Ann to Windveld, and what follows is really a reconstruction of their encounter by both Ann and Wilhelm, and if I've taken the liberty of touching up the scene here and there with details from my own imagination, it's only because I can see it so clearly in my mind's eye.

Wilhelm was in the poolhouse at teatime with Doreen, his father, his mother, and the children. He was completely taken by surprise when Ann showed up. He looked at her as though she'd shot him. Teddy Beresford played host. Wilhelm couldn't even muster up the pluck to say hello. Beresford had come off the polo field an hour earlier, so he, too, wore riding breeches. He was full of his own brand of bonhomie with its heavy overlay of sarcasm. He was a big man, blue-eyed, with a natural glower. His Hussar's frame now supported a coat of excess flab, but he was never what you'd call out of shape. He was tanned and ruddy from his workout on the polo field. He loved to brag about the great players with whom he'd ridden, men like Porfirio Rubirosa and Tommy Hitchcock, and to his credit it must be added that in his younger years he had been a great player himself. While

Wilhelm hovered in the shadows of the poolhouse interior, sipped his tea, and felt all the anguish of desire rise within him, Teddy took the initiative with Ann, introducing her to Doreen. They'd never met.

"And Willy I know you haven't seen in many years," Teddy said, and coughed into his fist as he said it, for he liked nothing better than to ruffle the conscience of his too virtuous and easygoing son.

"Oh, Ann, how awfully good to see you," said Wilhelmina Beresford, and she prepared at once to pour their sudden visitor a cup of tea, with sugar and lemon. That's what Ann had always taken, and Whilhelmina had made it a matter of principle never to forget how the Albrechts liked their tea, for although they'd troubled her and given her many sleepless nights, Wilhelmina Beresford worked smoothly, always for the benefit of her husband and his role as corporate servant, and in any event she was a superb and conscientious hostess.

Ann took her cup and grinned, swiftly, back at Wilhelm in the shadows. Doreen was great with child, played the alabaster beauty queen from Belfast, extended her hand up to Ann from where she sat, and Ann shook it with her own firm, slender grip. She dominated any scene at once: that was the frightening thing, at least as far as Wilhelm Beresford was concerned. He felt that he was at her mercy altogether, trapped in the back of the poolhouse, with nowhere to go, no secret exit through which to flee, no escape hatch; so he sat, head down, and stole furtive glances at Ann, who continued to stand, cup in hand, at the mouth of the cave, in the brightness of the golden summer afternoon on the veld, as though at center stage.

"Mother's *awful* housekeeper, Mrs. Keith," he heard Ann

say in her slightly skirling voice, "and that's not the worst thing about it. Lansing is going hunting after all with Mrs. Drayton, so we're going to *India* next."

What was she doing to him? What was she doing this to him for? It was the single-minded intensity of her pursuit that he felt without being able to exactly comprehend the motive lurking behind that purposeful tracking, and it made him uneasy, despite his own longing for her, because he thought of her as blind; she had about her the uncanny, smiling brightness of one who is in pursuit of an inner vision.

She took a sip from her cup of tea, glanced Wilhelm's way, then dropped her eyes, none of it observed by anyone but Wilhelm. She was touched, gilded by the afternoon sun over the Transvaal, which gave her a light golden aura. No one saw the thing that passed between her and Wilhelm, from sun to shadow, not quite a look, even, so evanescent was it, her trace of a smile concealed by the cup of tea she held to her lips, an unresolved love thing. In the teatime bloom of summer it was the most fleeting exchange.

Two servants moved about the poolhouse with trays of sweetmeats and sliced tomato sandwiches while Wilhelmina directed them from her wheelchair. She wore a loose shimmering green Shantung top and pressed white linen slacks, severely elegant black hair. She was serene now after many years of her own particular torment. Beresford stood with Ann and glowered into his teacup as though in there he might divine his own future: he swirled it, held his pinkie crooked, and sipped the last drop. Doreen sat at an angle to Teddy's vacant chair, her feet up on a hassock, looking lush and radiant with what she called "this marvelously gross business of bearing little babies." She was too exuberant to be at all dampened by Wilhelm's gloom, tended anyhow to belittle his dark moods as somehow unimportant in the larger, glorious scheme of getting on with things in life.

How long did he sit frozen thus in the wicker chair? How long did time freeze while Ann stood and chatted with his parents and his wife? He pretended to be occupied stroking the head of the Great Dane mastiff, which they'd acquired to keep the askari company on his nightly rounds and which Wilhelm had christened Rosencrantz, only to have his father thereupon refer to the dog as Guildenstern just to fan the embers; and the joke would never end, he knew, even after Rosencrantz had died, years hence, and gone to dog heaven.

"I daresay Willy wouldn't object to escorting you up to the stable," he heard his father say, and there was hardly any excuse he could rustle up to countermand that veiled order. In rank, in seniority, in every way the elder Beresford commanded his domain, and Wilhelm had never been able to find the appropriately graceful means to elude the very watchful, calculated form his father's oppressiveness took; so with heavy, pounding heart, he rose to escort Ann back to her mount. No way to get out of this one. He didn't look at her as they walked side by side up the steep lawn. The sun was lower now. He would not walk her all the way. They did not touch. His knees felt like weights as he took his measured steps.

She stood, Ann, at the top of the lawn to face him. She was almost his height when she stood this way, slightly above him on the lawn. Down below, in the distance, the others were making their slow progress across the lawn to the house, to bathe and dress for cocktails and dinner. So they had a moment, up there, by the hedge.

"Come to the ball," she said. "Please do that one thing. I must see you."

"I can't." Confronted this way by Ann, he could say very little. Instead he gently took her shoulders, intending to give a benign, school principal's speech about love and duty, but instead he kissed her. He held her to him and kissed her deeply. Somewhere, beneath her blouse, beneath her tender, soft breast, a faster heart than his was beating. He could feel his passionate sex press upward against her thighs.

"Look," he said. He held her now at arm's length. He looked into her eyes. "I want only to try to make some sort of go of my life at present. I can't take any risks. I mustn't."

She smiled.

His memory afterward was of her standing there pale, golden-haired, against the yew hedge in the late-afternoon shadow. She said nothing. She looked at him, her face lit up with radiant joy, then left him, with her darkling smile, a tentative wave. He watched her stride swiftly away through the bright sunlit flower garden of hollyhocks and foxgloves, of pinks and blues, through to where the stable was.

Just a quick word about Craig Court: this was a Regency-style mansion that might have been lifted right off the Long Island Gold Coast of the nineteen twenties and set down on the South African veld. It was rather obvious in the same way those houses were before they'd had a chance to age: no trees to grace them, they looked too crudely newborn. Yet it wasn't ugly. Mrs. Stoddard had done extensive work on the house to bring it up to Albrecht standards. She'd put striped awnings over all the terraces and introduced terra-cotta pots of gardenia trees to stand sentinel by the glass French doors into the living room. She'd persuaded the maharajah of Jaipur to obtain for her a copy of the little marble elephant that stood

at the entrance of the Rambagh palace to place at the front
steps that led from the porte cochere up to the entrance foyer,
which she'd done in simple black-and-white-checkered marble, and she had put down a deep green velvet pile carpet in
the living room as an extension of the lawn, just as she had
done at Cavemoor. The marvelous thing about this pile of
masonry, which had been erected to shelter the first Skene
baronet, was the skylit atrium. Stoddard had transformed this
strange inner court into an arboretum, filled it with tropical
plants, and fixed it up so that its sunken marble floor could
be used for the dances the Albrechts always gave when they
descended out of the summer sky.

The South African international set loved and hated the
piratical Albrechts. They hated them because they had swept
onto the scene and taken precedence over the other outland-
ers. This might have been acceptable by itself, but unlike
those other lords of the Rand, the Albrechts never saw any
need to actually live there. They weren't doomed to an existence in the faraway antipodal provinces, a life of exile lived
out in splendid aridity under the rule of Dutch Reformed
churchmen whom they despised and ridiculed. The Albrechts took what they wanted out of the ground, and they
came and went as they pleased, flying in aboard _Nightrider II_
with a jetload of partygoers, and threw a series of dinners and
luncheons and dances during their brief visits to which an
invitation was as good as a command. Members of the local
plutocracy loved the Albrechts for their parties. They loved
to show off their finery and to hobnob with one another in
opulent surroundings, for although they feared the undercur-
rent of black rage that ran along the surface of the veld like
the tremors of some distant seismic warning, partygoing was
one of the few pastimes available to them. Art and theater

and other manifestations of the cultural life of Western civilization they had to seek out on their restless jaunts abroad. They lived for the excitement and romance of parties. They loved to put on jewelry and makeup, to gossip and flirt, to arrive in their bronze and silver vehicles dressed for an afternoon at Royal Ascot and be served cocktails in the soft summer wind off the veld, moving from immaculate lawn to impeccably brushed carpet as the white-suited black men in their scarlet sashes, worn crosswise from shoulder to belt, passed among them deferentially with silver Georgian salvers of hors d'oeuvres. Best of all, they loved the annual Albrecht New Year's ball.

Everyone came. The party began while it was still light. The atrium had been cleared of potted trees, and as the guests began to arrive, music from the twelve-piece orchestra that had been assembled at one end drifted to us out on the terrace, where one of several bars had been set up. Out in the pale evening Gretchen Albrecht greeted her guests. The terrace filled slowly with people. Hetty and Duncan Erroll were among the earliest to arrive. Hetty Erroll was a deep-throated elegant old war horse. She and Duncan, a golfer and an aristocratic Scot with a terrible temper, lived down on the coast of Natal between Port Elizabeth and Durban in a yellow villa overlooking the Indian Ocean. Duncan Erroll—one wants to call him Sir Duncan Erroll, yet for the most part, unlike the Chinese merchant princes of Hong Kong, these barons, lords of the Rand, went untitled. They were of a more maverick stripe, men who had made their fortunes and staked their claims in a bastard land, and even the titled nabobs were bastards. In his own way Teddy Beresford was the biggest bastard of them all. He arrived soon after to pay his obeisance to Gretchen. The Ricelys were there. He was

Meyer de Groot's lawyer, a red-haired, temperamental man who'd made his reputation as a legal genius of corporate finance. The terrace filled with color as the younger guests began to arrive in their Arabian Nights fantasy clothes. Alicia de Lavillade came on the arm of her father, as always. She was a flirtatious, unstable, buxom girl who always added a dash of excitement to a party because you never knew who would have the privilege of taking her home, for the old general never stayed at any soiree past his bedtime. The three Clives had arrived with twilight and stood chatting on different sides of the now packed verandah sipping champagne: Nigel number one, the young son of a duke who had been sent down from Cambridge and was in "Coventry" in Johannesburg, working for de Groot; Nigel number two, dressed as a Zouave this night, who with his dark brown eyes and slick, almost Spanish good looks was considered to be one of the most eligible bachelors in all South Africa because he had been given the job of ADC to Spencer Marx, the local movie baron, who was present with his angular, ravaged-looking wife and their two daughters; and Nigel number three, a sweet, somewhat crushed young financial management consultant whose wife had run off with his best friend. Odd people showed up in South Africa, and one of the oddest was Tommy Devlin, the ill-starred former husband of the duchess of A. He was still a striking-looking man as he sat, sleek and silver, on the brick retaining wall with Daria Sinclair, the sister of Nigel number three, who was now his official date, although she was at that time having an affair with Nigel number two. Sir Rupert Skene's six daughters were all there with their husbands, horsemen every one of them, polo players of the front rank. Meyer de Groot, the greatest Rand lord of them all, was now dying, yet even he insisted on being there, in his wheelchair, where he sat in his double-breasted tuxedo, in a pair of dark glasses with blue lenses, his knees covered by a laprobe, puffing on a black cigarette holder in between seizures of coughing. He was suffering from the advanced stages of emphysema.

Wilhelm had indeed intended by leaving for Hong Kong immediately after Christmastime to gracefully sidestep the Arabian Nights ball and thus avoid an encounter with Ann, but I am not altogether convinced, as he is, that had he stuck to his resolution things would have turned out differently. Who knows? He might once and for all have escaped into the redoubt of the Nepalese Terai, free forever from the lure of Albrecht wealth and the single-minded pursuit of Ann. After their brief meeting at Windveld, however, he couldn't bear to leave her behind without one final rendezvous. It was so easy to do. It wasn't like running off to Morocco or something. He easily found an excuse to stay over at Windveld until after the New Year. I don't know whether he'd been goaded into it at all by Teddy or whether it was his own idea, but I suspect he'd come to his decision all alone.

Nobody recognized him. He was the mystery guest. Nobody put two and two together because he'd already said good-bye, and supposedly he'd flown off to Honkers. He'd filched his mother's hair rinse and dyed his hair jet black, and he'd taken the added precaution of wearing a Lone Ranger mask with the silver caftan, which he'd bought in Marrakesh and never given to Doreen. I don't think it mattered in the slightest degree, really, whether anyone recognized Wilhelm or not. The mood at Craig Court was entirely liberated.

The music from the orchestra in the atrium made a terrible racket. By the time Wilhelm arrived, most of the guests over forty years of age were in there dancing up a storm to music from _Kismet_ and _The King and I._ The older crowd wore conventional evening attire, black tie and floor-length extravaganzas. The Arabian Nights motif was for the hotter, younger guests, the _jeunesse dorée_ of South Africa and twenty-five or thirty young New York and San Francisco jet-set friends of Ann and Lansing Noble, who introduced a note of immediacy that was entirely novel in that remote place, as though some miracle had occurred to bring the world of fashion and fun to this last outpost. I think this was the party at which certain drugs were introduced to the local social scene for the first time. Mrs. Stoddard had done the entire downstairs part of Craig Court as a Casbah, complete with Persian carpets and hundreds of bright silk pillows that she had imported by the gross from the Thai Silk Company in Bangkok. The lighting had been done by a local set designer who'd used different-colored gels of green and amber and rose and violet to create a psychedelic effect that cast everything in a slightly surreal light, so that wandering through the downstairs you could actually get lost, as you do in a Casbah even though you keep returning over and over to the same place, where you see the same people over and over again, without ever getting your bearings. This was a funhouse Casbah, maddened by the roar of guests who were abandoning themselves to the hallucinogenic light trip and the music piped live into every corner, and the running flow of liquor. There was the thrill of anonymity, too. I kept seeing people I'd met in other circumstances who looked strangely familiar disguised as caliphs and sultans and Salomes and grand viziers and pashas and slave girls and Bedouin sheikhs and whirling dervishes and Aladdins. The spirit of promiscuity ran rampant.

Ann was Scheherazade. She was dressed in pantaloons made of blue silk printed with little gold stars, and she wore gold slippers. She also wore a gold lamé halter and a see-through blouse that was designed to fit snugly just above her midriff, the sort of thing a belly dancer wears to expose her undulating pelvis when she performs. I was Sinbad. Ann and Wilhelm and I kept seeing each other throughout the night in varying shades of purple, green, red, and orange as we moved from one thronged room to another. They were together all evening. When the lights in the atrium had turned low and slowly stroboscopic, they could be seen in each other's arms moving to the rhythm of some Italian torch song, "Quando Quando," or "Una Lacrima Sul Viso," some sulfurous erotic prelude music like that, which permits almost stationary dancing. Then later they dallied in the seraglio, decorated by Mrs. Stoddard with billowed tenting of maroon-and-white-striped cotton and low divans, dimly lit by the rose glow of a glass lantern that hung by a silver chain from the ceiling. This was where Ann and Wilhelm brought in the New Year. I peeked in to see them there, reclining in a corner with a bottle of champagne in the cozy tent atmosphere. Other couples lay about on the divans, spooning. You wouldn't linger in that harem chamber very long without a companion. Then they disappeared altogether up the back stairs at Craig Court, where they had made their way to one of those marvelous rooms with a view out over the Transvaal. I like to think that it was perhaps to be closer to the starry heavens that Ann had asked me for the temporary use of my room for her night of love with Wilhelm. I never had the poor taste to ask her if that was so. Some things, I think, are better left to conjecture.

The thing that delighted Ann more than anything was that under his caftan Wilhelm wore nothing at all, had come indeed with the single-minded purpose of finding Ann to make

together a night of everlasting rapture. She loved to run her
hand up under the caftan while they spooned. She loved to
feel his hard-on pressing unrestrained against her as they
danced. They were oblivious to anyone who might have been
watching them. Once upstairs, what Wilhelm wanted to do
first was to hold Ann and kiss her and run his hands all over
her body and feel her body pressed to his, one with his, to
slake his thirst before he even began to satisfy his deepest
desire, before he could stand it no longer and slipped down
her pantaloons, gently unbuttoned her blouse, and before she
could undo her halter got down and began to eat out her hot,
moist vagina so that she stood, impatient, legs apart, and ran
her hands through his slick black hair until she began to feel
the onset of an orgasm in waves that ran up her belly and
made her legs weak while she began to swivel her hips as
indeed you have seen those belly dancers do in their erotic
climax faster and faster sitting now against the end of the bed
back on her elbows thighs wide moaning and then pulling his
hair, pulling it up, trying to get more of him inside her which
he tried to do still in his caftan getting his lips pressed against
the mouth of her mooncave while she pulled up her thighs
begging him to do something, do this do that.

He wanted to take her like that. He wanted to take her in
his robe. She, weak, lay back to let him do it. He looked
down, like a priest, not at her face, but with the devotional
humility of a slave, at the very act of sliding his stiff cock
between her legs and into her tight, deep sex, and then drew
her toward him so that with new strength brought on by the
indescribable sensation of having him in her all she wanted
was to clasp his buttocks with her legs and hold him deep
within her as she rose and fell on his poniard, now writhing
her body, smearing her hands on her breasts, turning her

head this way and that in the confusion of mounting heat as
he began to buck and then, positioning his feet wider apart
for better purchase so that he could hold his balance, draw
back and then thrust up, more difficult each time to do because she tried to hold him in her, clasp him to her, and at
the same time turned her waist to get the slick torpedo cyl-
inder of his ever-upthrust piston to spin ever upward pulling
back made her gasp, she gasped for sex. He loved this one
thing most (orchestral strains of "Baubles, Bangles, and
Beads" faintly drifted to them from the atrium below, the
soft velvet night air breathing on his bare buttocks in their
constant fluid movement back and forth): he loved precisely
the crystal sugar ecstasy along the barrel to the tip of cock he
felt exquisite pulling forth to never stop oblivion and this was
what he got from Ann. Glitter sex that made him pow pow.
There was nothing wrong with Ann. He liked to see her suck
her stomach in despite herself as he withdrew, then see her
arc her back to get him into her as far as he could go while he
withheld, and held her hips, and got to go, go to batter go,
but nice and long not short and gasp still fluid strokes. They
must go on. They must not come. She come, not he. He
hold, she start to cold water gasp. Then frantic pull him down
he climb right over on top they just like tiger lovers him slick
viscount engine piston back and forth, now lets her pull his
neck down up go her thighs she sucks his neck and holds
down his angel wings and presses him against her breasts
heaves them up and presses open mouth commingles tongues
slakes her thirst on his mouth wetness reaches down to hold
his buttocks in and pulls them wide to force him in to feel
his huge plum dick lodging in her thing, batter dull and short,
the middle place, so she can try to make him split to diamond
splinters, spew his sex milk come, her legs down now let her

hips levitate, gently kiss his ear and feel a thigh tickling thick hot pole between her legs, rub her thighs on warm pole to make her come go humming on, and slide her fingertips so lightly back and forth along the inner rim, push the button, make him gasp, "My God," his stomach muscles convulse quite without his wanting them to do so and pulling out he felt the scarlet rush and shot the moon and thrust again, pumped up inside her, saw her grinning diamonds, they rode the thing together to a wild second screaming come.

But one thing more. They left the light on. Ann liked to gaze upon her lover's body. She made him lie against the pillows with the bedside light on so she could watch him while she kissed him down his belly and reawakened his desire with her tongue (all within the gardenia scent the zephyrs carried to them off the lawn). It's one thing she liked to do. She liked to watch his body come alive with desire. She liked to feel his balls tighten in the palm of her hand when she gently tweezed them, and she liked to lick his dick while he lay there idly stroking her bare ass. He liked the way she put her mouth around the crown and made tight lips and nibbled gently with her front teeth. She liked to tongue the base of his crown and kiss his balls. It got him quite excited, quite attentive once again, so he moved aside one thigh, rolled from being on his side to lying on his back with one knee raised, legs spread apart, and arched his back enough so she could suck down his cock with her lips while her tongue caressed the crown and then more businesslike herself she got on her knees, pressed his upraised knee down, and really went to work to keep her slave enraptured—all kinds of things she'd like to do and felt she could do, getting on him, for instance, and feeling him within her or forcing her asshole onto the upstiff round slick orbus—but she liked the hot feel of it in her mouth and did the job at hand caressing his stiffened balls and sliding finger up divide and pushing anus banus button there to make his stomach once again convulse and pull her tightened mouth up now full of gluey glee juice what she wanted was to put all of Wilhelm in her mouth and swallow but instead he felt one hand upon his belly while she licked him down and felt her mouth around his tightened balls now, so he closed his eyes, lay back, and felt the coolness of the veld upon his slightly drying cock. This, precisely, was the moment Mrs. Drayton finally found them. That was *her* job. To track down animal screams. She was looking in on Ann, and who was that young man naked and erect upon the bed, with jet-black hair? Sitting arms spread, beatific face, hands upturned, eyes closed. It only took a moment to find out. She never would have guessed otherwise, but Ann looked up: they saw each other briefly but for an eternity there, the hunter and the tigress, alerted at play, Mrs. Drayton in the doorway, white-faced, stricken with the excitement of what she saw. She stood with her arms at her sides, eyes very wide, mouth tight. She wore a white, flounced skirt. She wore a black bodice. She wore a dog collar of pearls on her neck. The expensive Mrs. Drayton.

"Wilhelm," Ann said. "Quick, the light." She flapped her one free hand.

That was it. Lights out. Mrs. Drayton pulled the door shut softly as on two sleeping children.

Isn't that the oddest thing, she thought. I could have sworn he used to have blond hair.

Cantonment personnel were frankly amazed by the glorious figure that Captain Beresford cut. He seemed to grow in energy and vitality before their very eyes. He had enormous charm to start with and a splendid physique, good looks that were humanized by a touch of homeliness: the slightly bulbous nose, the small, merry eyes that twinkled, Wilhelmina's eyes, and the pumpkin grin that everybody loved. He was also very bright and a sober, dutiful officer who made himself available to the brigadier general for all kinds of work and also play. He was a good tennis player, a competent horseman, a bridge player. All these social assets were useful to the commanding officer of a cantonment, for the onerous chores he was called upon to perform of a social nature included the wining and dining of dignitaries who came down to Dhahran to avail themselves of the opportunities that the cantonment offered for rest and relaxation.

The cantonment was situated in the great Nepalese plain known as the Terai. It provided a peculiar, semitropical oasis of convenience in that impoverished mountain kingdom. It functioned as the British Gurkha command post in Nepal and as the recruiting depot for the Seventh and Tenth Gurkha regiments. In addition, the British operated a small but highly efficient hospital within this sanctuary; a farm resettlement project and courses in bricklaying and carpentry were provided within the compound for retiring Gurkha soldiers and officers; welfare and pensions were administered to retired Gurkhas and their dependents out of the cantonment; and it was a place of employment for about five hundred retired Gurkhas. The cantonment was contained within an area of about one and a half by two miles and protected from the outside world by a high metal fence topped off by lines of barbed wire tautly strung and canted slightly inward. It was built by the British between 1957 and 1960, the site having been chosen because it was near an Indian railhead. They'd brought elephants up from the railhead to clear the compound, and then they had put in the metaled road that ran between Biratnagar and Dhahran, through a forest of sal trees that bordered the south end of the cantonment and was said to be dangerous at night because predators, human and beast, lurked in the jungle.

The cantonment was the work of a qualified landscape architect, a National Service officer who happened to be stationed there at the time, so that it resembled a well-ordered suburban estate with ample parklands, one, perhaps, that had been converted into a private institution. In some ways it was like a private sanitorium. Indeed, the hospital dominated the cantonment. It was the only truly well-equipped medical unit in the entire kingdom of Nepal. The British ambassador regularly flew down to Dhahran for weekend sojourns, and other Englishmen who found themselves out there, members of Parliament, business people, made their way to the airport at Biratnagar by the Nepalese airline, RNAC, which had been dubbed by one cantonment wag "Rarely, Never, Also Chaos," and thence to Dhahran by the new road, either because they needed to make use of the up-to-date facilities there or simply to rest up from the exigencies of travel in the Third World (or, as another cantonment wag sometimes put it, the Turd World).

The single-storied bungalows that housed the offices and barracks, the officers' mess, and the residences of married personnel were set off from the neat lanes that wandered gently upward to the north end of the compound by hedges and tall trees and gardens. When he sat on the verandah of his bungalow, Wilhelm Beresford found himself gazing out at a scene that could have been an English country garden during an exceptionally fine summer afternoon: a vista of lawn, a park of tall trees that made a carpet of green shadows and bands of lighter, sunlit green; a dignified quiet prevailed within, pierced by chattering birds in the high treetops, while above him, the deep blue Nepal sky showed through the bowers of rain trees.

Wilhelm was the regimental trump card of the Tenth Gurkhas, and his lovely wife, Doreen, provided a stunning accompaniment. She possessed the all-around talent a beauty contestant must always have in this day and age to win a major national contest. Doreen, as queen of Ulster County, had achieved the semifinals of Miss United Kingdom before she was knocked out by an obscure festival princess from Lanark, Scotland. In some ways Doreen outshone her husband. She knew how to pattern her own handmade clothes after the designs of Mary Quant and Jean Muir. Consequently she was the best-dressed officer's wife in the cantonment. She played the harp. She cooked a marvelous soufflé when called upon to do so.

She and Wilhelm were clearly a contented couple, and one key to their success was generally understood to be the money that enabled them to spell one another. They got away from the stifling inbred life of the cantonment at regular intervals, and Wilhelm's highly polished royal-blue Lancia could be seen frequently barreling between Biratnagar and Dhahran, to and from the airport, where either he or Doreen might have been arriving from or departing for Hong Kong, Delhi, or Katmandu. And then it was also pointed out how clever Wilhelm was to have the old man come up and look after his wife and children while he was off trekking, or sowing his wild oats in Bombay, or gambling in Honkers. He managed to find excuses to get down to Hong Kong every two or three months, often on official business. Wilhelm was one of the officers in charge of the dispensation of pension funds, and four times a year he was called upon to trek into the foothills of the Himalayas to visit the villages of Gurkha tribesmen who had served as soldiers and officers and were now retired and receiving regular payments from the British army; it was part of Wilhelm's responsibility to look into the welfare of the ex-Gurkha soldiers, to take complaints, and generally to look after their needs even in retirement.

He met with Ann. He'd started seeing her once again as soon as he had settled comfortably into cantonment life and found some pretext for a visit to Jaipur, where Ann had gone to stay while Lansing Noble and Mrs. Drayton had gone off on a tiger hunt. She seized the chance at once to introduce him to the high-stakes social world to which the Albrechts had access in the East. They owned a flat in Hong Kong, a beach house in Bali, and a hotel suite in Bangkok, all of which were available to Wilhelm whenever he wanted to use them. The House of Albrecht, Wilhelm discovered, was available to him whenever he wanted to use it, regardless of whether Ann was around or not. She made this very clear to Wilhelm. He could use it exclusively, like a private club, for his own pleasure, whenever he wanted, so that whenever he felt the urgent need, the chance to snatch a few days here and there, he had the use of an Albrecht facility. This sudden discovery was a revelation that filled Wilhelm's soul with joy. He was quite astounded by the possibilities available to him. He and Ann were, of course, having an affair. He had to admit that his love affair with Ann was part of the arrangement. Yet even when she wasn't able to join him, he took the opportunity to make use of the Albrecht hospitality, flew down to Bali from Hong Kong for a long weekend or stopped off in Bangkok for a night or two en route to the Gurkha camp on Brunei, where he was sometimes called upon to go.

Wilhelm fulfilled his conjugal responsibilities with diligence, did his job as he was required, oversaw the welfare of the men for whose responsibility he was charged. Yet at all times now the dazzling thing, the real life, awaited him on those occasions when he could take leave of the cantonment and find himself in the embrace of beautiful Ann for an exquisite torchlit forty-eight hours of passion in Hong Kong, or Bangkok, or an extra five days of gratification in Bali at the Albrecht Water Palace. This pleasure house had been constructed by a local king out on a lake beneath Mount Agung on the edge of the Java Sea with one enormous room under a high-peaked roof. It was open on three sides to the sea breezes. I would sometimes meet Wilhelm here, and we would lounge around in sarongs and listen to the music of the gamelans, those gentle Balinese tympanic orchestras that sounded like nothing so much as a breeze running through wind chimes, which you hear no matter where you are on Bali.

Wilhelm and I were both by now addicted to sexual pleasure, and it was almost impossible not to submit to the coconut-oil massages supplied by local Balinese girls as we lay on the verandah under the eaves of the floating palace. And then there were the French and Australian girls who came up from Sanur Beach with Bobby Song, the Albrecht factotum who co-owned the Water Palace (for legal reasons, because on Bali property had to be owned by Indonesians). The foreign girls Bobby Song brought up there were avid to experiment with drugs. We all ate magic mushroom omelettes one evening, and then, loaded with psilocybin till our eyes were racing out of their sockets, we wandered naked by the Java Sea, swam in the phosphorescent waters under the impression that Balinese magic had transmogrified us into Black Sea crocodiles. Shimmering and gleaming in the blue moonlight, we had a crocodile orgy on the black volcanic sands.

"The crocodile orgasm lasts at least a hundred years," Wilhelm cried out from the water's edge over the passionate operatic sighs of his crocodile mate, with whom he was flailing and flapping on the moonlit shore. The sex, it's true, seemed never-ending at the time. Later, in the cool predawn, as we came off the steep slopes of hallucination, we shed our reptile skins and, naked, climbed a hill above the Water

Palace to watch the blood-orange sun slowly burst upon the world in all its glory. How could we ever have guessed on the beach at Fishers Island that one day we would be reborn, whole, from crocodiles, on the slopes of Mount Agung?

Wilhelm possessed an enormous capacity for the life of the abundantly rich, and by his very hedonistic, joyful, glad, sun-dwelling nature, he was suited to enjoy the extravagant possibilities of the very rich life. He loved fine clothes, he loved having servants, he loved flying around on private planes. He loved gold. On Bali, he always wore at least one gold chain with a gold coin that glinted on his tanned, oiled chest. He was, with respect to jewelry and clothes, a willing idiot. Once you have known all these pleasures of the rich, once you have in your youth experienced the intoxication of great wealth, as Wilhelm had, the ease and command of it, the utter ongoing fun of it, the grandeur of swank, you don't lose a taste for it. You do not fit happily back into a less exalted way of life. It had taken Wilhelm great effort and discipline to do this. He had chosen a way of life, one deliberately suited to a more severe, shadowed disposition than his own, as a necessary antidote to the man he might otherwise have become. Yet the other Wilhelm was there. Ann knew this. She knew her man. He was the one who'd got away. Gretchen had permitted this to happen. It had been so stupid of her. This was what Ann had always thought, and she'd never quite forgiven her mother for expelling Beresford, even though she understood that her mother had expelled the freebooting South African British privateer because she saw him quickly gaining too much wealth and power. Wilhelm was the golden prize. He was the magic treasure, the golden prince who'd come and gone across the Albrecht frontier as he pleased. Now at last she was getting him back. He'd been recaptured by Ann.

She had dazzled him, confused him now with sunlight and the disorder of freedom and her own passion.

Wilhelm moved, through the Albrechts, in a rather exalted circle of people in Hong Kong, India, and Malaysia. In some cases the Albrecht circle overlapped with the regimental life. In Hong Kong, through Ann, he met the Chinese merchant princes, the titled British taipans, and the Portuguese gold-trading aristocracy, all, like the Albrechts, great pirate families made respectable through commerce, on the whole a chic crowd of racing people. He saw them on Bali. They were in and out down there. Ann also knew the princely Indians. In Bangkok the Albrecht cicerone was Bobby Song, who was often there, when he wasn't on Bali, and who knew the same Hong Kong people. Whom else did Wilhelm see? He saw Lansing Noble. They never spoke about Wilhelm's love affair with Ann. They got along quite well.

"The two Gurkha volunteers worked out," Lansing Noble told Wilhelm. "There wasn't any problem. The papers came through without any hitch."

"Where are they now?" Wilhelm wanted to know.

"Ivan's got them on Corfu," Lansing replied. "He moves them around. He wants a couple more of them, at least, maybe more. Can you help us set it up? I'd like to go up and do the recruiting myself, but you'll get the commission. We'll work on it together. Same deal. Fifteen percent."

"You needn't." Wilhelm reddened. Actually, he needed the money badly. The expense of running with the Albrechts was taking its toll on his exchequer. He was in debt. He had considerable gambling debts outstanding in Hong Kong and Bangkok.

"Why not?" Lansing wanted to know. "Let me advance you the percentage to a Swiss account. Nobody's going to know. It's no sweat off my back. You can use it as playboy money if you want."

The very expression for some reason enraged Wilhelm. It was the presumption of it. He resented the implication and perhaps even feared that the playboy in him had gotten the upper hand. Yet he quite agreed. Why not? He raised his eyebrows. After all, I'm fucking your wife.

"Why not?" he said.

It was not really all that hard to arrange. Wilhelm's task would be simple enough. He had to organize a trek and take Lansing up to the Gurkha villages, where he would select the men he deemed suitable for Ivan's needs, such as they might be. Wilhelm understood that they'd be used in the campaign to take over the House of Albrecht that Ann had tried to rope him in on, but that was none of his affair. He'd already helped them once by sending them two failed recruits. He welcomed the prospect of organizing a trek for Lansing Noble, so that for once he could demonstrate that as a British officer, he, too, had an empire. He looked forward to dispensing a little patronage of his own. The only other thing he'd have to do was some paperwork, and then he'd have to make sure their expedition coincided with the timing of one of his own seasonal treks.

Wilhelm rode down in the late afternoon from the transit center to the great house where the Noble party was staying, and as his Gurkha driver steered the Land Rover up the gravel driveway to the Palladian entrance, he was shocked to see Ann Albrecht out on the lawn playing in the sunlight with her whippets. What was she doing here? No one had told him that she would be coming along on the trek; he'd expected to leave in the morning alone with Lansing Noble and two bearers at the very most. Now here was Ann. She came toward him in her blue velvet slacks and a pink sweater that was decorated with many tiny pearls. She was quick to defuse the panic that rose within him. She looked at him from under the visor she made with her hand against the glare of the afternoon sun that shot down through the tall trees rising darkly behind the eastern wing of the house.

"Hi, Wilhelm," she said. "I couldn't resist coming along just for the exercise. It gets so goddamned cold here, though, after four o'clock. Is it like this everywhere in Nepal?"

Wilhelm grinned. He had to. "I daresay," he replied.

It was true, the days in Katmandu were often radiant with the warmth of sun, and then at night, even now, in early November, the air got cold, and inside the dimness of Nepalese-lit interiors it was difficult to find any warmth at all, even in this palace.

She took him up the wide front steps, arm in arm. The next thing he realized was that the Nobles had brought along their own servants. Lansing Noble's Filipino valet, Orfeo, was waiting for them in the entrance hall in his white jacket. This made Wilhelm uneasy right away. Ann told Orfeo to take the dogs out to the palace courtyard and feed them. Then she informed Wilhelm that they had chartered a plane in Bangkok for a month because in case they needed it in Pokhara, where they had rented a chalet, they could always have it there to fly them down to Katmandu or even send it down to Thailand for supplies.

"You know?" she said to Wilhelm. "Maybe we'll run out of mangoes." They were standing in the half-light of the hallway. The sun fell on the carpet like lamplight. Ann stood very close to him and said in a conspiratorial tone of voice, "It makes me nervous not to have a getaway plane."

"I've missed you," Wilhelm said. "Very much."

"I kind of missed you, too," Ann said.

Lansing Noble and I were in the library taking tea. It came as something of a shock to Wilhelm when he discovered that

I was present. He'd somehow not expected to find me there. He told me later that he'd never thought I'd ever do anything so energetic as to make a two-week expedition into the foothills of the Himalayas on foot. I explained that it was a great society-page story, which to his horror he'd come to realize was true.

We were in the nineteenth-century Balkans. That was how it felt to be in this palace in Katmandu. There was, in this room, which was already deep enough in gloom so that table lamps had been turned on, a character of something more than mere ancien régime. It was *ancien* Transylvania. It was a drafty, damp room that smelled faintly of mildew, of rotting library books. Gray light from the palace courtyard came to us through the antiquated, uneven glass panes. The furniture was all the same heavy Victorian darkwood stuff, rather like the upholstered couches at Cavemoor, only dowdier, perhaps because it was tasseled and less grandiose, and it had probably all been ordered at the time from some London department-store catalog. Full-length portraits of the men of this princely family hung from the walls between the window casements. They looked like movie poster matinee idols of Ramon Novarro vintage in full military regalia with mustachios and heavy-lidded eyes.

Our host rose to greet Wilhelm; his wife, a plump gray-haired woman in an Indian sari of black-bordered gold silk, came forward also. Lansing, as usual, was standing where a fire would have been raging had there been a fireplace at all. He wore a green tweed jacket, cavalry twill trousers, and a tattersall vest. He introduced Wilhelm to his friend Damian, a guitarist from Singapore. Damian wore a jacket, a polo shirt, blue jeans, and loafers and spoke articulate English. He was a Malaysian. Wilhelm mistook him for one of our host's sons.

He only discovered Damian's connection to the Nobles when Ann and I gave him a tour of the upper stories after he'd taken a ritual cup of tea with our hosts.

Ann wanted to show him the layout. The palace was built around a quadrangle in which much of the domestic activity of the household took place: the washing and drying of clothes, the care and feeding of pets, and the peeling of vegetables. Lansing Noble had taken over the ground floor of the western wing of the palace; Ann had taken over the top floor of the western wing; I was occupying a room on the eastern side of the house on the second floor. Ann occupied a suite of rooms from which she could look out over the palace grounds onto a walled-in vegetable garden and beyond that to an uncut field of high grass that ended at a brake of eucalyptus trees. She slept in a great double bed under a musty, tattered fringed canopy that had faded out to a pale lavender hue, although it had been the color of lilac once or a deeper plum red. She took us back to show us where her personal maid, Esperanza, was staying. Then she showed Wilhelm the door that opened onto the back stairs. Here we could look south through a window above the landing to the Monkey Temple towers, which shone dully in the late-day sun across a ravine, and southeast to the shadowed, terraced low hills that ring the city of Katmandu, and behind them, suspended like floating icebergs in the sky, the rose-tinted peaks of the Himalayas. The stairs descended two floors to Lansing Noble's quarters. Ann did not take us down there. Instead, we stood at the top of the staircase and peered down into the shadows of the stairwell. Ann said she was afraid of the bats down there.

"He sleeps down there with Damian," she told Wilhelm.

"Damian?" Wilhelm asked her. He looked taken aback.

"He's the boy with the Afro you met downstairs in the library," Ann said.

"Oh, that chap," Wilhelm said.

"The very one," Ann said. She grinned fiercely at him. "He's a hippie drug-addict musician from Singapore. Lansing met him one night on Bugis Street. That's where all the transvestites hang out. He's quite sweet. He's coming with us to Pokhara tomorrow. He goes everywhere with Lansing," she told him. "Lansing tells everyone that he's his private secretary, which is quite divine, you've got to admit. They put a bed in Lansing's dressing room for Damian, but he gets scared at night, which isn't too hard to do in this place even after three or four Seconals. So he only pretends to sleep in the one they made up for him next door. He sleeps on a couch in Lansing's room with his teddy bear."

Wilhelm stayed with Ann. That's the way it was. He was supposed to go back up to the transit center that night, but he never did. He didn't have the will to do it. Our hosts prevailed on him to stay for an elaborate feast that lasted well into the early-morning hours and entailed the discreet sniffing of cocaine, which Lansing Noble produced from a snuff box he carried in his tattersall vest, not to mention the imbibing of champagne and Scotch and four-star brandy. Our host wouldn't dream of letting Wilhelm go back to the transit center so late at night, on the very eve of our departure for Pokhara and the trek from there up into the foothills. I persuaded him to accept their offer of a room down the hall from my quarters, from which, thanks to Ann's guided tour, he was able to make his way up the back stairs to her room without even awakening her maid. He didn't care, though. He was quite high. He didn't care what anybody knew at that point. But it felt strange to him to sleep on that canopied bed, between cold sheets, on a horsehair mattress, making love to Ann. He would have felt more snug in his bed at the transit center. Yet there was something compelling about the mood in that palace. It cast a sort of spell, like the magic mushrooms we had eaten together on Bali. Wilhelm felt as though he were back at Cavemoor. Or so he told me. Back in that guest room on the second floor.

Dully, dimly, however, Wilhelm was not altogether
satisfied with the arrangements that had been made, without
his approval, for this expedition, by Ann and Lansing Noble
with the assistance of our princely host. His own expectation
had been that he would take full charge of the trek once
Lansing Noble got to Katmandu. He'd intended to organize
the trip to Pokhara, to find accommodations there, to arrange
the hiring of porters and a guide. He had planned to use
equipment from the warehouse at the brigade depot in
Pokhara for their trek. He had agreed to give Lansing all the
help he needed, had cabled Lansing once he'd returned to Nepal from Hong Kong to say he was all set; he couldn't wait to

help him, couldn't wait to do his part, to play the role of host, and he'd timed his meeting in Katmandu with Lansing to coincide with his own trek in the foothills in November to visit local tribesmen and to make a reconaissance of Gurkha rejects, from whom he intended to select a small number, four or five, for Operation _Zephyr Echo_.

He had not, however, made arrangements for such a large party. He'd expected this to be at most a group of seven men, counting the porters. Instead, Lansing had arrived by chartered plane in Katmandu with Ann, myself, Damian, Orfeo, Esperanza, a Chinese cook named Mr. Lau, four whippets, two standard poodles called Whisper and Truffles, who traveled everywhere with Lansing Noble, and thirty-seven pieces of luggage, so that three automobiles and a small van were required to ferry us from the airport at Katmandu to the palace of our princely host. It further developed that Lansing Noble had made a previous trek to Annapurna Base Camp, knew the ropes, and was far better equipped for a trek than the British army. The Nobles had flown in futons, tents, cooking utensils, a battery-operated electric range, a portable refrigerator, and a full set of heirloom silver in a case made of Honduras mahogany, which they customarily took with them wherever they traveled together. They had also imported gaspowered reading lamps, canvas chairs, portable heaters, and inflatable rubber bathtubs.

The size of the trekking party required the use of a number of porters that would have far exceeded what Wilhelm was prepared to provide through the brigade. Our princely host, unbeknownst to Wilhelm, at his own expense had already supplied bearers from his staff of servants who had often acted as porters on Himalayan expeditions. He had donated his own majordomo to supervise the household of the Nobles' chalet in Pokhara. For convenience of transport alone to the point of the trek's origin, it was obviously far more sensible to fly everyone up in the prop jet, which Ann had christened the *Bouncing Bunny*, than to make an arduous overland expedition in a fleet of hired cars.

Wilhelm had to concede that Ann and Lansing Noble were hardly in any need of his assistance or direction when it came to outfitting themselves for this trek; he was forced to admit, furthermore, that they needed no advice from him when it came to organizing the daily route they would take. They had already studied a map of the area through which he had been intending to take them, and they had employed the services of Mr. Joshi, a professional guide whom Lansing had found through the Explorer's Club in New York. They had rented the lakeside villa in Pokhara through an agency in Hong Kong. They had brought along their own cook. So you see Wilhelm found himself immediately absorbed by this enterprise and en route to Pokhara without any clearly defined authority. In status, he was afloat somewhere between a guest and an exalted servant, like almost everyone else on board the *Bouncing Bunny*, myself included, for after all, I was the court photographer.

He had no authority. Accustomed though he was to the business of soldiering and to the command of Gurkha enlisted men, in this party Wilhelm's right even to order the servants around was severely curtailed, for these men were employed by our princely host and answered to the majordomo, who had been loaned to the Nobles for the duration of our trek. When we reached Pokhara, Wilhelm decided that it would be better for him to avoid the depot there, even though the officer in command expected to see him on his way through. He didn't want to have to explain things. He asked Mr. Joshi to go up there on his behalf to tell them that he'd be stopping in on his way out of the foothills, instead.

There was something pleasant, he found, about his truancy. He enjoyed the enforced idleness of it. He was being brought along as a recruiting officer. That was how he saw it. That was his task. No one told him so, but clearly, apart from his social role as Ann's playmate, it was the only job available to him. That was something he could perform only when we got up to the villages where the potential recruits lived; so, while we lingered in Pokhara over the final preparations for our trek, Wilhelm did the sensible thing: he relaxed and enjoyed himself with the Noble Albrechts, as they were sometimes called, down by the lake.

Ⅰt was Lansing Noble's concern for Damian's comfort and well-being that delayed the departure of our caravan from Pokhara, for Damian developed some form of dysentery, imaginary or real, and Lansing Noble refused to budge until Damian felt well enough to travel. This meant waiting around down at the chalet. Wilhelm and Ann spent part of every day boating on the lake, and often in the afternoon they conspired to meet in Ann's room for a siesta of love play, while downstairs Lansing Noble ministered in the dark to Damian's needs by bringing him herbal teas prepared by Mr. Lau.

Nothing was too good for Damian as far as Lansing Noble

was concerned. He treated Damian with the kindness and consideration he might have given to a treasured only son, although the very nature of his attentiveness was of the sort more often bestowed on a cherished concubine, for he liked to keep Damian in the utmost comfort. All our living arrangements were determined by the needs of Damian, who though lean and wiry was of a somewhat fragile disposition and inclined to come down with ailments. He always had to sleep on the ground floor, because it was his belief that the air was better on the ground floor and because a ground floor was apt to be darker than the upper stories, and adequate sleep, of all natural activities, was uppermost in the catalog of creature comforts that Damian required. He became emotionally unstable unless he could sleep for ten hours every night in a slumber mask.

Ann called him "the monkey." He had an Adam's apple of some prominence that moved up and down when he sang. He had a crisp crown of black, curly hair, protuberant eyes, heavy-lidded, beneath arched and spidery-looking black eyebrows, a finely articulated nose, and a space between his slightly buck teeth. He had a way of dancing when he walked that enabled him to carry on several conversations at one time, his dark eyes, with pupils dilated from drugs, sparkling and wickedly animated. Lansing Noble dressed him in freshly stone-washed blue jeans every day and Indian cotton shirts and Italian loafers without socks, and kept him in silver bangles.

"But as for what they do in the privacy of their downstairs room, it's a mystery to me." That's what Ann said to Wilhelm, who wondered what Lansing Noble was up to, for there was nothing in the comportment of Lansing Noble to suggest that he was anything other than a statue that could walk. Did he like to wear lipstick in private? It was possible to imagine him with lipstick that had been applied by some impudent street urchin. Damian only rolled his eyes at any such speculation. He called Lansing "my best friend." Whatever his sexual inclination may have been—and he made it a point never to address the subject—Lansing Noble to his credit made no attempt to hide the affectionate care that he lavished upon Damian, the patient efforts to help him procure hashish at a hippie hangout in the village above the lake, his efforts to make sure that Mr. Lau cooked separate meals for Damian that would not trouble his digestion.

When, finally, our caravan began to thread its way up into the foothills along paths leading up peat-covered slopes and wound its way westward on the narrow trails, it took less than a day for Damian to develop trouble in one of his legs that prevented him from being able to walk. His problem was a bad knee, which he'd twisted on a slippery upward path, because he'd insisted on wearing his Gucci loafers instead of proper walking shoes, and his foot turned sharply on the slippery instep when his loafer lodged in the mud. This delayed our party for half a day while Lansing Noble treated the swollen knee and bandaged it and arranged for a palanquin to be constructed so that Damian could be carried aloft by our porters, taking turns two at a time. Damian rode for the rest of the journey on a litter of pillows, which made him so happy that he serenaded us with pop ballads, which he crooned in a voice that was surprisingly deep and mellow, so that he sounded like Charles Trenet. He accompanied himself on the guitar. By night he stayed wrapped in blankets beside the heater in Lansing Noble's tent, where he was served by Lansing Noble with the special stir-fried vegetarian meals that Mr. Lau concocted for Damian in his wok. He used his elegant long shiny fingers to pick up items of food and, throwing his head back on his neck, would drop whatever vegetable morsel it happened to be into his rippling throat. He grinned at Lansing Noble when he sang, and winked. He claimed to have learned English by reciting the ballads of Bob Dylan. He always referred to himself in the third person, as Damian, and as we walked along the trekking path on our mountain journey, he sometimes tapped Wilhelm on the shoulder.

"Damian would adore a chocolate," he'd say, extending an elegant hand from his sedan chair, with its makeshift canopy of bright red cotton, and Wilhelm would oblige him with an oblong of the bitter chocolate he always carried with him on his treks.

Ann took the presence in our lives of Damian without skipping a beat. I never heard her criticize Lansing for keeping a catamite, or having a male Malaysian lover, if such he was, and none of us was prepared to say so for certain. She never expressed exasperation about the money Lansing Noble lavished on Damian or the time he devoted to Damian's comfort or the sleeping arrangment he seemed to have worked out with Damian, or Lansing Noble's patient, devoted attention to Damian's needs when the balladeer was under the weather. Of Damian I only heard her say, "He's Lansing's _copain_." That was how she saw him, evidently, although there was an implicit criticism of Lansing for having to find his _copain_ in a monkey and not in another human being, even though she, too, liked pets, and had insisted on bringing her whippets along on the trek, while Whisper and Truffles remained back at the chalet in the care of a servant. The whippets dashed ahead on the trail and confounded the donkey caravans of Tibetan merchants we encountered coming down from Lhasa, who had rarely if ever had the opportunity to lay eyes on this breed of Western racehound. The whippets were far more of a nuisance than Damian and had no real talent to entertain as he had, and they dashed around the camp in and out of the tents, urinating on the mattresses and rugs that the porters had laid out on the tent floors. Ann nevertheless compared them to Damian.

"They're high strung, like the monkey," she informed Wilhelm, who found her dogs especially annoying. They were racing around knocking over our plastic glasses of Chablis one day during a lunch stop. Then she flashed a grin at Wilhelm. "You're *my copain*," she said. It made him laugh.

In the daytime Wilhelm walked in the middle of the caravan by the side of Damian's litter or with Ann. It was her belief that he would be better camouflaged that way than if he walked up at the head of the progress with Mr. Joshi and Lansing Noble, who for all his solicitousness of Damian was not especially interested in keeping the singer company or even listening to his ongoing musical performance. Wilhelm strolled along with Ann and helped her by offering his arm when they had to climb especially precipitous hillsides or make an arduous descent down a steep green hillside, and he always sat with her at lunch and served her, much as Lansing Noble served his *copain*. It was the expected, gallant thing to do. We always stopped for an hour at eleven o'clock for tea and then again at two o'clock for lunch, and for the day altogether we came to rest sometime around five. Ten men working together were usually able to assemble the camp by nightfall, which came very suddenly in the foothills. We often ate at sundown so that we could retire early for a good night's sleep to the soft, Spanish-sounding serenade of Damian strumming his guitar in Lansing Noble's tent, wherein

Lansing Noble could be seen silhouetted by the inner glow, perusing the works of Sven Hedin or some other Western explorer of the Asian steppe with whom he might identify himself. Ann and Wilhelm always found their way to one another's arms once the lamps had dimmed.

We rose before dawn, drank tea in the cold mountain air, and walked at least an hour once we had performed our morning ablutions in the hour before sunrise. When our porters and other servants had caught up with us, we stopped along the trail to eat a hearty breakfast. We were a long, strung-out contingent on the trail, so that the sheer numerical size of our party was not readily apparent to other trekkers. Occasionally we passed a similarly, if less grandly, equipped trekking party. The mountain trails were busy indeed with sophisticated travelers, including a small, elite trek _gastronomique_, the bearers for which labored along under crates of gourmet food. Once, Wilhelm was spotted.

"I say! Beresford!" It was Trawick from Dhahran. Wilhelm had known that Trawick would be up and about on the trails. He had not expected to run across him because the Noble trek was due to end just as Trawick's was getting under way. Unfortunately, due to Damian's indisposition, we had left much later than planned. It was bad luck. He couldn't duck Trawick. The other officer made a wide-eyed appraisal of our retinue and the elaborate gear the porters carried on their bent backs.

"Isn't this rather four star?" Trawick asked him point-blank.

Captain Beresford was, occasionally, seen at the races in Hong Kong and even as far afield as Bali by fellow officers, but it never worked against him. There was after all a certain latitude in what the officers' unwritten code permitted one to

97

get away with, a prevailing spirit of live and let live. In the case of Beresford, who had a reputation for moving in rather swank company, a legend was already growing, and Trawick's wide-eyed question was really, I must say, more of a comment on what he gathered was Beresford's good luck than any kind of censure. Even so, Wilhelm was rather nervous. He looked around.

"I'm up here on a reconnaissance," I heard him explain patiently. Then he and Trawick went off for a discussion that must have lasted a good ten or fifteen minutes. Neither Ann nor I could make out even the gist of their confab from where we waited while the trekking party went slowly by, but it was evidently not a light, easygoing chat. Trawick was explaining something now to Wilhelm, and every so often, with a dim and rigid expression that I'd seen on his mother's face when she was under some duress, Wilhelm glanced in our direction, although I don't think he really saw us. He was taking in what Trawick was telling him. They then saluted one another and broke off the conversation, and Trawick started off down the trail in the direction he'd been trekking with a quick backward glance at us.

"Nothing important," Wilhelm said once he'd rejoined us. "Just setting the chap straight about our trek."

Still, it looked as though Trawick had been giving him some important piece of news, and Ann was worried enough about running into other Gurkha officers that she made Wilhelm lie low during lunch and stay close to her tent at Ulleri, the day before Wilhelm was scheduled to arrange for the recruiting of men. She didn't want anything to interfere with that. She made Wilhelm wear aviator sunglasses with mirror lenses.

The next day we met with a former Gurkha whose name

Wilhelm had found in a file at the cantonment of men who were deemed reliable and eager to serve as security officers in private service now that they were retired. We met in the house in which this man had been living ever since he'd retired from the brigade. He was, like all the former Gurkha soldiers whom Wilhelm visited in their mountain villages, extremely prosperous in comparison with his fellow tribesmen. He wore a pink crew-neck Shetland sweater and a Seiko watch. He owned land down below his house and spent his days drinking _raksi_, a local grain alcohol the excessive consumption of which had caused slush to appear in the corners of his eyes.

It was Wilhelm's task to drink with him and talk him into helping us recruit the young men we needed. By the time we had returned from our trek farther north, he had obtained a selection of eight young men, who were examined, not by Wilhelm, but by Lansing and Ann, who chose four of them, although not the four Wilhelm might have selected, because even though as physical specimens they were admirable looking, as material for soldiering they left something to be desired: one had rickets and was therefore of unsound health; another had flat feet. Wilhelm's job, then, turned out not to be that of a recruiting officer, but merely that of expediter, one who made the contacts and dealt in Gurkhali with the former soldier, who was finally induced to accompany the boys to Pokhara, separately, and instructed to wait there with them for the Noble party to arrive.

Our trek went well. We made a wide loop of it, from Korakomuk to Alse, from the Dorali Pass to Tulka and then to Landruk, where we descended to the Modi River and then mounted to Gandrung on the opposite hill, where we joined the Jomson Trail and trekked to Ulleri, thence to Ghorpani, and up to Poon Hill. We made our negotiations for recruits, by night, at the hut of the former Gurkha soldier who agreed to act as master sergeant and to accompany the four new boys back to Pokhara to await further orders. Wilhelm was in captivity without being aware of it. He let Ann feed him delicacies she had brought along on the trip. They sipped away at Aquavit at night in her tent. They read passages to one another from the *Arabian Nights*. They discreetly partook of hash brownies that Damian had thoughtfully brought along from Pokhara, and these gave their lovemaking an added euphoria in the exhilarating mountain air.

Damian sang to us by day as we descended along the mountain trail, sometimes beside leaping streams, through ferny groves, always within sight of the majestic white peaks of the Himalayas. No one who saw us would have divined the nature of our caravan or guessed that in our midst, striding along beside the sedan chair upon which was borne the gay young Malaysian minstrel, Wilhelm Beresford's wrists had been bound by invisible rope, that he was being force-marched to certain captivity at Pokhara, where he continued to believe he would bid a fond farewell to Ann and return to Dhahran, perhaps to meet with his childhood sweetheart sometime again in the future and perhaps not, for he had more pressing matters on his mind and was beginning to think that he should cut the affair off for all time, once this entire extravaganza had come to an end.

We pitched our camp on the return trip below a village called Trikhadhunga. We broke open the champagne by the Burungdi River. It was like a wide highland trout or salmon stream as it raced down the valley, leaping around the big white boulders that blocked its course. At night the moon came up full in the dark, moody sky and filled the valley with a cold light: the river ran black with silver-white rapids where it churned up against the blanched rocks. The sound of strong running river rushed past us all night long, accompanied by the chorus of crickets. In the morning we ate Tibetan bread and watched as the sun slowly forced the shadows of the mountains up the valley and illumined the riverbed with amber light.

The last night of our trek we walked down from Lumle toward a spectacular view of the mountains, gold and lavender in the contrasting glow of the fiery setting sun. Way below us we could see the Pokhara Valley and the bright sheen of Phewa Lake. We established ourselves for the night after dark in a field at the edge of a deep valley. Across the chasm, which plunged into vaulted darkness below us, the spectral mountains seemed uncannily close in the night. The bright snow made the ridges and slopes and what appeared to be mountainside trails in the slick glacial walls stand out with the clarity of an etching. We thought we could hear snow blowing up there in the night air, in the silence of the night.

Then the problem was how to get the men out of Nepal and where to take them. Wilhelm's idea had been to fly them down to Katmandu and have them registered there and provided with passports. This was the usual procedure. Once again he was overruled, this time by Mr. Joshi, who had already obtained passports for the recruits through contacts of his own. Suddenly Wilhelm hated everything about the situation in which he found himself: the overcast, humid, druggy atmosphere of Pokhara at the end of the trek, the lazy, disorganized manners of the Nobles, the flies, the food left about uneaten, the silly Damian, the smell of shit from the clogged toilets in the chalet. He wanted no more to do with any of them. He was enraged. Simply furious. He was disgusted. Beneath it all was the despair of deeper disquiet about Ann. The whole affair: the trek, her behavior, the way the enterprise was taken out of his hands, the oppressive smugness of Lansing Noble, which matched, somehow, the drugged Pokhara mood, finally got to him. He exploded when his instructions were disregarded by the even-tempered and insistent Mr. Joshi. He stormed out of the guide's office, and without so much as even saying good-bye to Ann or any of us, he made his way directly to Dhahran. Later, it was given out that he'd gone directly down to Bangkok and simply disappeared, but this was not the case.

The conversation between Wilhelm Beresford and Trawick, his fellow officer, took place on a nasty, wet, cold day up on the trail, where it was impossible to get warm even if you sat over a fire in some villager's thatched dwelling, for the houses of the Gurkha tribesmen were without chimneys, and the windows remained open at all times to allow the smoke to escape. So it was to begin with a demoralizing sort of day, and everyone was out of sorts, and then along came jolly Trawick.

His converation with Trawick left Wilhelm with an uneasy, empty sensation in the pit of his stomach. From Trawick he received his first intimation that all was not as he might have hoped it was down at the cantonment. To be more precise than that, Trawick, I should like to suggest in all innocence (though truth to tell Beresford had provoked enough envy in his fellow officers to inspire a certain amount of malice, and Trawick could indeed have been motivated by a certain indignation, I do not know), managed to inform Wilhelm that not only was his father presently paying a visit to Dhahran, but he was raising eyebrows by his affectionate familiarity with Wilhelm's wife, which was of a sort not considered altogether paternalistic. It was all inference. He said nothing specific that Wilhelm could challenge, but the implication was that the old man was plugging away at his daughter-in-law while Wilhelm was off on a trek, and it was not the first time this had happened. The whole thing had become something of a joke, obviously. It was Trawick's way of putting Wilhelm in his place for trying to shut him up.

Wilhelm had no way of knowing that I was the one who'd given the go-ahead to Teddy to go up to see Doreen. He had no idea that I was Teddy's man in all of this. He came to me about it to ask me what I thought he should do. He was quite concerned, he said, that Teddy was roosting in his nest: that was how he said it. I replied as smoothly as I knew how: "Quite honestly I've never heard anything more preposterous in my life." You see, Wilhelm thought perhaps he should leave the trek then and there to go back down to Pokhara and thence to Dhahran, and he was counting on my advice to help him decide what he should do. Had he left the trek at that point, it would have made our efforts far more difficult, would have put Teddy on the spot, of course, and could have blown the whole operation to pieces and lost us Wilhelm into the bargain; so I worked very hard to assuage his worries there and then. He wasn't happy after that, but I think he was really more at ease. The weather cleared, up there in the foothills, where, when the sun shines, the world is a different place: it's glorious, the hills look green, the mountain streams sparkle, the jagged peak of Machupuchere glistens white in the brilliant sun, and the air has a kind of zest, a mountain tang. In this reinvigorated atmosphere it was hard to brood on anything so improbable as one's wife's alleged adultery with one's father.

Wilhelm kept his apprehensions well under control. He mentioned nothing about them to dear Ann, who was not herself aware of this particular angle and if she had been would have found herself at a loss, temporarily, about how to handle the situation, probably because it would have seemed to her so boorish and stupid of Teddy Beresford to have been so concupiscent when he was already so greedy for money. She had never liked Beresford, considered him naught but a lowly butler or some such thing, at best a stupid Englishman who was too conceited to be trusted. I was able to tell her all about it, however, once Wilhelm had stalked off the scene down at Pokhara without saying good-bye, so that she was not too disturbed by his sudden angry departure. His rage was partly due to the tension of his anxiety as it had grown during the last days of our trek, bottled up within him as it was; the unbearable part of it to Wilhelm would have been the knowledge that everybody down at Dhahran knew about Teddy's cuckolding but him, that he was during all his time at the cantonment something of a joke, one perpetrated of all things by that bastard father of his. It gave him a quickened pace, a more agitated manner—a more preoccupied manner, I should say—as we descended from the foothills down to Pokhara. It would have made him most impatient with the obstinacies and idiocies of the Nobles and their entourage, for it's one thing to idle away one's days in the company of the very rich as though there would be no tomorrow, and he was quite capable of that, yet another thing to feel entrapped within that company, to chafe at the realization that one is really a captive, a prisoner of indifferent and powerful forces whose appearance of concern is something of a patronizing mockery at best and only accentuates the dilemma. For I have noticed one thing about the very rich, and that is while they may appear concerned about the sudden hardships of someone in their midst, they are actively hardening themselves, armoring themselves, I should say, against any uncomfortable feeling of guilt or sympathy that could possibly interrupt the ongoing fun and even-tempered high that being rich enables them to experience indefinitely, and Ann was no different from any of her rich ilk in that respect.

Actually, when I later informed her of the situation down in Pokhara when we got word from Mr. Joshi of Wilhelm's sudden departure, she was terribly titillated, I think would be the right word, quite excited by the news, which spiced up the anticlimax of our return to the chalet and the always trying matter of "what next?" Now the next act was under way, and everyone was keen to settle down to find out what was going to happen when Wilhelm got back to Dhahran. Initially Ann had planned to try to talk Wilhelm into flying directly down to Bangkok in the *Bouncing Bunny*, then maybe somehow getting him to come along to Corfu with the men, though like all somewhat lazy people I don't think she'd figured out a plan, exactly; I think she thought she owned Wilhelm by then and could borrow him from the queen whenever she wanted, even though there were occasions when he might find it rather hard to do that. Blackmail wasn't at all beyond her ken as a means of persuasion. Now she didn't really have to worry. She'd sit it out in Bangkok and wait for him to come to her, which he was pretty sure to do, once the fireworks began. "So marvelous of Teddy," she said to me. "So much fun of Teddy to know exactly what to do. I guess he really has his uses after all."

He was prepared. I'd sent him off a signal, so he was waiting in the bungalow for Wilhelm to show up, which he did, in the night. He was at his thundering best when Wilhelm came racing up the road in his Lancia and charged up the front steps of the bungalow the next afternoon. He didn't wait to hear what Wilhelm had to say. It was as if Wilhelm had come barging unannounced into his, Teddy's, house, which in a way it was. It was Teddy's love nest. "You yellow-bellied deserter," he said to Wilhelm, "coming back like this to interrupt my session with Doreen. Just what's the meaning of this outrageous kind of behavior when you know you have to call up first to say you're coming—it's a matter of manners, which I can see you've probably forgotten."

Wilhelm, nonplussed, wanted to burst into tears right away. Doreen was angry, too. They'd both gotten worked up. "If it wasn't for Teddy, you wouldn't even have a cushy job like this at all that lets you run off to Bali and Hong Kong with Ann Albrecht and all those racy friends of hers," Doreen declared. "It's true. He's your grubstake, who do you think you are?"

"Well," Wilhelm said, "I'm the father of your children."

He'd said it that way intentionally just to get her reaction. Teddy laughed about it later in Hong Kong, where he'd gone with Doreen en route to Windveld. "They aren't bloody yours by a long shot," Doreen spat back. "Not all of them, at any rate. They're his, if you have to know the truth."

The whole thing shot to hell for Wilhelm. It shattered all

his hopes for married life, happy or not, on a British military stipend. This is just what Ann, and I, had figured up at Pokhara when we were trying to decide what to do. Naturally I had plans for Ann she didn't know about, but at that time I was all prepared to let her sit it out and wait for Wilhelm. We knew he couldn't stay at Dhahran. He could have stayed at Dhahran, but not in his bungalow with Teddy and Doreen, and it would have been most unlike him to skulk around the cantonment with them up at the house behaving like a pair of love birds. It wasn't handled awfully well. Teddy could have been the one to leave right away, with Doreen, but he was a respected figure there and a pillar of the regiment who gave money every year to the pension fund, no small amount, indeed, so that while Wilhelm may have been a captain in the regiment, his father was a regimental force and an almost unassailable figure.

Besides, Wilhelm hated scenes.

"I should have you reported," he said quietly to his father. "You have absolutely no right to be here and to be doing this. It's simply wrong. You haven't heard the last of it."

The fact of the matter is that Beresford had always been insanely jealous of Wilhelm. He'd chosen every possible opportunity to try to destroy his enviable charm and appeal. He was a Cronus if ever there was one, and he'd dealt Wilhelm the ultimate insult. Wilhelm was shocked and hurt. He had nothing further to say to either his father or his wife, who by then had begun to have misgivings and had started to make certain placating noises before she was silenced by Beresford. At that moment Doreen was torn between father and son, not because she loved Wilhelm, although she was in her impatient way fond of him, but because she suddenly perceived the end of everything, saw what a ham-fisted blow

Teddy Beresford had dealt to what had become all around a suitable arrangement.

Wilhelm did not wait around, however, to hear the end of it. He was purposeful at all times. He turned and left the bungalow. He left his aging father and his bride standing together in the brightly lit living room and strode out onto the verandah, down the steps, and up the path to his car, through the scent of night jasmine and the silence of the moonlit garden. He drove back to the airfield at Biratnagar, where he remained until morning. He was white with fury, I'm told, shaking with rage, but unable to think very clearly. He'd not made a connection between Teddy and the Albrechts. Teddy, it seems, was angry at Wilhelm for walking out on Operation _Zephyr Echo_ prematurely, but Wilhelm had no way of realizing this.

Yet he was not disposed to go and find Ann. He'd come to an end of the whole thing, you see. He was not going to look back once. Oh, I know we all cherish a little hope in the back of the mind that they'll call to us, laughing, begging our forgiveness, saying, "It was really only a joke, we were just kidding, come on back." Still, Wilhelm was staring straight ahead. He happened to have a pair of aviator sunglasses so that he could conceal the glare of his eyes from his fellow travelers. He was in mufti still. He was equipped with plenty of cash and traveler's checks; he always was, for, after all, he was not broke. He could walk away from everything, and still he had that Swiss account with Lansing Noble's contribution to his welfare deposited within it.

He was sorry for the mess. He was sorry about the botched career. Here was the thing, though: Wilhelm was a real person. He had a basically sound mind. He was, furthermore, capable of assessing how he stood in relation to reality: the inner man and the outer world. He was not by any stretch of the imagination a ruined man. He flew, not to Katmandu, which he never cared if he ever saw again in his life, but south, to the Indian border; stayed a couple of nights there in a hotel to gather his wits; made his way to New Delhi; flew from there to Hong Kong, where he checked into the Peninsula Hotel. I'm not sure anyone knows besides Wilhelm how he chose to spend those few days. He sat down and wrote out a letter of resignation to his regiment, with apologies, and made no effort to implicate his father or his wife. He was basically too good-natured to wish them any harm. He was unable to take the blows of life too seriously. He also wrote a highly charged personal letter to the brigadier. The honorable thing to do would have been to go personally to see the brigadier at the Hong Kong HQ, but he'd taken a good long look at Honor and decided to play hard to get with that vicar's daughter. He cast a doleful glance at Prudence, also. Then he went to ground in Macao for a while to do what he really loved to do, which was play cards.

Beresford handled the whole business of Wilhelm's departure from his regiment in such a way that would if anything reflect some credit on himself and none whatever on Wilhelm. The main purpose of his efforts was to hush up the matter of the illegal recruiting that Wilhelm had been engaged in up on the trek with Ann and Lansing Noble; I don't doubt that Teddy Beresford was quite capable of believing that he was really protecting Wilhelm's hide by painting a picture of him to the commanding officer at the cantonment that was hardly comlimentary, although it was not without certain touches that Beresford might have liked to claim for himself. For instance, he actually called Wilhelm "a rakehell." This was a sobriquet he'd always rather fancied for himself. He confirmed what all the officers in Dhahran and Hong Kong already suspected: that Wilhelm was a terrible gambler, a womanizer, a hedonist, and ultimately too much of a playboy to stick it out at a hardship post like Dhahran, because it was a known fact that Wilhelm had been down to Bali, Bangkok, and Hong Kong on other than regiment business.

Teddy Beresford was overbearing and convincing in his presentation to the senior staff officers. None of them seriously entertained the rumor that had circulated among Trawick's set of Beresford's cuckoldry with Doreen. This is not to suggest that they had known such a rumor was in the air. It simply didn't square with what they knew of Teddy Beresford from the days when he had served on the staff of the Supreme Allied Command at the HQ in Ceylon. He'd been a stiff and upright officer of unimpeachable integrity at that time, although to be honest he'd annoyed a good many people with his priggish conceit. He'd outclassed a good many other men to get the ear of Dickie Mountbatten and in so doing had ruffled not a few feathers, but he'd never been known to cuckold a comrade-in-arms. This story was just another cross that Teddy Beresford had been called upon to bear in his campaign to uphold the honor of the regiment. He was the sort after all to marry the vicar's daughter. He was already the darling of the wife of the commander for being such a long-suffering husband to his wife, Wilhelmina, who so many years ago had been paralyzed in an automobile accident and confined to a wheelchair. She had been a dancer with Sadlers Wells when just before the war the young Beresford had met and married her, and wasn't it just one of those dreadful ironies that a dancer of all people would lose the use of her legs, when so many others . . . But here the logic of discourse vanished into mist and reappeared with yet another encomium for Teddy Beresford: "How difficult for him to have a lifelong cripple for a wife, and now this."

Older men and men who have not yet reached the golden mean of middle age see things so often from opposed positions. Quite obvious it was to Trawick and Wilhelm's young fellow officers at Dhahran that in Wilhelm's absence the old fox was showing up to poke his wife because why, for one thing, would he only come to stay when Wilhelm went away? Why those long evening walks together on the cantonment lanes? And why had Wilhelm's wife made those clever needlepoint vamps for Teddy's black velvet evening slippers that showed a devil with a pitchfork before a roaring fire? Wilhelm's cohort was not without affectionate envy for their brother officer. They saw Doreen as an almost irresistible vision of female desirability, a ripe peach of a woman, whom childbearing had only enhanced. Wilhelm was regarded as a bit of a fool, really, for leaving her alone so much at home, but, I say, can't one even trust one's own father? For Beresford never hesitated in the mess to pull rank on younger officers, to brag about his own regimental glory; he gave no evidence of any humility whatever, which is the graceful way to lord it over your juniors. He carried on, pontificated, and ordered the servants about and in the end was universally detested by the younger men, who thought of him as certainly slovenly enough to shack up with Doreen in Wilhelm's absence.

Doreen never made any real effort to conceal her affections for the old bastard, either. She got great excitement from being in bed with him and probably overstrained the weighty Beresford with her demands. In other words there was a stench of scandal emanating from the Beresford cottage that smelled obnoxious to a man like Trawick, who now that he'd abruptly resigned his commission was inclined to feel sympathy with Wilhelm while suspecting that his father had all along been behind the disgraceful business, without exactly understanding why. The older contemporaries in the brigade of Teddy Beresford sniffed at handkerchiefs doused in eau de cologne and smelled nothing, while Teddy lingered on at Dhahran, no one knew quite why, although he'd said at the time that it might be easier on them all if they could wait it out through Christmas and then pack up and leave, and he'd received assurances that this was quite all right. So Teddy Beresford, imperturbably, remained at Wilhelm's bungalow with Doreen for another month and could be seen out on the lawn in the late afternoon with his grandchildren playing croquet; together he and Doreen appeared for movies in the mess and otherwise were seen about, to all appearances unconcerned about anything at all.

This was odd. Another odd thing was Wilhelm's resignation. What, after all, had been the purpose of that? people wondered. He had done nothing himself that could be considered reprehensible. He was a good officer. His performance in the course of duty was exemplary. No one took very seriously his excessive visits to Hong Kong and Brunei. So what if he'd been seen in Bali? So very what indeed!

The truth was that Wilhelm wherever he went in life added a touch of glamour, a brightness that never seemed to be at the expense of anyone else, or his obligations, and when he was seen at the race track in Happy Valley or in the company of Lansing Noble at a party on a royal barge in Bangkok, he only added luster to the regiment and by association the brigade itself, which had a reputation to maintain and was not averse to a certain social public relations. So he was missed.

His debonair soul conferred upon the cantonment a certain sophisticated magic, because Wilhelm was happiness incarnate. He might vanish, but he could not be extinguished. Rumors began to grow up about his disappearance and disgrace among the younger men of the regiment. He was said to have been despondent upon the discovery that his father and wife were having an affair during his absence and that he'd gone out to sea and drowned himself at night off the coast of Borneo. Then there was the matter, also, of his considerable gambling debts. He seemed to have run out on these altogether. He was last seen, as far as anyone knew, by Trawick, on the Jomson Trail. Had he gone up into the farther reaches, then, of the Himalayas and plunged himself into a chasm of ice? This was entirely irrational speculation, as you can well imagine, since his letter of resignation, dated well after Trawick's meeting with Wilhelm, had been postmarked in Hong Kong. Shame, that was the only motive anyone could find to ascribe to Wilhelm's departure from the regiment; shame had driven him to vanish. It caused a certain sadness among those who appreciated the element of swank, of verve. The man most held responsible was, of course, Teddy. After a time—a week, ten days—the chill that Wilhelm's father encountered, and the opprobrium Doreen herself experienced from the other officers' wives, was all but forbidding, like a relentless, stiff wind, an autumn wind cold enough to make them want to stay inside, which is what they did. They ventured forth at night to dine with the commanding officer and his wife when they happened to be entertaining guests from Katmandu, but after a time the myth of Wilhelm's disappearance came in from the outer world to make even those forays somewhat less than clement.

They did not, at first, know exactly where to go or what to do. They were awaiting word from me, or Lansing Noble, to say that we had Wilhelm with us and were now en route to Corfu with the Gurkhas. We were down in Bangkok, waiting for Wilhelm to show up. This was Ann's idea. She could not imagine that Wilhelm would not arrive posthaste to join us there, especially since it would have been unlike him to abandon the recruits altogether; certainly we were expecting to hear from Wilhelm. We had no idea that he had summarily resigned from his regiment. We had no knowledge of what had happened in Dhahran. Had we understood that Wilhelm had bolted, and why, we would ourselves have decamped for

Corfu at once with the recruits. Naturally Wilhelm's disappearance created a suspicion somewhere of wrongdoing, certainly his resignation would have made people ask questions, and the vanishing act provoked head scratching that Teddy Beresford all by himself up in Dhahran could not altogether prevent, with his scornful bad-mouthing. We were festering in ignorance down in Bangkok—actually, by this time we had removed ourselves to a retreat Damian knew about in northern Malaysia called the Beach of Passionate Love, where the Gurkha recruits could be more safely held. We were therefore no doubt somewhat hard to reach. We still had the *Bouncing Bunny*.

When Teddy Beresford finally reached Ann by telephone from the cantonment, I think she was really very fed up with him; perhaps she began to understand why her mother had finally decided to fire the man. He was impatient with her for not getting in touch with him herself, as though it had been her fault, not his, that somehow their scheme had become derailed, or I should say our scheme, since I was implicated along with all the others. He was enraged to find himself sitting in Wilhelm's nest, which he had fouled, without knowing where to go next, or what to do, and blamed it on Ann for letting Wilhelm out of her clutches prematurely. I must say that on this score he certainly had a point. The rich mishandle personal relations out of a kind of arrogance, and it always blows up in their faces. He told Ann that he'd been waiting for her signal that Wilhelm had arrived and *Zephyr Echo* was on course.

"How could I send a signal like that when I haven't seen Wilhelm in ten days?" Ann screamed over the bad connection. "Jesus Christ, if Wilhelm had come here, we'd be in Europe by now."

In the end they could wait no longer. It was all a damned inconvenience as far as Teddy Beresford was concerned. Now he was saddled with Doreen and the children, which hadn't been his idea at all, even though it greatly appealed to Doreen, even though he'd sired two of the children himself. The last thing he wanted was to have another family on his hands. The whole idea had been to have his cake and eat it, too, so that Wilhelm would shoulder all the responsibilities and he would enjoy the fruits whenever he felt so inclined.

He was sneering and impatient under these conditions; Doreen found him distinctly odious to be with now, although she had no other choice. Her options were severely limited. She managed to pack up her household in a week, while he shuffled through the bungalow in his velvet slippers with their needlepoint reminders, and complained about this and that, and drank too much Scotch. The ayah looked after the children. Or was she an amah? I have trouble keeping those two designations straight. Teddy went about with his nostrils pricked, as though he were constantly trying to identify the particular stench, which was like a really bad fart, that had enveloped their household. Nobody ever called. The house was silent now at night because Doreen had packed the record player and shipped it off along with all her other worldly goods to Windveld. They had decided that Doreen and the children would move permanently to Windveld, to the cottage, and remain there, under Teddy's protection, until things sorted themselves out. They anticipated that Wilhelm would seek to obtain a divorce. They anticipated that Ivan, Wilhelm's disappearance notwithstanding, would move against the House of Albrecht. When he did, Teddy would fly to Zurich and take over as chairman. That is what they anticipated. Doreen and the children would live in Zurich.

Teddy, as always, would commute to South Africa to Wind-veld to stay with Wilhelmina. Teddy and Doreen discussed all this in an even, low conversation at the dinner table by the fire while, after dinner was taken, Doreen knitted and Teddy sat staring into the fire, which cast a glow on his face and touched to bright gold his fierce tufted blond eyebrows and the gold forelock that fell across his brow. He heaved a great sigh. He was overwhelmed, now, by the vanity of the enterprise. Doreen was not surprised. He'd betrayed his son, his darling Wilhelm. He'd sold his son to the Albrechts. He'd shoved his son into the furnace.

Wilhelm Beresford, it seemed, had disappeared for good. There was some speculation that he'd gone to live in New Zealand, although in the regiment it was generally thought that if he'd gone anywhere, he'd have migrated not to New Zealand, but rather to Australia, which just goes to show how unimaginative most of his colleagues in the Brigade of Gur-khas were, because Wilhelm Beresford would never have gone to live anywhere so déclassé. Not that he was a snob. He was nothing of the sort. He was merely a man of the world. To go and hide out in the land of the marsupial wasn't his style. He liked to touch base in any of several dozen smart places all around the world, and if he was going to have to go to ground, he'd have to do it in such a way that would allow him the maximum opportunity to travel. It had not, however, been his intention to altogether disappear from the world. At least I don't think that would have been very much like him. He was by nature full of self-respect, though he wouldn't have put it thus; he was gregarious, also. To hide was not natural to him. The fact is he hadn't decided what to do, although he'd considered taking a job as an executive with a tobacco exporter because he liked to smoke.

He was indifferent to occupation. He would have worn a
fedora, I imagine, if he'd ever gone to work for the tobacco
company, but it would not have changed him in the slightest.
He was also considering accepting a job with one of the hotel
casinos on Macao. This is the kind of routine consideration
anybody would give the job market once they've been prevented from practicing their chosen vocation. Both positions,
either position, would have allowed Wilhelm the opportunity
to travel. There was a woman on Macao who loved him very
much named Linda. She was just right for him in many ways;
she was a nice, tall, dark-haired woman who worked there in
a bank. Of course he couldn't marry her.

He was in love with her, of this there is no doubt. He'd
had the excellent good luck to meet her in the casino where
they were both playing _vingt-et-un_. That was what Wilhelm
called it. He never said "twenty-one." It's what his father
had always called it. Linda was quite svelte and had a past of
her own, nothing seamy—quite the opposite, in fact, for
she'd been a convent girl who'd entered a religious order with
the intention of becoming a nun and just at the very last
minute had bolted. So like Wilhelm she, too, was on the lam.
She was tall, almost his height. They began to have a very
good time together, and before long they were stretched out
in bed together. Linda was one-half Portuguese, one-half
Chinese; she was thus a full-bred Macanese. They lived together after a time in Stanley Ho's big hotel on Macao. Wilhelm had plenty of money to draw on for his gambling sprees.

He was more drawn to gambling than he was even to sex.
He was, however, a man of heart, and he needed—nay,
preferred—the love of one woman, although he'd had mixed
luck before his encounter with Linda. He particularly liked
Linda because she gave him the maximum opportunity to act

out his mysterious melodrama. She asked him no questions he would not have wanted to answer. Besides that, he liked her long legs and her pointed nipples. She was stylish in just the way he liked. Being on the lam from the nuns gave her the necessary license to be naughty in her own earthy way, and let's fact it, we all need a little pornography to spice up the act of love from time to time. It doesn't have to be a daily diet. The porno of our times just happens to be necessarily seedy, that's all: someday we'll all be looking for a big-enough asshole to stick our heads up into just to escape the banalities of television, eh what? Wilhelm found the proper seedy touch in his hotel room on Macao, and for over two months he never left the hotel. He commuted between his penthouse room and the casino. Linda brought him Chinese food every day for lunch.

It just happened that he decided one Sunday to zip over to Hong Kong aboard a jet foil for an afternoon at the races. He'd dyed his hair black once again. He was smart enough not to be caught by any of the British Gurkhas, but even if he had been spotted, it would have made no difference to Wilhelm because he could get out of any situation when he wanted to. But the last person he ever expected to run into, face to face, was Francesca Drayton, mother of Amber, whom he'd known on Fishers Island and who had always admired Wilhelm from afar. She recognized him right away with his slick black hair. It was how she remembered him best; it was not, I should quickly add, such a very great surprise to Frankie Drayton to see him there, for she was a hunter and forever on the prowl these days for any kind of trouble.

She looked slightly different from the woman Wilhelm had remembered her to be, the reserved, unsmiling, composed wife of a New York stockbroker. For one thing, she'd clipped her hair so that it was boy short and silvery blond, which gave her the appearance of a gamine. Had she also had a face lift? He couldn't tell. Her skin was taut, polished. She no longer wore that cross expression he'd observed on the Fishers Island ferry. Also, she was dressed in a short white sharkskin skirt and a matching jacket, so she was really Hong Kong chic, not Fishers Island clean-cut, but something a little glittery; he recognized the full mouth and the sportswoman's physique, however, when she addressed him in the wide seventh-floor hallway near the Jockey Club betting window at Sha Tin.

"Billy B.," she said, and whipped off her dark glasses.

"Why, Mrs. Drayton, fancy meeting you here," said Wilhelm.

She spoke quickly. "Not at all," she said. "Eternal Prince is entered in the fifth race. Is there somewhere we can talk?"

Wilhelm accompanied her to the box that at the moment she was using—it belonged to one of the merchant princes whose acquaintance he had made with Ann and which, as it happened, she had the exclusive rights to use as an Albrecht representative. Had she been sharing it with any other guests, he'd simply have suggested they go somewhere together off the track to talk, but it wasn't necessary. She offered him a glass of bubbly; he accepted. They toasted one another.

"Divine, isn't it?" said Frankie Drayton of nothing in particular, but Wilhelm got her drift and quite agreed.

"You know, in spite of everything that's happened, you seem to be in a very good mood," said Amber's mother. "I wonder why?"

Said Billy B., "Why not?"

"I don't know." His hostess sipped a little Piper-Heidsieck

and put her glass down to fetch a cigarette. That's the generation she belonged to, what someone I know refers to as the Hemingway generation, although she was slightly younger than that; even so, she drank and smoked. "I guess you aren't aware of what's been going on."

"Well," said Billy B., "I don't know. Fill me in. Perhaps I am and perhaps I am not, but we shall never know until you speak."

He lit her cigarette. He was not, just then, in a mood for one of his own. She felt excited to be here with him like this. She blew the smoke out through her nose and said, "They're looking for you, Wilhelm, everywhere. Not just here. They're scouring every continent trying to find you."

"Who is they?" said Wilhelm.

"Your father, Ann Albrecht, Bruce Fox, the Gurkhas. Your wife, I guess. I don't know her, but I understand you left her to run off with someone else. The fifth race is about to begin. Why did you just run out like that?"

Such talk naturally made Wilhelm impatient. What did this woman know, after all, about his recent revelation that his father had been sleeping with his wife?

"That's a leading question," Wilhelm replied. "I gather you don't approve of people who run away."

"Not awfully, no," said Mrs. Drayton, and she sipped some more champagne. "I have rather old-fashioned principles."

Wilhelm snorted. "Even if your knees do happen to be showing," he said.

They both laughed.

"The Ivan thing has kind of ruined me for elopement in general," said Mrs. Drayton.

"Even though you do seem to have come through it rather well, rather happily, and well, I should say," Wilhelm said.

This made something of a strain between them.

"I happen to have a job to do," Mrs. Drayton told him. "That's why I'm here, you know. I'm not just playing hooky."

"I never intended to imply that you were," said Wilhelm. "But you must admit that you do appear to be having a rather less dowdy time of it than you were when last I saw you on Fishers Island."

"Gretchen Albrecht has been very kind to us both under the circumstances," Amber's mother replied. "It's been extremely trying. We've had to live with the knowledge that we may never see Amber again. That may not be the case. What I'm trying to tell you," she said now to Wilhelm, "is that for our present jet-set mode of life, we've paid a very steep price."

Wilhelm looked at Mrs. Drayton. He regarded her without a trace of irony. "I say, you don't mean to tell me you've given up the ghost."

Frankie Drayton couldn't suppress a rueful smile at Wilhelm's apt selection of phrase. "What do you think?" she said.

"I think," said Wilhelm, "that you are absolutely mad to have let Ivan have your lovely daughter, Mrs. Drayton. I know him very well. We used to call him Ivan the Terrible."

She'd finished her glass of champagne but didn't feel like having another one. "That was a long time ago," she said. "In another country. Now I work for Gretchen Albrecht. I have no choice."

Wilhelm was sitting on a sort of lawn chair or upholstered deck chair. He put his head back and closed his eyes. Mrs. Drayton beside him did the same. Then, still with his eyes closed, in a rather quiet, low voice, Wilhelm said: "In a few days, in a week, I don't know how soon, Mrs. Drayton, but soon, you can count on it, Gretchen Albrecht will be out of a job, and so will you."

Frankie Drayton did not move a muscle as she sat there. She kept her eyes closed, too. This was precisely what she had come to Hong Kong to hear. She wanted to hear it clearly and precisely, because she knew that if she didn't get it right this one time, she'd lose her chance to get it at all.

"The Gurkhas," Wilhelm said. "Do you know about the Gurkhas?" He waited for her small voice to reply, "No." Then he continued. "I think you ought to know, for whatever use you can make of it, my dear Mrs. Drayton, that Lansing Noble and Ivan Albrecht, I daresay with the assistance of your daughter, Amber, not to mention Ann Albrecht and very likely Bruce Fox, are going to take by force the Albrecht factory in Turin, using six or eight Gurkha recruits whom I helped them to select and to take from Nepal to Bangkok by plane. Having indulged in this bit of terrorist shenanigans, or whatever you'd like to call it, I decided to resign my commission, although I might add there were some further circumstances which I believe made the decision easier to make, though I see no reason to get into any of that."

The fifth race had been run in the course of this revelation, but neither Wilhelm nor Mrs. Drayton had troubled to watch it on the video console suspended before them from the ceiling of the private steward's box. They could hear the roaring of the spectators way below, however, and they could hear that roar simultaneously in miniature on the console.

"Where are they now?" Mrs. Drayton wanted to know.

Wilhelm held on to the arms of his deck chair. "They are undoubtedly somewhere in Asia with Lansing Noble," he replied.

There was a silence between them. The Albrecht pony, Eternal Prince, had won the race. The news was piped over the public address system wired into the box where they sat together in silence.

"So what's our plan?" Francesca Drayton wanted to know. "I gather we have to act now or not at all."

"Well," Wilhelm said.

Still they sat with their eyes closed. He'd bet five hundred Hong Kong dollars on Eternal Prince at five to one. This gave him a good feeling. It made him calm, and he relaxed his grip on the arms of the deck chair. He hadn't given any thought to what they might do to frustrate the sabotage.

"You'd get those Gurkhas back safe and sound to Nepal," said Mrs. Drayton. "That's one thing. For another," she said, "you and I, we could take the whole thing over ourselves, couldn't we. I mean, really, Billy B., I hate to say it, because it sounds so boastful, and I was really very well brought up, though it seems as though it's been two hundred years since I graduated from Miss Hewitt's. It sounds so common. Still, I know just about everything there is to know about what's going on in the House of Albrecht, and I've spent most of the last six or eight months running it. You didn't know that, did you?"

Wilhelm shook his head. He had to confess that he had not known that.

"Gretchen's let the whole thing go to pieces. No one knows just how much except me because, you know, I'm her _copain._" Frankie Drayton snorted. She sat up. "I guess that horse won."

"It certainly did," said Wilhelm. "And so did I."

Mrs. Drayton stretched. "Divine," she said.

"So what's the plan?" said Wilhelm.

"Okay," said Frankie Drayton, "here's what we should do. You can shoot?"

He nodded.

"You know the Gurkha tribesmen."

He nodded yet again.

"We'll steal a march," said Frankie Drayton. "I'll show you how."

THE
MOON

One never saw the Albrechts. They were always somewhere else. What one saw instead, if one had the temerity to investigate the grounds of the Albrecht estate, say, on Fishers Island, was a garage of Albrecht cars, facing out, glittering in the half-light, waiting to be used. A maid, or the caretaker on duty, would have to explain to one that the Albrechts were not on the island, were not expected to visit that month. At Cavemoor the Albrecht standard flew in the breeze over the capacious roof, and within the house a mood of subdued anticipation prevailed; but whenever they were present, one was not, oneself, on the premises to see them. One knew they were in residence by the increased amount of traffic at the gateway to the Albrecht estate. One might, if one's luck was running high, actually pass an Albrecht limousine on the road leading past the Albrecht estate, but that was all. When Albrecht executives from abroad went to Cavemoor now for dinner, the Albrechts were not present. Others filled in for them, wined and dined the servants of the Albrecht empire: Monsignor Cathcart was very often among the resident guests, and the vicomtesse de Roissy was frequently called upon to play the role of hostess, but Mrs. Keith, the housekeeper of the Albrecht domain, was also in attendance and could be counted on to preside when all else failed. There was a sense then of characters without an author banding together to create a spirit of warmth in the vast dark night. Often, in London, the Albrechts had just departed by private jet for the north of Scotland, or else they were in seclusion at Great Wyke House in Buckinghamshire. In Paris they were there, but one wouldn't see them because where they went most other people couldn't go. Perhaps they were at Roissy, at the château, where the Albrecht Arabians were stabled and trained by Hubert de Roissy. Their appointments were always private. They attended private luncheons in the salons of people who only existed in the columns of newspapers, people who rarely if ever showed up in public places. Gretchen Albrecht, a master of public relations, coincided her public appearances with the winning race of an Albrecht horse, and at such times her husband was always believed to be nearby, in the private Albrecht box, but one never saw him. They were mythical people of fabulous wealth, whom one heard about and rarely, if ever, had the opportunity to see.

One heard about the Albrechts at length from Monsignor Cathcart. He liked to chat at lunch about the Albrechts. He invariably paid one the compliment of assuming that one knew more than one really did about the Albrechts. He then expressed shock to hear that one had never laid eyes on Henry Albrecht. Then he would say, "But of course that makes absolutely perfect sense because I don't suppose Henry's actually been here a *great* deal, although it does seem odd. He *does* come in and out. He's down at El Parador right now. He moves about at night. But it's true he's *deep* in the English countryside four-fifths of the time, which is an *awful* strain on Gretchen, who has to commute. And she *loathes* England. You can quite see why." He implied things about Henry Albrecht but became very grave when he did so. Henry Albrecht was a potentate. He was, according to the Jesuit, quite obscenely obese, rather killing himself in the style of a Roman emperor, gorging himself on meals in the predawn hours prepared by his personal Belgian chef, Gaston, and being carried about his English country house on a sedan chair. "Which is another frightfully compelling reason to live *there*, rather than *here*," Monsignor Cathcart would then confide, and roll his eyes in mock horror, "because he's frightfully heavy, and you see there are no *stairs* at Great Wyke. God *only* knows why. The architect simply had no use for stairs." There was, evidently, nothing that Gretchen Albrecht could possibly do to alter her husband's appearance, according to the monsignor, but she could, and did, keep him from being interviewed by the prying gossip columnists and photographed by the *infinitely* resourceful paparazzi, which, he would then assert, was no mean feat. She could control the staff, which was sworn to secrecy and vastly overpaid, one was given to understand, and kept under the strict supervision of the vigilant Mrs. Keith. Gretchen Albrecht made a *tremendous* effort, the monsignor liked to say on her behalf, to open the Albrecht mansion to garden club tours and luncheons, to loan her name to cancer benefits, and to preside over the distribution of funds for a great range of charities. She was also photographed on occasion with the duchess of Windsor. She made a great effort to create through the skillful management of information about her husband and family the appearance of a very busy, even hectic, but altogether happy family household.

The Albrecht children one almost never saw. One saw, one had met, Ann Albrecht, who was otherwise engaged. Ivan one only heard about. One heard about how terribly difficult Ivan had been, even as a small child. "I mean, it's *really, truly awful* when you think of what they have to put up with from Ivan," Monsignor Cathcart had been heard to lament, "and yet there's simply nothing they can do." He had, Cathcart, a reproachful, or rueful, expression and the worried eyes of a basset hound even when he laughed. "It's really outrageous," he'd say, "when the richest man in the world is quite powerless to command even the slightest *degree* of attention or respect from his only son."

One was shown the beach on Fishers Island where Ivan almost drowned. Ivan had been sent to five different Swiss boarding schools, each of which had dismissed him for disciplinary reasons, although one never learned exactly what these were. The Albrecht children spent Christmas in Europe and a large part of the summer somewhere else, and even when they were there on Fishers Island, one heard about them but did not necessarily see them. Ivan was there but was not allowed to leave the house. Later on, when he was older, one saw Ivan waiting down at the Fishers Island aerodrome without knowing him, saw a tall, moon-faced, pale, dark-haired wraith. He'd be waiting, one supposed, for the arrival of an Albrecht jet craft. He'd be slouched in a black leather jacket against the green-black Cadillac convertible he drove at such high speeds, recklessly, up and down the two-lane island road. The Albrecht party always flew to Fishers Island. The senior Albrechts were always preceded by their children, by a reinforcement of domestic help, and by their summer guests, Albrecht functionaries mostly, and permanent members of the Albrecht entourage, Monsignor Cathcart, Colonel and Mrs. Stoddard, who had done such an enormous job on the interiors of all the Albrecht houses, and of course, for as long as he remained in the employ of the House of Albrecht, Teddy Beresford, accompanied by his family. The Albrechts senior, Henry and Gretchen, were always rumored to be imminent. One knew that they existed. One had seen them once, Mr. and Mrs. Albrecht, at a distance, on the deck of the Pompeiian cabana on Chocomount Beach, where Ambassador and Mrs. Noble entertained their guests for lunch. He had been wearing a sombrero to keep out the sun, white trousers rolled up to his calves, and a bright yellow shirt open at the neck. Gretchen Albrecht, very blond at that time, had worn for the occasion a white sailor top, white trousers, and enormous dark glasses.

Ivan Albrecht was an object of people's speculation on Fishers Island to a far greater extent than his parents ever were. They never seemed to put in an appearance there, whereas Ivan was seen, fleetingly, in the low-slung chariot with its deeply dyed interior of red leather upholstery that he preferred to drive above all others in the Albrecht garage behind Black Pond House, the Albrecht summer palace. He could be seen, Ivan, briefly, on the edge of the Nobles' lawn that looked out from its bluff to Orient Point across Long Island Sound. His dark figure was seen on occasion roving about inside the Nobles' cabana, set back from the beach in the lee of the cliff below their house. He was known as Ivan the Terrible, although what, exactly, was supposed to be so terrible about him no one really knew for certain. He was rumored to have been barred, permanently, from entering Italy for having murdered a pimp on the edge of the autostrada outside Rome during an altercation concerning the services of a prostitute. It was all adolescent speculation. It was said that he never bathed, if he could avoid it, that he lived in darkness, and it was true that he was never seen on the beach, and that his bluish, sunless pallor and black locks contrasted unfavorably with the gilded looks of the Fishers Island youth.

The last summer he visited Fishers Island, when he was nineteen, Ivan was seen always in the company of Amber, who was the comely, tanned, golden-haired daughter of a member of the New York Stock Exchange named Francis Drayton. Amber was fourteen, although tall for her age, and on the very threshold of early bloom. Ivan found her while prowling in his car one morning down around the Fishers Island ferry building where Amber had gone to accompany her father to the early Monday ferry. She was walking home. He'd offered her a ride, snapped her up, and that was it. She was captive from that moment on to the strange spell of Ivan Albrecht. It was an altogether subversive and somewhat scandalous affair conducted in the privacy of the Albrecht precincts by day, which Amber could easily reach from the beach where she ostensibly went every midday to swim with her friends. By night, under cover of darkness, in the warm leather interior of Ivan's chariot, Ivan and Amber masterminded the burglary that they together believed would finance their flight to Europe, and freedom. They plotted to break into a castle on the north end of the island, which they had ascertained was not in use at the time because its owners had decided to spend that particular August in Scotland. It was really Ivan's idea. Amber was utterly under his spell.

They were supposed to perform the robbery together, but at the last minute Ivan, whom one must presume was overwhelmed by a sudden enthusiasm, jumped the gun. He was alone in the house when the burglar alarm installed by its owners against just this eventuality began to shrill, not in the house Ivan was stealthily ransacking, but in the police department headquarters in New London, on the Connecticut mainland. Ivan was alone when a helicopter descended out of the night sky and spotlighted him as he ambled down the road from the burgled house with a small Degas canvas rolled under his upper arm.

Gretchen Albrecht materialized soon enough, within twenty-four hours, by jet, in New London, to save the day. One did not see her, but it was understood that she donated a Degas of her own to the city of New London and swiftly committed Ivan to an exclusive private sanitarium in Westchester County. Amber was never implicated in the foiled crime. Her mother never knew that Amber had considered herself a full-fledged accomplice. Amber had long since learned how to circumvent her mother while appearing to be the very soul of innocence and good conduct. Her mother had issued an edict forbidding her daughter ever to "go out" with Ivan Albrecht, and she was vastly relieved to hear that he had been removed, finally, as a menace to her peace of mind and worried only that Amber had lost her appetite, now seemed rather pale for someone who spent every waking hour in the sun. She was quite concerned. She was glad when Labor Day came, uncharacteristically relieved to pack up and return to New York, where Amber was enrolled in a fashionable private day school for girls on the Upper East Side of Manhattan. Neither she nor her husband had any inkling, really, that Amber was altogether lost to them already.

Legend would like to have it that Ivan Albrecht ran off with his child bride, Amber Drayton, on board a yacht and took her away forever and a day from school and family to sail the seven seas. Like any legend, this one contains elements of the truth, although the real story is more complicated.

When Amber returned to school in the fall, she took up a passionate correspondence that Ivan had initiated with her from Echo Zephyr, the posh place in Westchester County to which he had been committed by his mother and where Ivan found himself in the company of some exceedingly smart mental patients, among them a well-known playwright who was the manic-depressive author of a string of Broadway comedies, each one a dazzling piece in its own way of theatrical legerdemain now somewhat out of fashion. This second-generation Philip Barry arranged for the exchange of love letters between the conspiratorial lovers through the intermediary services of his private secretary, who used to visit him at Echo Zephyr every Friday afternoon between the hours of three and five. The playwright was keenly excited by the fancy that he was nurturing a real-life Romeo and Juliet during his enforced respite from the business of writing plays. Furthermore, he was very taken with Ivan Albrecht. He was aware of the fabulous Albrecht fortune and considered it an excellent piece of luck to have been placed in such close proximity to the scion of this mysterious house. He really became somewhat infatuated with Ivan Albrecht.

This is not surprising. There were people who formed a passionate attachment to Ivan Albrecht often without wanting to know why. He was compelling. He went about with an air of purpose. No single gesture of his appeared to be without meaning, part of some larger design that he alone was capable of understanding and so altogether urgent that he could rarely allow himself the frivolity of laughter, except when the irony of circumstances called for a certain low, shuddering chuckle, which he emitted with a sardonic smile.

Ivan was entirely engrossed in the seriousness of his private mission. He talked the playwright into bankrolling his escape from Echo Zephyr. He met Amber by prearrangement at the bus depot in White Plains, and together the young lovers took flight. They rode all night by bus to Montreal, where they had booked passage by prearrangement through the good offices of the playwright on board a Polish freighter bound for Gdańsk and sailed to Europe with passports secured for them by Ann Albrecht, who delivered them to Ivan on a visit to Echo Zephyr in the company of Bruce Fox, who at that time was one of Ann's aspiring beaux. The yacht came later.

Amber did not return. Mr. Drayton could appreciate the irony of his predicament as well as anyone. He and his wife, Francesca, who was known as Frankie, had long aspired to the company of the very rich, although they were not financially equipped to do so, for well-heeled though they most certainly were, they were not in a class, economically speaking, with people like the Albrechts. Nevertheless they cultivated the very rich. They had gone to shoot big game in East Africa with the Nobles and were not above indulging in a certain amount of discreet name dropping at the Big Club, where they consorted with the merely rich, people like themselves, investment bankers and stockbrokers, Wall Street lawyers and life insurance executives from Hartford, Connecticut. Indeed, when Amber first informed her mother that she had formed a friendship with Lansing Noble's friend, Ivan Albrecht, Frankie Drayton experienced a pleasurable, though restrained, rush of adrenaline through her viscera. She was momentarily inspired by a measure of anticipation until she actually got a good look at Ivan Albrecht one afternoon as he stood on the street side of his Cadillac convertible, insolently sprawled across the black canvas roof in conversation with Lansing Noble, who was standing on the sidewalk. She had never taken the trouble to find out what sort of young man Ivan Albrecht was, or how he looked, even though Catsy Noble had expressed some dismay about the friendship that had sprung up between her son, Lansing, and Ivan. Now, as she beheld that unnaturally tall young man with his prison pallor and his lank, unshorn raven locks and the inexpressibly disdainful sorrow of his eyes, his black leather jacket and his tight black leather pants, Frankie Drayton was stricken with dread. She forbade her treasured child to have any further social exchange with Ivan Albrecht, she did not care who he was. He was a killer. She was a killer of sorts herself, very skillful when it came to using a gun, and she knew a killer when she saw one.

The sight of Ivan Albrecht as he stood there outside the liquor store in conversation with Lansing Noble jolted her soul with fear and loathing. Amber was her only child, her jewel. Her plan was to marry Amber off someday to someone like Lansing Noble, some very rich, well-brought-up, good-looking blond young buck from Long Island, but not to Ivan Albrecht. She drew the line well short of anyone like that. She was a tense mother, though even-tempered and capable in the privacy of her daughter's bedroom of a mirth all the giddier for being so repressed. At such times, when her laughter rose in waves from her belly in barely controllable spasms, she showed a rictus of perfect white teeth. Otherwise she was the tense, attractive woman one saw on the Fishers Island ferry, lean, quite tall; she possessed fine hair of a white-gold color, worn simply parted at the side, pinned above one ear by a gold barrette, and combed to an inward curl at the nape of the neck. She was the athletic Mrs. Drayton of simple chic, who wore a single strand of pearls on the ferry transit, a kelly-green crocheted sweater, a gold bracelet, Tretorn tennis shoes, and modish, tortoiseshell dark glasses of a cat's-eye design. She was often called an upper-crust Grace Kelly. She tended to speak through clenched teeth. She was out of the classic mold, square-jawed, with good facial bones, and she was always tan from her life as a sports-woman, one who preferred the manly recreations of golf, deep-sea fishing, and shooting. She laid down the law to

Amber that under no circumstances did she ever want her to see or be seen with Ivan Albrecht again, and that was that.

Francis Drayton backed up his wife one hundred percent on this issue, as he could be counted upon to do on all matters having to do with rules and regulations. He was an easygoing man who in his youth had been a top-seeded doubles player with a national amateur ranking even as a Yale undergraduate. He had quit the tournament circuit only after his marriage to Frankie, the daughter of a prominent Park Avenue physician. Drayton had done quite well for himself, thereafter, as a Wall Street investor. He eventually inherited a seat on the New York Stock Exchange, but he was rather too much of a drinker to make a real killing, which would have required of the man a hunger he did not possess. He was a martini drinker. He now worked half days and came home to his Gracie Square apartment after lunch at his downtown club. He occupied himself with activities that were compatible with drinking: social tennis at the River Club, the reading of spy novels, the very serious study of the spy novel as a genre, and backgammon, which he played whenever and with whomever he could. He referred to Frankie and Amber as his "cheering section." When he and his wife went big game hunting in Africa or in the Canadian wilderness, or pheasant shooting in South Carolina, or deep-sea fishing, Francis Drayton took along a canvas bag full of spy novels and stayed behind to read while his wife went off to match her wits and her will against the wild game and the game fish. He had no interest in killing anything and said so in a very agreeable tone of voice when asked. He was called Saint Francis of Drayton by his friends. Killing was the special province of his wife. She was also good at growing flowers and arranging them, and the Draytons had constructed a greenhouse on the terrace of their Gracie Square apartment so that she could busy herself with flowers during the day. Big game sport, flowers, Amber, and the judicious management of her husband's drinking habits were the occupations of Frankie Drayton's life.

Mainly, Francis Drayton liked to be at home without altogether being present in the lives of his women, as a sort of bright-faced leprechaun, chuckling from behind his _Wall Street Journal_, taking issue with the issues of the day, for he was also an avid consumer of newspapers and news magazines. He loved to read them and to expatiate at great length during the extended cocktail hour on current events. He scored high on the weekly news quiz in the Saturday edition of the _New York Times_. The only tense part of his day was the hour between five in the afternoon and six o'clock in the evening. He was inclined to be somewhat snappish in that final sixty-minute revolution of the clock's long hand before his next round of martinis was scheduled to be ceremoniously mixed, for he was very strictly called upon by Frankie Drayton to observe a four-hour hiatus between the lunch hour martinis and whatever else he liked to drink at midday, cognac very often followed by coffee, and his more serious nighttime quotient, three being the limit imposed by Frankie Drayton, although he often somehow managed to fit in four or even five martinis, despite the ever-present vigilance of his wife, who sipped judiciously away at a Scotch on the rocks while she watched him. It was all Francis Drayton could do to occupy himself in the interstice, and at this hour he was wont to cavil at the beautiful golden child he had sired, whom he desired, and whom he was permitted to kiss only once in the evening, just before she went to bed, more often than not in the presence of his wife.

This, in the opinion of Francis Drayton, was the chief irony: that in their hour of deepest grief, and only then, the Draytons finally and irrevocably attached themselves completely to people possessed of a wealth great enough to suit what they considered their due, and even then, irony of ironies, the superrich by whom they were adopted, to wit the Albrechts, had to be considered at least indirectly responsible for the Draytons' great loss. They were taken up at once by Gretchen Albrecht. She would not have had it any other way. She made it clear to the Draytons that no people should have to suffer so terribly at the hands of her monster son, the one she'd always tried to keep locked up, without receiving from her immediate solace and any amount of recompense. The instant that word reached her of the flight of Ivan and Amber Drayton, she sent a car to Gracie Square to fetch the Draytons and bring them out to Cavemoor. She insisted there and then that they move in with her for the duration of what she could not believe would be a waiting period of more than a week, if that, before the lovers were chased to ground.

At first the Draytons lived at Cavemoor in a state of luxurious emergency. They had packed quickly for a weekend. Frankie Drayton, when five or six days had passed, made a move to return to Gracie Square, but this was checked by Gretchen Albrecht, who wouldn't hear of it, on the grounds that solidarity was of the essence. To the great surprise of Frankie Drayton, her husband, ever the very personification of good-natured common sense, took the side of Ivan Albrecht's mother. They stayed put. An Albrecht car was sent to Gracie Square with an assistant to the Cavemoor housekeeper, Mrs. Keith. She soon returned with everything the captive Draytons would need for an extended stay, which perforce, given the style of life required by the vast Albrecht interests, included spontaneous travel of a kind that even in their wildest dreams the Draytons had never dared to imagine for themselves. At Cavemoor life was extremely pleasant and rarely dull. As Francis Drayton put it to his wife, if you have to wait out something that by its very nature is like the course of a dreadful disease, why not do it in conditions of the utmost comfort among people far better equipped than you to ease the pain of waiting?

M rs. Drayton was not as content to just lie back
and relax on the Albrecht hospitality as her husband so clearly
was. He found himself at home immediately in the Albrecht
atmosphere. He loved to chatter madly away with the Stoddards, for instance, about people they knew in common who
had served in the OSS. At *Chez* Albrecht, furthermore, he
could play backgammon morning, noon, and night with other
members of the Albrecht party who, like the Draytons, were
in a permanent state of waiting. The art of waiting, which
others in the Albrecht entourage practiced with great skill,
came quite naturally to Saint Francis, and to the surprise once
again of his wife, in the Albrecht ambience her husband al-

most immediately ceased to drink martinis. It no longer seemed to be necessary for him to bother with martinis. He drank champagne instead and never more than just enough. Had it not been for this unexpectedly tonic effect on her husband of the Albrecht scene, she undoubtedly would have attempted more vigorously to get him back to Gracie Square, where they might have ben surrounded with less opulence but where they might have devoted themselves with more urgency to the matter of recovering their daughter, whom Frankie Drayton still believed had somehow been forcibly kidnapped by Ivan Albrecht, that Rasputin, although she never quite dared to say as much within earshot of Gretchen Albrecht.

The Albrecht situation, and her role in it, gave Amber's mother migraine headaches. It turned out that this was not the kind of money she admired. There was much too much of it for her peace of mind. The Albrecht circumstances overwhelmed her. The very rooms at Cavemoor, the living rooms that the fabled Mrs. Stoddard had designed to perfection and indeed was employed to constantly update and reappoint, engulfed Frankie Drayton, made her feel terribly small. The great drawing room alone, which was like the public room in a lodge in one of those huge hotels in western Canada from which they sallied forth to shoot elk in the autumn months, contained five sets of different intimate groupings of chairs and sofas, for instance, each with its own fireplace. She could never feel entirely alone once she left the sanctuary of her bedroom and made her way down the thickly carpeted Cavemoor hallway and down the stairs. Lorenzo was instantly there, not to take an order, for never at Cavemoor or at any other Albrecht domicile were guests troubled with anything so vexing as a choice, but to place before her a butler's table of tea things on a silver Georgian tray, including such delicacies as clotted cream and raspberries, crystallized ginger and hot buttered scones, or else Mrs. Drayton's double tumbler of Scotch, accompanied by a nice hefty mullioned goblet and a miniature silver bucket of ice, equipped with a pair of silver Georgian tongs. Frankie Drayton mistrusted all this service, and despite her sweet tooth she disliked eating so much rich food. Dinners at the Albrecht table were exquisite repasts concocted in the kitchen by a man who had been *sous chef* at Grand Vefour, and he was not even the Albrecht master chef, the Draytons were given to understand by Monsignor Cathcart. Gaston, the Albrecht *maître de cuisine*, a Belgian pastry chef by training, prepared food exclusively for Henry Albrecht at Great Wyke House in Buckinghamshire, where he now lived in seclusion most of the time.

They never saw Henry Albrecht. This was another thing that made Mrs. Drayton uneasy. They always seemed to be waiting for Henry Albrecht to arrive. Gretchen Albrecht was the impresario of this particular waiting game. She was often heard to hoot, "I can't wait for you both to meet Henry because I just know you're all going to hit it off like a house on fire." But he never did appear. Otherwise they seemed to wait for Gretchen. They waited in the living rooms at Cavemoor; out at the pool down at El Parador, the Albrecht hacienda on the Gulf of Mexico; in the drawing room of the double adjoining suites the Albrechts permanently occupied at the Ritz in Paris. They waited for her in the living room of the Waldorf Towers apartment or in the VIP lounge of any number of private airfields used by the Albrechts when they traveled aboard their private jets.

They were waiting, at first, for word of Ivan and Amber. The overriding excuse that Gretchen Albrecht had impressed upon the Draytons for holding them indefinitely to the bosom of her private world was that the Albrechts possessed all the resources necessary to hunt the lovers down. That was one good reason. They also possessed the means to protect Amber's parents from the press, which had not yet gotten wind of the story. Gretchen Albrecht had taken possession of the Draytons at once. From Cavemoor she had directed them to notify the headmistress of Amber's school that they had withdrawn their daughter to take her on an extended educational tour of Australia, New Zealand, and the Far East. Gretchen furthermore bestowed upon Echo Zephyr a new croquet green—with an allowance for its permanent upkeep—and in return for this rather unnecessary gift exacted from the director an explicit promise never to speak to anyone of Ivan Albrecht's residency there, indeed to expunge from the records all evidence that he had ever been their patient. Every conceivable leak was plugged by Gretchen Albrecht, who knew how this was done. Unquestionably Gretchen did possess the means to find the lovers if anyone did, and so in exchange for a few weeks of Albrecht protection and care, all the time that anyone expected the process to take before the truant couple resurfaced, Frankie Drayton was willing to put up with being a forced guest.

She didn't like it. Somehow she felt humiliated. For perhaps ten days, she would be discovered by her husband in some corner of a Cavemoor living room, quiet as a church mouse, heaving with grief, her cheeks slick with tears. All she could say was that she was homesick for Amber. In these inimical surroundings, in the company of the chilly and hard-edged Albrecht household regulars, Frankie Drayton felt the loss of Amber even more keenly than she might have in the familiar cage of the Drayton flat on Gracie Square, while the Albrecht resort atmosphere seemed to make Amber's elopement easier for her husband to bear.

In time, she pulled herself together. Soon she was once again resolute and matched the well-appointed *froideur* of Mrs. Keith and Mrs. Stoddard with her own hunter's mien. At least she had her husband. She could count on him. They could wait it out together here like people on a cruise. Every day they rose full of guarded hope and descended to a sumptuous breakfast on the brilliant, perfumed Cavemoor breakfast terrace to await the latest word from Interpol and Scotland Yard and various Albrecht secret agents whom they supposed to exist in legion around the world. Then they moved out to the pool to wait there. Then they went to the terrace by the croquet lawn to wait there over canapés and drinks before lunch, and so forth. In the afternoon Saint Francis of Drayton played tennis with Colonel Stoddard. Frankie Drayton found a niche for herself at Cavemoor arranging flowers. After a time this came to be for her a kind of occupational therapy. It was one thing of which she could never have enough: the abundant variety of brilliant blossoms available for her work in the Cavemoor gardens and greenhouses. Gretchen Albrecht never failed to pay Frankie Drayton special words of praise for the quality of her arrangements, which never failed to send through Amber's mother a shudder of gratitude, against which she could never steel herself in time.

Gretchen Albrecht's plan was to make an acolyte of Frankie Drayton. Saint Francis of Drayton she saw at once would be an easy convert. She turned him over right away to the Stoddards, who made short work of him. He was almost immediately prepared to live at Cavemoor as a permanent guest for the rest of his life. Frankie Drayton was obviously an unwilling captive, on the other hand, someone who was apt to entertain subversive notions of escape in the privacy of her quarters, where, Gretchen was alarmed to learn from Mrs. Keith, Teresa, the Spanish maid assigned to the Draytons, had discovered nesting among the piled sweaters in the bottom drawer of Frankie Drayton's dressing room bureau a snub-nosed revolver. At least it _felt_ loaded, she had said to Mrs. Keith.

Gretchen Albrecht went to work personally on Frankie Drayton. She did not attempt to overwhelm her reluctant guest with false affection or a bravura performance of spirited gaiety, as she did often so successfully when she set out to captivate the powerful men and women of state whom she and once upon a time her husband had sought to control for financial purposes. Frankie Drayton was too wary for this approach. In terms of willpower she was a match for Gretchen Albrecht. She was actually dangerous. The gun was proof enough of that. Gretchen, instead, took Frankie Drayton into her confidence. She was brilliant when it came to knowing how to use people, and in Frankie Drayton she found a lieutenant. She placed Frankie Drayton under the command of her personal brigadier general, Mrs. Stoddard, the interior decorator who best knew how to put the talents of Frankie Drayton to work, but she also included Frankie Drayton in the strategy sessions she held with her core staff, made up of Mrs. Keith, Mrs. Stoddard, and Monsignor Cathcart. Frankie Drayton was present at the weekly sessions. Her opinion in those early days was never called for, and she was not encouraged to speak out, although in time her practical advice on social matters became unwritten law, but afterward, when the staff had been dismissed, Gretchen Albrecht often kept Frankie Drayton an extra five minutes in her bedchamber with only Monsignor Cathcart in attendance to discuss the matter of Ivan and Amber.

Frankie Drayton felt like an officer at the bedside of an empress. That was the effect Gretchen wished to achieve. Frankie Drayton sat in a comfortable straight-backed Louis Quatorze armchair beside the bed, impeccably dressed for the day in loafers, a soft wool skirt the color of butterscotch, a shot-silk shirt of dull bronze, a Hermès scarf at her neck, an ivory bangle at her flared cuff. Gretchen was tiny. She sat propped up against massed pillows in a quilted bedjacket of aquamarine satin about six inches above Frankie Drayton in a vast mahogany bed with four supporting pilasters under a tented Turkish canopy of fringed damask that had once belonged to Catherine de Medici. The interesting thing to Frankie Drayton about this performance was that Gretchen Albrecht already had been elaborately made up. She undoubtedly had already taken her morning bath. Her brilliant orange hair had been gathered up, combed out, brushed, and frosted into a glorious upswept coiffure worthy of a duchess, at least.

She was a woman of over fifty who looked a year under forty. She was captivating with that bright-winged smile and her black, sparkling, upward-slanting Slavic eyes. On the third finger of her right hand she wore an aquamarine stone the size and shape of a brick of Callard and Bowser's spearmint candy, only of a more deeply Brazilian hue and clustered with tiny diamonds. She wore the ring to match her jacket. Gretchen always called her lieutenant "Mrs. Drayton" in those early days and spoke to her in a respectful, forthright manner. "I just wanted you to know, Mrs. Drayton, that we are doing everything in our power to find the children and bring them back," Gretchen said. "We have no real leads.

The *sécurité* may be brought into the case, but this is a matter that ought to be left in the hands of Scotland Yard. Some false clues have been reported, and these take time to hunt down and discredit. It's just a long, grueling process. I know how hard it is for you, just as in its own way the whole business has made us all here at Cavemoor perfectly sick with worry."

It numbed Frankie Drayton to be in a room with someone who addressed her thus, from such a height. She forgot for the moment that she was in the presence of Ivan Albrecht's mother. She was temporarily blinded. Here was a woman she could follow to the ends of the earth. She had very few questions under the circumstances to ask Gretchen Albrecht. "I want to thank you, then, Mrs. Drayton for your patience," Gretchen said. "I know it must be tedious, this whole business *is* tedious, but it's something all of us will have to endure if justice is finally going to be served. I hope everything is being handled here to make your stay as comfortable as possible so that you'll feel it's your home away from home. I *love* the flowers."

Frankie Drayton took this as a sign that the audience was over, and she rose to leave and was escorted to the bedchamber door by the monsignor. By the time she was out in the hallway and the door had closed behind her, Gretchen Albrecht had already turned to other matters presumably as pressing as the one she'd just addressed.

Gretchen Albrecht had absolutely no intention whatever of using any international agency to track down the lovers and bring them home. She could not possibly hold open house for agents from half a dozen countries. No one over whom she could not exercise the strictest control was ever allowed to penetrate the borders of her domain. None but her immediate confidantes knew that Ivan had been placed in Echo Zephyr and subsequently eloped with Amber Drayton, with the exception, that is, of a very few other cognoscenti. Gretchen Albrecht had not decided exactly what to do once she had snatched the Draytons from their Gracie Square aerie, a bold and brilliant stroke in itself, but she was quite certain that things would follow their proper course, as they very nearly always did with her help. The main thing to do, she concluded after a strategy session with Mrs. Keith, Mrs. Stoddard, and the monsignor, was to take the Draytons permanently captive, make them as comfortable as possible, and convert them into Albrecht loyalists. They were, in a manner of speaking, the in-laws of her son. She had no idea where Ivan had gone with Amber. Ann, her daughter, who rarely came to see her, was customarily vague over the phone and probably didn't know where they were. Ivan was cunning. He was the only person in the world who could strike terror into the heart of Gretchen Albrecht.

"Where on earth do you suppose they've gone?" Monsignor Cathcart ventured to ask her at the initial emergency session they held in her bedchamber at Cavemoor the morning after the Draytons had been brought there to stay.

"That's exactly what I plan to find out as soon as I possibly can," said Gretchen Albrecht, and flashed her vixen smile at the monsignor. "I have my resources, as I'm sure you can very well imagine." Which prompted her confessor's own droll, heartbroken, adoring, rueful croak of mirth.

She summoned Bruce Fox to Cavemoor. She instructed Lorenzo to take him directly to the little writing
room off the entrance hall. She made her own appearance
shortly after that through a pair of closed double doors that
opened into the writing room from what Bruce Fox could
only guess was a corner library. She gave him a rough time
right off the bat.

"Just how serious are your intentions toward my daughter
Ann?" she demanded to know.

"Pretty serious," conceded Bruce Fox.

"It's not bloody likely to work out as a match. You know
that, don't you?" Gretchen said.

It was a morning interview on a smooth overcast day in March. She wore a suit of apricot silk and matching topaz jewelry, which complemented her hair, which was lustrous and on this day as always worn upswept like the flames of an orange fire. She had allotted exactly twenty-five minutes to her interview with Bruce Fox. She appraised him candidly. This was a good room for such a close inspection. French doors opened from it onto a beige gravel drive where Fox had parked his mother's Canadian Ford. The furniture of the room was of officious, burled walnut Empire design. Fox took note because it was not a room he had been privileged to enter on his visit to Cavemoor with Teddy Beresford or later, when he attended Ann Albrecht's coming-out party as a guest of Wilhelm Beresford. The chairs and the straight-backed settee were upholstered in a banded satin material of silver and maroon.

Ann was in Paris. "She's been claimed already," Gretchen told him. "She's about to announce the engagement. I know she's been seeing you, and I know how fond of her you must be. I wish I could be more optimistic, but I can't. Just between us I'm not *that* crazy about Lansing Noble, but he's the only boy I know who's rich enough to marry Annie Pannie. I've had you checked out, and you don't even have an income. The Nobles are utilities."

"I didn't think my odds were very good to start with, Mrs. Albrecht," Fox replied. He stroked, with one hand, the smooth satin material of the bench on which he sat, while he made this absurd confession and squinted up at her as he did so with a smile. He was sitting on the settee as though it were an armchair, slumped down, so that the collar of his blazer rose up around his neck. He wore dark gray slacks, loafers.

Gretchen Albrecht squinted back. She did not dislike the

presumption of Bruce Fox. He was engaging in his forward-ness, almost but not quite obnoxious in the degree of his self-confidence. She knew about him. She'd heard about his academic achievements from Teddy Beresford, who had al-ways spoken very highly of him whenever possible. She knew that he was the son of people who had run a cleaning estab-lishment in Newark. Fox was a scholarship boy at Wilhelm's prep school, and he'd made it through the first two years at Princeton. He knew more about the Albrechts than she quite liked, however, and perhaps it was this familiarity that put him at ease in her presence, gave him the confidence to assume a rather more intimate manner than she thought was correct in someone his age. He was almost too casual, the way he sat on the settee. He was a smart aleck. He had smart-aleck looks: he always seemed to have a smile poised on his lips, a quicksilver smile. She rather liked his slickness, though, and the wicked way his nose crinkled when he grinned. She thought she might even have detected a wink.

"How well do you know Ivan?" she asked him.

This insolent young man could possibly be of use. Ivan was her problem, and she wondered whether Bruce Fox had any inkling that she was insecure about her son. She hap-pened to know that Bruce Fox was someone to whom Ivan was indifferent but not ill-disposed. Bruce was no friend of Ivan, but the truth as she knew it to be was that Ivan selected the people he wanted to know for very specific reasons. Lan-sing Noble was his only confidant, and this was what made Gretchen Albrecht uneasy about his engagement to Ann. She strongly suspected that Ivan had put him up to the whole thing, and that Ann had gone along with it because she did whatever Ivan wanted. Gretchen Albrecht brushed aside Bruce Fox's equivocal reply to her question.

"The point is, do you know Ann and Ivan together well enough to be in regular contact with them? I'll tell you why I'm asking."

Bruce Fox actually rose out of his slouch to saunter forth and ignite Mrs. Albrecht's cigarette with a fat blue-and-gold table lighter embossed with a fleur-de-lis pattern that he'd discovered on the end table beside the settee. He stood before her while she inhaled to make sure the flame had caught. She blew the smoke out of her flared nostrils like a dragon.

"I don't know if you realize that Ivan has run away from Echo Zephyr with that child he met on Fishers Island, and I'm really rather worried, not about Ivan, but about what he's done with Amber, where they've gone, and so forth. He's supposed to be locked up, of course, but that can't be helped. What I need to know is where they are, and what role Ann and Lansing played in all of this. Frankly I don't altogether trust Lansing Noble, even though I've known the Nobles for simply ages. In some respects I think Ann would be much better off with someone like you." She gazed steadily up at the young man before her and boldly said, "You're obviously a very charming and capable young man. And you're smart. I like that. Anyway it can't be helped. She's going to marry Lansing."

"Well, I've known them both for a while," Bruce Fox said, looking out the window. So Ivan's run away with Amber, he thought. He had driven in the backseat of Ivan's Cadillac convertible between Black Pond House and the Fishers Island ferry landing, with Amber in the front seat and Ivan driving at breakneck speed, jouncing the low-slung car over the dips and rises of the well-worn road as he plunged the radio buttons one after another trying to get a decent station. He couldn't claim to really know Ivan. He was Ann's friend, really. He liked Ann Albrecht very much. She was pure blond, Nordic in appearance, and that appealed to him. He had managed to invite her to dinner, once. Her manner was wary, but she laughed in spite of herself, and under the laughter something seemed to be troubling her, so that she sent out a message for help that was entirely unconscious. This turned him on. He was excited by her mystery and had hoped to pursue her into the heart of her forest kingdom, which was how he thought of Cavemoor. She had never in-vited him past the threshold of the Waldorf Towers apart-ment, however, where he'd gone to fetch her the night he took her to dinner at a very expensive French restaurant well beyond his means and afterward to a Broadway play. "Ivan's kind of hard to get to know," he said to Gretchen Albrecht.

She wasn't absolutely sure what she had in mind, but this never prevented Gretchen Albrecht from giving the impres-sion that she knew, always, exactly what she wanted. Ac-tually, in her experience, the appearance of the right person sometimes created an opportunity for employment that had not revealed itself theretofore. She did not have any specific task in mind for Bruce Fox to perform. Yet she was radiant with inspiration, and it showed. Inspiration gave her a glow. She was dressed for glow, and she was assisted as ever by nature, which obliged her and drew back the coverlet of cloud and sent a shaft of sunlight through the French windows that suddenly bathed the room in warmth and light where Gretchen Albrecht and Bruce Fox were sitting. The sun picked out glints of fire in Gretchen Albrecht's coiffure and cast her face in brilliant warmth. It lit up her topaz earrings set in gold.

She crossed her ankles and tapped her cigarette in a little gold-scalloped ashtray on the table beside her. What was charming, Bruce Fox decided, was that in spite of all her efforts she permitted herself a little disarray, so that one wisp of hair floated free of her elaborately constructed crest. It was suddenly for him a form of transport simply to be in her presence, in this little antechamber. They might have been in France. For a moment he was in some confusion about where exactly he was. He wasn't any more a friend of Ann than he was, at this intimate moment, a friend of her mother.

"I know exactly what we'll do," said Mrs. Albrecht. "Obviously we can't stop Ann from marrying Lansing Noble, and we can't force either of them to lead us to the hiding place of Ivan and Amber, but I don't see what's to prevent you from continuing to be her friend. Don't you see? Why can't you just *be* there, where she is, from time to time?"

"Well, what about Lansing Noble?" Bruce Fox frowned. He was a conspirator already. She could see that. He was cautiously appearing to be troubled by what she seemed to be suggesting, but she caught a glimpse of the excitement he must be feeling. He reddened. "I don't think he'd be too happy about this, do you?"

"No, I think not. That's why we have to be careful. But you're a photographer, Bruce, *n'est ce pas?* Why don't you go over there to France and take some pictures of them for *Vogue* or *Harper's Bazaar?* I can set that up."

Bruce Fox colored, lit up, then became somber again. "There's Ivan," he said. "He won't want me around. He's the most intensely secretive person in the world," he confided suddenly, with feeling. "He won't let anybody get close to him. I got to visit him out at Echo Zephyr because Ann needed an escort. He didn't like having me there, though. He made me wait in the solarium with the zombies while he and Ann shut themselves up in his room."

"Listen, here's what I'm going to do." Gretchen Albrecht looked at her watch. The interview was almost over. She'd decided to hire him on a trial basis as a spy. "Don't worry about Ivan. I'm going to pay you a retainer to go over to France to get some good engagement snapshots for an album I want to put together to give Lansing and Annie after they get married. Don't worry about anything. We'll have a good look at the photos when you get back, ducks, and I'm sure we'll put the right ones together."

"Okay," he said. He nodded briskly.

That was it. They stood up. She wanted him to leave by the French windows, which she opened to let him out. He swiveled sideways to slip out the door, hands in trouser pockets. She followed him out onto the gravel, waited while he got into his car, and watched him until he'd vanished into the trees at the end of the long straight carriage drive where the driveway wound through tall ivy-clad woodland to the Cavemoor gate house. He could see her in the rearview mirror.

He could not believe his luck. He kept pounding the steering wheel with his fists on the way back to the city. This was what he wanted. He wanted to be in with these people. He wanted to be in with Ann Albrecht. His heart beat a tom-tom in his chest. This was his ambition. He wanted to be on the inside of the Albrecht empire. He could endure Lansing Noble under these circumstances. He understood, furthermore, or thought he did, what Mrs. Albrecht wanted him to do. He knew that he and Mrs. Albrecht had an instinctive understanding. She wanted him to spy for her on her children. This he was willing to do. He had been trained, as a class officer, at school, to spy on his classmates for the headmaster and to report to him his findings. It had been espionage in an honorable cause. This was no different. It gave him access, the luxury of access, to the private, secluded precincts of the Albrecht empire. They'd never be able to get rid of him now that he'd been taken on, invited in, by Gretchen Albrecht, he could promise them that, whether or not he ever married Ann, which he fully intended to do if he possibly could.

He was a perfectly rotten photographer. She could tell at once. He'd spent three days with the couple in France. He'd shot some inferior pictures at the Ritz, and then the worst ones by far he'd taken out at Roissy. Of course she could understand why. They had probably treated him like shit out at Roissy, made him feel nervous and unwanted. This was the result: his picture of Ann in her riding habit made her look as though she had just thrown up, which was perfectly likely, since, as Gretchen was the first to realize, she was hardly happy about marrying Lansing. Lansing, also in riding clothes, appeared in most of these photographs in a green velvet hunting jacket, grinning. "His gums don't look too good," Gretchen pointed out. "You would never want to see gums like those reproduced in *Vogue*."

It was after nine o'clock at night. The house was silent. Night, black, stark, was not altogether effectively shut out of this room, the library off the antechamber where they had held their first meeting. He waited under some strain while she held each photograph up to a lamp on the table behind the sofa on which she sat. It was tense. She had not offered him so much as a cup of coffee. He was compelled to watch her while she examined the prints. The ones she thought she might be able to use she carefully placed beside her on the couch. She made her occasional comments over the rims of her spectacles and gazed over at him where he sat stiffly in a straight-backed chair. Then, with a shrug, she resumed her inspection of the photographs in hand. The close-ups were the most insulting. Some of the heads had been partly cropped. He had no eye for composition, either. It was hard for her to believe that anyone could be a worse photographer. When she finished looking at the pictures, she took off her glasses and sat back against the sofa.

"What did you find out about Ivan?" she asked her spy.

"Not a whole lot," he said right away. There were only three lamps on in the entire library. He could feel the gloom of the room, which was also a trifle cold, although he may have acquired this impression from the surrounding silence of the house and the wind outside that tore on the night. "Just some leads. He wasn't there, if that's what you mean."

"I didn't expect him to be there," Gretchen said. "Good grief. He has more sense than that. I just wondered if anybody said anything about him. What did people say?"

"They think he's in Poland," he said quickly.

"Poland!" Gretchen shrieked. "What in God's name are they doing there?"

"Hiding out, I assume," said Bruce Fox.

"Don't assume anything," Gretchen said vehemently. "If you don't know what he's doing, don't try to imagine, because Ivan is cunning. He could be anywhere. He could be right here now. He's very restless. He's completely unstable. He and Ann work together, you know, and now there's Lansing." She sat around on the couch, picked up her spectacles, and looked once again at the grinning Noble with his bright red gums. "Lansing is in on it, too. So attractive, really." She rapped the photograph with her long fingers. She looked right up at Fox. "Okay, Snoopy, how about it?"

"What do you mean?"

"You want to sign on?"

"As what?"

"These pictures are pretty awful. We'll sign you on as court photographer if you promise to take some lessons. You can go anywhere you want. You can stay at the Waldorf Towers in one of the maid's rooms. Mainly we work together, ducks. I want you to be my espionage agent. I want you to spy on Ann and Lansing and get as much information on Ivan as you possibly can. Never telephone me directly. Mrs. Keith takes my messages. I'll see you in the city. Do you know what the vicomte does for a living?"

"No," said Bruce Fox.

"We stable our horses at Roissy. He and Juliette are on the payroll. Still, they forget sometimes who they work for. Especially Juliette. Don't you ever forget that, if they ever give you a rough time. They work for me. The same goes for you."

In London, Ann calmly asked her mother what Bruce Fox had been employed to do.

"Why is he living at the Waldorf?" she wanted to know.

"I hired him to come and stay," Gretchen replied.

"And?"

"I don't know why I have to stand here at a cocktail party and explain why I've taken on an extremely capable young photographer."

"He's also kind of a spy."

"I know that." Gretchen took a deep drag on her cigarette and squinted. "That's in a way why I hired him. First of all I wanted him to take your wedding pictures. I also thought it would be good to have him on the payroll. He's quite furry."

"Nobody wants to hang out with Bruce Fox," Ann said. "I don't think anyone needs Bruce Fox in the House of Albrecht. I really don't like him," she said. "That's why I stopped seeing him. He's just a prick, Mother, if you have to know." She kissed her tiny mother on the forehead. "Thanks a lot."

She hated Bruce Fox. She hated her mother for bringing him into the picture. She never would have consented to spend three days with him in Paris and out at Roissy if she'd realized what her mother was up to. She considered it a direct invasion of her privacy, an insult that filled her with passionate resentment. She considered Bruce Fox to be the worst kind of prying social leech. She decided, however, not to report her conversation with Gretchen to Ivan. Instead, she flew to New York, where she invited Bruce Fox to join her for lunch at the very expensive French restaurant where he had once taken her for dinner. Her approach was to confront him head on. She was cross with Fox.

"I can't believe that you've taken a job with my mother," she told him. "Do you have any idea what she's like?"

"I'm beginning to get an idea," Fox replied. He was amused by the way Ann expressed herself. "I guess I've always known you had problems with her."

"None that I can't figure out how to handle on my own, thanks. We're talking about you. What on earth are you doing for the duchess that could constitute full-time employment?"

Bruce Fox was embarrassed. He was not without a certain pride, even though he was not blessed with any outstanding talent.

"She wants somebody full-time, to take pictures, to handle her personal publicity, to travel. Besides, I went out with you, and maybe that makes her trust me more."

"Nobody knows where Ivan is," Ann said. "Get that straight. Nobody _sees_ Ivan. Present company included. So don't get the idea that just because you work for the duchess you're going to get in touch with him."

"What do you mean?"

"I guess you _are_ slow. She's using you as a _spy_ so that she can keep herself informed of Ivan's whereabouts and activities, such as they are. Don't pretend you don't know that because I'm not an idiot. How much is she paying you?"

"Just about what I'd be getting if I took a job with an ad agency, plus rent, which isn't very much. I'm doing it because I've always wanted to be part of your family, you know. I told you I wanted to marry you. I still do. Since you won't marry me, I've got to think up other ways to get into the House. You tell me what I'm supposed to do."

"Why don't you find a job with an ad agency? It might be easier on your ego."

"Hard to get the work," Bruce Fox said. "Besides, as I told you, I want to be a part of your gang. I don't have one."

"This isn't a gang, Bruce. This is a family, of sorts. But I think you might be happier if you didn't get to know it any better than you do because it's not a happy family, as I think you've guessed. Ivan does not happen to know that you are on the payroll of the House of Albrecht. That's a good thing.

If he did know it, he'd kill you, he really would. You don't know how lucky you are to be alive. He hates dumb spies. You don't even begin to understand what the situation around here is, do you?"

"I'm a little new to it," Fox said. "But I'm learning. I know more now than I did ten minutes ago."

"What do you want, Bruce?"

"I want to marry you. I told you that before."

"Look." She smiled wanly at him. It was the one thing that filled her with dread. The only man she really loved was Wilhelm. She happened to be engaged to Lansing Noble because Ivan had promoted the union, and she had gone along with Ivan's dictates, always, because they existed in a world beyond the border of time and the reality of people like Fox, and all she really cared about was getting Wilhelm Beresford back and sealing up the frontier. This hired spook was trying to muscle in on the act, and she didn't know what to do to get rid of him, so she decided for the moment to accept him. Not forever would she tolerate his presence, but she would lead him on. She decided to ignore his highly personal statement of intent. "I don't want you to get hurt," she told him. "This is a pretty rough scene, I don't know if you realize how rough it is. It's because we've got this money. Ivan doesn't like to have people on the outside looking in, or even on the inside looking in. You'd better be careful. The duchess can really fuck you over. She knows how to do that, a lot better than I can. She's done it before."

"This doesn't make much sense, does it," he said. "Here I am, right where I want to be, and everybody tries to give me a rough time. So tell me what I'm supposed to do?"

"You're such a feckless Jew," she said, and laughed. "You're such a fucking stud. That's all you're really good for.

Still, I can think of worse things to be. Why don't you be my spy, too? It shouldn't be so hard if you really love me the way you say you do. We've been trying to keep Jews out of our family for three generations, you know. That's another thing I don't think Ivan would really like. I mean, you weren't even supposed to be on Fishers Island. They have a law there. Anyway. You can spy for me on my mother. How about it? That way maybe you could do us both a service, I mean you and me. You could keep yourself from getting killed, and you could keep me au courant on the duchess."

"Okay," said Bruce Fox. The insolence of it! He was up for any betrayal at all. She was half inclined to report his easy defection to her mother right away. She didn't like him. He was too eager to please. Yet she was just as amused by the situation as he was. He was cool. He was shaking across the table from her in merriment. He'd eaten a very rich veal chop for lunch. He ate too much rich food too greedily, she could see that. "So," he said. He wiped his mouth with his white linen napkin. "What do we do?"

"Just keep in touch," said Ann. "I'm not around too much, but if you have anything you want to tell me, just leave a message with the answering service. You can always reach me that way. It's a private, unlisted number. Don't ever let Lansing know you're trying to reach me, though, because he might get the wrong idea. We're very discreet, you know, about our private lives. He's very fond of cock and might get jealous."

He was comfortable living in the Albrecht empire. He fitted in harmoniously from the very beginning. He was variously known as the house Jew and the court photographer. Nobody actively disliked Bruce Fox. He was altogether too congenial to dislike. Furthermore, he was perfectly suited to the atmosphere of subdued waiting that prevailed in any Albrecht establishment, because he was exceptionally good at doing nothing. He had all but achieved his ambition in life, the not inconsiderable feat of being adopted by Gretchen Albrecht, even though his trophy continued to elude him, and bagging Ann was in his estimation just a matter of time, of waiting it out. Meanwhile he found at his disposal all the recreational pursuits he needed to remain pleasantly occupied most of the time. Bridge he did not very much care for, because the game demanded of its players far too much mental rigor, which was not at all beyond him, but rather more exacting than he wanted anything to be. He wanted to relax, was indeed a person of whom it could be said in all apparent truth that he had not a care in the world, which made him excellent company for the Saint, with whom he spent part of every day playing backgammon out at Cavemoor, when he was in residence there, or down at El Parador, which was always a great pleasure to visit, as far as Bruce Fox was concerned, on a par certainly with Cavemoor, but even more laid back because tropical, although for sheer ease it was his opinion that Craig Court was hard to beat. He was a successful ingredient in the Albrecht social recipe, mainly because he contributed an appealing element of youthful attractiveness, which theretofore had been missing. Nobody awfully much minded that he was a Jew except Mrs. Keith, who called him a Jew boy and found it difficult to be civil to him at the dinner table, something he had no great trouble adjusting to, since in any case she was clearly not very well liked by anyone herself, more perhaps in the end to be pitied than despised. He was far too satisfied with his lot to take issue with someone like that, as he explained to the Saint, who thought he had a point. Furthermore he hit if off with the other older women, Mrs. Stoddard, Mrs. Drayton, and Gretchen Albrecht, when she was around, for older women were a specialty of his.

Nobody else besides Mrs. Keith found it especially reprehensible that he was a Jew because he was also a photographer. This was the reason sometimes given by those who, like Mrs. Drayton, were not otherwise comfortable in the constant company of a Jew, day in, day out, no matter how attractive he might happen to be. Bruce Fox could be regarded, however, as someone who was professionally employed to take pictures from time to time, and for that you obviously hired the very best available talent, as long as it was not of the colored persuasion, to borrow a term from Saint Francis of Drayton. Luckily for Bruce Fox, not a soul at Cavemoor knew anything about photography as a profession, with the possible exception of Mrs. Stoddard, who used it in her work as an interior decorator; but she always took her own pictures with a Polaroid anyway, and these were generally worse than the ones Bruce Fox took, also with a Polaroid. His work never got any better, either. He made up in quantity what he failed to provide in quality and flooded the Albrecht scene with candid snapshots. It was true, as he'd once been told by a world-renowned *Life* photographer, that if you took enough pictures all the time, a few of them were bound to be first rate, not that anyone at Cavemoor ever cared two hoots about it one way or another. It was festive just to have someone around taking fun pictures all the time. It was another of Gretchen Albrecht's little *divertissements*.

After a time, everyone got used to Bruce Fox. He was constantly there. He was mostly to be found down by the pool, either on the chaise longue he preferred beside the Olympic-sized Cavemoor indoor pool with its glass wall looking out onto the lawn, which Henry Albrecht had paid some huge amount of money to an Italian contractor to install some years before, or else down at the new outdoor pool, when the weather was good. He found that he was even more acceptable to the Cavemoor residents when he wore a bathing suit and sat around in the seminude, available at any time for a game of backgammon and a rum drink Lorenzo knew how to make using lemon juice and sugar and something else, some special ingredient no one had ever quite been able to isolate, although the vicomtesse adamantly insisted that she had seen him micturating into the pitcher once behind the poolhouse bar and refused to drink any cocktail mixed by Lorenzo after that. Whenever he was present at Cavemoor, Monsignor Cathcart, once he was freed from his matutinal duties as Gretchen Albrecht's confessor, would invariably make a bee-line for the poolhouse, to bask in the proximity of Bruce Fox's young physique.

He also, Bruce Fox, liked to travel on assignment for Gretchen Albrecht. He told his employer about his lunch with Ann at La Caravelle. "Obviously, she's on to me," he told Gretchen when he next saw her in London, at Claridges. "She knows I'm working for you," he said.

"Of course she knows that, darling. I told her you were working for me. I'm paying you. She knows all about that."

"Not that I'm your spy."

"No, I never told her that directly because you weren't, exactly, hired to be a spy. I took you on to snap delicious photos of all things Albrecht, and I'm absolutely delighted with the work you've been doing, it's terribly exciting. Honestly. If you reward me with a morsel of sorely needed gossip every now and then, I'll be more than happy. You see how it works."

"The situation may have grown a little out of hand," said Fox. "By the way, did you know that she calls you 'the duchess'?"

Gretchen released a sharp laugh. "That's divine," she said. "Ann has always been very good at nomenclature. You see, you are a spy whether you want to be or not," she said.

"Yes, I guess I am, and now guess what?" He lit Gretchen's cigarette with his own, new, gold Dunhill lighter. He did not smoke himself but found the accessory useful.

"Tell me." Gretchen had a few minutes to spare.

"I think Ann would like me now to go to work for her."

"I think that's a very good idea." Gretchen regarded him thoughtfully. "Why *don't* you do that. You might find out something really useful for a change, instead of what derogatory nicknames my children think up." She looked suddenly resentful. "We still have no word on Ivan. What are you planning to do about that, if I may ask?"

"I'm on my way to Switzerland now," he lied. "There's a rumor that he's been seen in Geneva."

"Good, that should be fun," Gretchen said. "You can be Ann's spy, too, you know. It's quite all right by me. It's all the same family. I can't imagine what there is to tell her that she couldn't get straight from me, though. Whereas, who knows? There might be quite a lot of stuff you can find out if you stick around her long enough. If you can manage to keep track of her, she moves around so much."

He was really working for Teddy Beresford. That, to Bruce Fox, was the best joke of all, his most private joke. He was a Beresford man. He'd been chosen by Teddy Beresford while he and Wilhelm were in school together and off and on through school and even when he and Wilhelm had gone their separate ways—Wilhelm to Sandhurst, Bruce Fox to Princeton—they'd stayed in touch, and he had spent one summer in the south of France at a villa Teddy Beresford had rented in Cannes. He recalled the crowded beaches of the south of France, the sultry air, the cluttered hillside behind Cannes, the palmy evenings. That was the summer of Teddy Beresford's great humiliation, when he'd been summarily fired by Gretchen over the telephone from New York, and Beresford's outrage.

He'd been selected by Teddy Beresford to be a future ADC: Teddy was a great one for plucking some young man out of a pool of contenders and giving his protégé every special advantage. He'd spotted a good acquisition in Bruce Fox, had brought him into the bosom of the family and picked up the cost of his college tuition. He'd even hoped, when he was running it, to bring the young Fox into the House of Albrecht, but that had not worked out. Instead, Teddy Beresford was out of the House of Albrecht altogether, and Bruce Fox was on the grounds of the Albrecht domain. This was not mere good luck as far as Teddy Beresford was concerned. He'd helped set it up to some extent, encouraged Bruce from afar to keep his eye on Ann Albrecht. Now that he was inside, Bruce Fox repaid Teddy Beresford's patronage with his loyalty. He knew a great deal. He knew that Henry Albrecht had been murdered. He knew that Teddy had helped to dispose of Henry Albrecht's body in the abandoned poolhouse in the Cavemoor woods. He knew that much. He knew about the poolhouse, even though he'd never actually gone out there to visit the site.

He knew enough, Teddy Beresford had made certain of that, so when the time came and Gretchen Albrecht finally summoned him to Cavemoor, Bruce Fox had all the confidence he needed to enter a high-stakes game. He had no purse, but he was playing with a distinct advantage of his own because he knew what hands some of the other players held. It gave him an impudence that was like an open challenge. For someone who was the size of a jockey, Bruce Fox was sexually provocative. He had a naughty snicker that was sexually suggestive. He carried his trim body with a swagger. He wore neckties of brilliant hue, like plumage, that advertised his cocky self-esteem. He liked to fondle a very good, long, richly brown cigar between his lips in front of men who

were much bigger than he was, after formal dinner parties at
Cavemoor, when the men gathered in the library to speak of
manly things. He liked to tell the servants what to do.

He stayed in touch with Teddy Beresford. He it was who
brought Teddy Beresford into Operation *Zephyr Echo*. He
gave Teddy Beresford the all-clear sign to go and see Ann
and Ivan Albrecht in Rome on his way back to South Africa.
He met with Teddy in the lobby of Brown's Hotel in London
after he and Ann returned with Wilhelm from Corfu. He told
Teddy that Ivan was prepared to help him get his millions
back from Gretchen in return for his assistance, and although
Bruce Fox couldn't, or wouldn't, tell him what they wanted
him to do, Teddy Beresford saw it as the invitation he'd been
waiting for to get back into the game. He'd briefly entertained the hope that Wilhelm might oblige him by marrying
Ann, but things had gone awry there, hadn't they? Wilhelm
had eloped instead with Teddy's mistress. Better still, Teddy
thought, was this new scheme, presented by Bruce Fox. Of
course it meant that he'd have to deal with Ivan, but Ann
would be along. Besides, all that was long ago.

Ivan wore a brown bomber jacket with a sheepskin collar.
Ann wore a sable jacket. They sat across from Teddy Beresford in the back of a bar on the Via Babuino. What struck
Teddy Beresford was their twinness: Ivan with his shoulder-
length black hair that gave him the look of a beautiful Val-
kyrie, and Ann, platinum blond, were both white-faced, and
like the children of inbreeding he had seen, they both possessed high, wide, domed foreheads. Ann's diamonds glittered on her fingers in the candlelit interior of the bar. Ivan
said to Beresford:

"So you know about our plan." He had a prim, crafty face.

"I do," Beresford said, "insofar as I have been in communication with Bruce Fox. I must say at the outset that I'm not all that keen about children's pirate games."

Ivan lowered his head as though in silent prayer.

"Cut the crap, Teddy," Ann said.

"Oh, Ann," Ivan said as one mumbling the rosary. "Let it go."

"I will not. You," she said to Teddy Beresford. "You killer pirate, you killed Henry Albrecht, so don't be such a cunt."

Teddy Beresford got red. "My, my," he said.

"Ann, Ann, Ann," said Ivan now as though she were causing him pain.

"No, it's true," she said. "It's time to tell the truth, you butler cunt. My brother saw you. Mother always tried to make it look as though he did it. He did not do it, and you know it. You're a hired butler killer."

"I'm afraid it's his word against mine," said Teddy. Something nasal crept into his voice. "Isn't it? My good steadfast trusted word against a ranting madman. You were lucky they took you away," he said to Ivan. "The butler never does it," he sneered to Ann.

Ivan raised his eyes to look at Ann to see what she would say.

"A henchman, then," she said. "Let's get our language straight. A henchman killer pirate butler cunt."

"Why?" Teddy Beresford ignored Ann. He held the palms of his hands up and shook his head, postulating amazed laughter as he addressed himself, red-facedly, to Ivan. "Dear boy, if you *saw* me do it, as you seem now to claim, then why the bloody hell didn't you notify the town police?"

Ivan fiercely regarded the nails of the fingers of both hands, turned both his palms upward to do it. He clenched his jaw in furious concentration. Then he looked at Teddy Beresford with the abused hauteur of a great, proud, beautiful whore, battered but unbowed before the law, as though he'd practiced this for years.

"Pirates settle things among themselves," he said quietly to Teddy.

"It's over," Ann said abruptly to block any further elaboration on that theme. "It's time for you to get us Wilhelm," she said to Teddy.

"Get Wilhelm?" Teddy Beresford said. "Get Wilhelm? What on earth do you mean?"

"We want Wilhelm. You have to help us get him. That's the deal. You get us Wilhelm, you get the money. It's a trade-off," she said. "We need him."

"But why?" Teddy wanted to know.

"To run the private army," Ann replied patiently, as if the whole thing ought to be perfectly clear by now. "Didn't Brucie tell you anything?"

Ivan said:

"Teddy, Ann loves fucking Willy. Loves to fuck him. That's all. She's Lorna Doone. He's just too shy. You know that? He's a wild bongo. You have to entice them to a feed. They don't eat," he said, and revealed his gums obscenely, like a camel, to Teddy Beresford, to make his point. He was clearly on some kind of drug.

"Perfect rubbish!" Teddy Beresford exploded.

Ivan grinned at Ann. "You see?" he said.

"No, it's not 'perfect rubbish,' " Ann said to Teddy. "Forget about the fucking. Sure, I like to do it. But I need Wilhelm, Teddy. I need him, we need him to come help us sabotage the company. We've got to get our clutches on his little ham hocks before he disappears into the Hindu Kush or wherever it is that he's going. Nepal. He's gonna get away.

We need your help. Let's forget about the business with the kukri. Okay?"

Teddy Beresford looked stricken.

"What about my money?"

"You get your money. Fifty percent of the preferred stock, plus all the cash you tried to steal that's in New York. You get that back. You do, you do. We'll give you a title," she said. She was excited. Her voice trilled. "Lord Killer Butler-Cunt," she said, and laughed maniacally. "How's that? You can help us run the show. Really."

"Stop this cunt talk," said Teddy Beresford.

"Oh, Teddy," Ivan said. He had a silken voice that matched the white silk scarf he wore at his throat. "Be a sport. We know you want that money. You want to take that succulent cunt of Wilhelm's to Palm Beach." He flashed his winning hand at Teddy Beresford with a smile of astonishment at his own good luck.

For it was true. What got him in the end was not the money, it was his lust for Doreen. He never would have agreed to pitch his son into the Albrecht furnace had it not been for Doreen. He wanted Doreen for himself. He wanted her back. They were a natural pair, Doreen and Beresford. They were the king and queen of hearts. They were big brazen people with enormous appetites for all the worldly things, and they each had something the other wanted: Doreen had a beautiful, luscious body, a certain glamour, marvelous sense of adventure, and speed; Teddy Beresford had it nearly within his grasp to set her up in a very grand way. Teddy Beresford did take a good look around, first. He gripped the arms of his throne in the manner of someone who is strapped to the electric chair. His eyes bolted from Ivan to Ann. Gretchen's twins stared at him with matching, eager

177

faces. White petals on a dark, wet bough. Please, Uncle Teddy, say you'll do it. He was a startling purplish color, richly pressured as he was by the grief and lust that ran through his veins. His eyes glowered from under his blond and tufted eyebrows, lips pursed, a big man picking up a rotten stench through whitened nostrils.

"Very well," he said.

The Draytons were now permanently, one might also say rapturously, installed at the Albrecht court. Frankie Drayton adored her work as chief flower arranger under the direction of the bullish, white-haired Mrs. Stoddard, who made her feel so gay, so carefree, once again, like a vibrant little girl. Saint Francis was in heaven. He never seemed to do a great deal that was obvious to the eye, but then he never all that much liked to do things. Even playing tennis after a while became something of a trial for him. What he really liked to do was travel with the Albrecht entourage. He considered himself retired. He liked to read. He continued to devour spy novels. One day, when she was passing through the living room where Saint Francis was reading from a stack of novels by Alistair Maclean, Gretchen, who was on her way to London, cried out: "We'll have to buy a writer for Saint Francis who can turn these things out by the hour!" She whooped with laughter, was gone. He was still red with merriment days later at the very thought.

The Draytons loved the travel and the hoopla of takeoff and arrival, the rustle of tissue paper when they unwrapped the presents from Gretchen that always awaited them at their destination: an ebony box inlaid with mother-of-pearl and ivory for Frankie, inside which she found a diamond-and-sapphire scarab pin, for Saint Francis a pair of gold cuff links set with little jade pre-Colombian Mayan faces, and a leather set for each of them, gold-embossed with their initials, containing little silver flacons of eau de cologne, toilet water, and talcum powder from the Albrecht accessory specialist on Bond Street. Things like that.

This kind of treatment they absolutely relished. They were now part of the inner circle, members of the team that entertained the guests who were brought into the Albrecht fastness either by plane or by private car. This in particular was the function served by Saint Francis. He was simply there, at all times, prepared to entertain the Albrecht guests with the most spirited gossip and badinage. He loved to talk about all the people he'd known on the tennis circuit during his youthful twenties. He was a master of the dropped name, a whiz at cocktail talk. He was a voracious consumer of all the newspapers brought to him in the morning in a flower basket by old Lorenzo. He liked to read the *New York Times*, *The Wall Street Journal*, the Paris *Herald Tribune*, and the London *Times*. He also read, from cover to cover, *The New Yorker*, *The Atlantic Monthly*, the *Manchester Guardian*, *Newsweek*, and

Time magazine. It would have been difficult to be more con-
versant on the subject of current events than Saint Francis of
Drayton, which was invaluable to Gretchen Albrecht as a
service when she imported the president's wife to El Parador
for the weekend, or brought the French ambassador to the
United Nations out to Cavemoor for lunch, or, down in South
Africa, when she invited the leader of the opposition down to
the Albrecht lodge at Timbavati.

Together, also, the Draytons made a handsome couple.
Her appearance was really the virtue of Frankie Drayton,
socially speaking, in the opinion of Gretchen Albrecht. She
also made an excellent fourth at bridge and a good golfing
companion to the occasional business tycoon Gretchen
brought in for a visit, and she went out on board the jet-
powered Albrecht cabin cruiser to fish for marlin with the
president of Mexico while Saint Francis entertained his wife,
Carmen, at a luncheon served al fresco at the El Parador pool.

Nobody ever mentioned Amber. The Draytons no longer
used their house on Fishers Island. They put it on the market. They also sold the apartment on Gracie Square. This
was Gretchen Albrecht's idea. Too many painful memories
of Amber. They had never gone back there after their departure the night an Albrecht limousine had come to fetch them
in the rain. Gretchen handled the whole thing through Adrian
Gilbert, her estate manager, who got them an extremely good
price.

The money was useful. The House of Albrecht paid for
everything except tips and the presents, or tribute, that the
Draytons discovered they were expected to bestow not only
upon Gretchen and the absent Henry Albrecht, but to all
other members of the extended Albrecht family. Gratuities
ate up the yearly Drayton income, and for tribute they were

forced to dig into capital resources. The choosing of presents took up a part of every day whenever the Draytons found themselves away from Cavemoor. It required their joint ingenuity and imagination to think up new gifts. It meant keeping lists, comparing them constantly to make certain they didn't repeat or overlap. They pored over catalogs from Cartier and Fortnum and Mason. They browsed hungrily through the antique bazaars of London, Paris, Rome, and Madrid to stockpile treasure against the day they might be caught shorthanded.

A competitive spirit of gift giving prevailed at *Chez* Albrecht. The Albrecht people scrutinized their presents with a practiced analytical eye, and in time the Draytons developed a similarly shrewd sense. If you gave a mink-lined cassock to Monsignor Cathcart, furthermore, you had to be sure that the golf cart you proffered Colonel Stoddard bore a somewhat higher price tag, not because the colonel was of higher domestic rank than the Jesuit, but because his wife, who was, might decide to take offense.

The Draytons' brief, rushed visits in Manhattan were spent on buying sprees with Mrs. Stoddard or Mrs. Keith or young Bruce Fox, who never had any money of his own to speak of and so had to be helped along by Saint Francis, who thought of himself as bearing an easy, avuncular relationship to the photographer. On such occasions they took lunch in a party at "21," visited the theater in entourage, and consequently seldom caught more than a glimpse of old good friends or relatives, which was a relief, really, because that way they avoided any difficult questions concerning the whereabouts of Amber. They found that they could do very well without most of their old chums, fond of them as they may have been, although it was always possible to fit them in at the hairdresser or the barbershop.

They never met Henry Albrecht. They had at one time eagerly anticipated the day when they would meet him, but that expectation finally waned. They heard about him. Gretchen Albrecht constantly quoted him, referred to his authority, and she was always coming back from England with fresh word of his existence, but they never saw him. Monsignor Cathcart drolly assured them with his basset hound rue that if they actually saw Henry Albrecht, they wouldn't be in any doubt at all of his existence.

"I mean, he's enormous," he groaned. He'd really become quite a good friend of the Draytons. They often sat together out beside the pool, at El Parador, at Cavemoor, at the Mamounia, at Craig Court. It was the one time he did not have to be present in their lives as a priest. He wore a pair of bikini briefs out by the pool to bronze his chaplain's pallor, and he liked to play backgammon with Bruce Fox and the Draytons, sip Lorenzo's rum drinks by the hour, sometimes attired in a terry-cloth gown to prevent his skin from turning a profane shade of brown. He it was who filled the Draytons in on all the inside Albrecht family gossip. Really he gave them all the lowdown, including the scandalous excesses of gluttony to which Henry Albrecht was profoundly enslaved. "I mean, it's become far more of an illness in the true sense of that word than *anyone*"—Monsignor Cathcart loved to exaggerate the sound of words with an almost theatrical emphasis and roll his eyes—"in their wildest imaginations ever *dreamed* possible, and it's quite frankly one reason *I* think that Gretchen more or less runs the company. I mean, it's *quite* extraordinary how much she really does run the business. All ex-post-Beresford-o," he said with an agonizing groan of mirth dragged up from the depths of his esophagus. "For it was Beresford, let's be honest," he said to Saint Francis, who was red-faced and agape with rapt fascination in the sun, "who

183

after all put the Albrecht consortium"—he pronounced the word *consorshum*—"on the global scene, carto*graphically* speaking, and I daresay *truly truly* adored Gretchen, as you can see even now whenever he comes over here for lunch. She just kicked him out. He *really* had to go. He was *quite* high-handed. I think he'd purchased at least half the pre-ferred shares of Albrecht for his personal account *right* before they were issued, which was *simply* unpardonable. You cannot imagine how that infuriated Gretchen, whom you've got to admit is really at heart *quite* generous with the people who work for her, and of course Teddy never got to realize the sale of his stock." Monsignor Cathcart told Saint Francis of Drayton that Teddy Beresford's Albrecht stock, worth mil-lions and millions of dollars, was still sitting in his name creating dividends that were forever impounded in a New York bank where he couldn't get at the money because Gretchen Albrecht had arranged to have the SEC freeze the account until the matter of the Albrecht shares was settled. "But you see he won't *dare*," Monsignor Cathcart explained to Saint Francis by the Craig Court pool, "come to New York to fight it out in court because she'd have him put in jail or some such *awful* thing because she's capable of *the most* ex-treme measures when sufficiently aroused. Ivan is a case in point." Here again the monsignor raised his eyebrows in a knowing way. "Because he really was a trial, I think, abso-lutely from *day one*—I mean, the moment he stuck his no doubt already grizzled head from between her legs, let's face it—at which point she really *ought* to simply have crossed her thighs or done something like that because he never *was* normal."

Monsignor Cathcart on the paved terrace beside the black marble Craig Court pool sipped at his rum drink, which was replenished from a gold pitcher by a Bantu servant in a white uniform crossed at the torso by a green silk sash. He proceeded to fill Saint Francis of Drayton in on Ivan the Terrible. "Which *is* an appropriate name if ever there was. *Really.*" He groaned. "It took three people to supervise Ivan when he was growing up. I mean, you simply haven't any *idea* what it was like. He killed Miss Pym. I mean, it was said to be a hemorrhage, and I haven't any doubt in my mind at all that it *was* a hemorrhage, but caused by what, I ask you? An *enor*mous brass paperweight shaped like a heart that fell out of the sky on her head from nowhere. And she was *not* Ivan's governess, technically speaking, she was Ann's. I mean *really.* You know that's really why Henry went to England. It had nothing whatever to do with Teddy Beresford *au fond*, although Gretchen *does* want people to think so and you can quite see why because it's plausible, but if that's the case, then why did Henry move to England *before* Teddy Beresford was expelled and not after he left?"

"He's such a *hunk*," said Frankie Drayton. She was cutting the stems of freshly harvested yellow roses at a glass table under the pool canopy nearby. She'd met Teddy Beresford only the night before, at the Arabian Nights ball.

"He was absolutely *the* best polo player at Windsor before the war," the monsignor informed her over his shoulder from the mat where he lay on his side before the backgammon board. "He was already a commissioned officer with the Brigade of Gurkhas, and then, you see, he had a very good war. He was attached to the HQ of the Supreme Allied Commander, which put him right on top, and then after that he came to the Rand with *enor*mously good credentials and got right in with Henry and Gretchen, who really rather used him, I must say, but I *do* think they would have treated him better in the end if he hadn't been quite so frightfully ambitious. I don't think Wilhelm's ambitious at all. It's quite true that Henry *was* very fond of Teddy Beresford, and when they parted company he was absolutely *grief*-stricken, but after all, by then he was in England, and I do to this day think Ivan did it. I mean, you know in the *end* Ivan lived at Cavemoor all alone." This information elicited a gasp from Frankie Drayton, who'd never heard it. Neither had Bruce Fox, who had just thrown double sixes and was about to take the game. "It's true. With Ann. Ann they never *could* do much about, although they sent her off to school. Finally," he groaned, "with great effort they got Ivan into one of those rather posh but quite second-rate Swiss boarding schools at Locarno. Henry *never* saw him again. I think he *simply* went away," the monsignor said with a little flick of his fingers, "vamoosed. No one *ever* sees him. That's not *strictly* true, but you know what I mean. He sees the people in England, and of course he sees the vicomte and the vicomtesse, who's so divine and *truly truly* loyal, and then he sees the vet, who gives him shots, and all sorts of *rather* shadowy men he wakes up at four in the morning on Threadneedle Street. They come roaring out to Buckinghamshire when he calls. He doesn't shoot. He shot all those elephants in one day down at Timbavati, which was an awful scandal because you really *aren't* supposed to do it, and after that he stopped. *Everybody* got a standing lamp made out of an elephant's trunk, but the awful trouble was that you couldn't really put lampshades on them." The monsignor groaned and rolled his eyes.

"I've gammoned you," said Bruce Fox. "At last. It's taken me all day."

Gretchen Albrecht had not at this late hour in her life expected to fall in love. She had experienced love once in her life, as a child, and she therefore very well knew what it was, considered it to be a disease, could sense the symptoms of it at a very great distance, and had developed a battery of defenses against it that had kept the illness at bay for forty years. It had not been necessary for Gretchen Albrecht to resort to the use of a chastity belt to protect herself against the charms of sexual intercourse, in which she had permitted herself to engage often enough with Henry Albrecht to keep his lustful nature satisfied. His method, or style, of sexual congress was entirely self-serving, for which

Gretchen had always been grateful. He had never sought to bring her sexual passion into play through artful and prolonged coitus and the seductive provocation of foreplay. He had never been of an especially experimental nature, greedy as he had always been, and indeed he made love to her very much as you might expect a man to do for whom plunder was a way of life. He never wasted time on what he wanted; Gretchen collaborated in the satisfaction of his lust. She never experienced therefore any of the humiliation attendant upon sexual submission. She never surrendered herself to the oblivion of orgasm. The Catholic Church and the Holy Fathers had greatly helped her to know how this could be done. Later, before his premature demise, Henry Albrecht had come to feel that sex was essentially unrewarding and found that food satisfied his lust as well as anything could and soon enough ceased to trouble his wife for conjugal favors whatsoever. This left her secure in what she considered her bastion of chastity, a state of being not without allure for men of an adventurous spirit like Teddy Beresford, who assaulted the bastion at their peril and found themselves brutally impaled upon the jagged rocks below; for while her eyes bewitched and her fragrance bewildered the men she wished to dominate—nay, ruin—below the neck she carried herself as one armored in cast iron. Few men would really dream of trying to seduce Gretchen Albrecht. She was too forbidding. She herself could not imagine such a thing ever coming to pass. She was not even on the lookout for it. Apart from her personal maid, who was an ancient Carpathian crone, no one ever saw Gretchen Albrecht naked, except God, for whom she had been saving herself, and, once, quite by accident, Monsignor Cathcart, who was visibly shaken by the experience.

Perhaps what finally happened was a failure of vigilance, for, having quite forgotten altogether that God had after all created her as woman, and being out of touch with the visible manifestations of concupiscence, she made the error of actually inviting Bruce Fox to hook the back of her dress one evening when she was meeting him at Claridges in the drawing room of her suite—the maid was out, it was a last-minute thing—and thus offered him the chance he took not to hook the Balenciaga gown, but to zip it down the back, slip those nimble fingertips, warm they were, up her bodice as at one and the same time he put his mouth on the side of her neck and gently moved against her hips in such a way that might both hint at the truly ardent nature of his desire and distract some of her attention from the manual play about her surprised and stimulated breasts and the swift things that followed, so that desire rushed before affront, and she permitted herself just that one moment of pleasure, stood, head thrown back, to feel those thick fingertips flying about her nipples, moved, in fact, her head to one side to give the sucking mouth as much purchase on the tender, somewhat loose flesh on her neck as it could obtain, allowed, in that one fraction of a minute's abandon, her buttocks to graze the unsprung arc of passion in his youth's groin.

Bruce Fox! His gift was quite confounding. His assault was so keenly alert to that one brief flicker of indulgence that he'd got her skirt not off but up, high up, and slipped at once her underwear down just far enough to send one fleet hand down there: it was not a gift for the sensitive romantic gesture as anybody's mother might have thought it was rather a boy's shrewd understanding of the purely erotic thing to do with the back of his thumb on the inside of her leg around the lip of her vagina and the way he was pressing his own now naked, stiff organ like a hot rubber knout against her now writhing backside as she struggled with confusion, for if he was as miniature as she then could he be so strong? What was she doing? Love rushed in, years and years of it, so fast, so turbulently, she could hear it crying like twenty little school-girls running out of class at last to play, all crowding out the door together, at once; her joy tumbled out with tremendous force that robbed her of just the trigger reaction she needed to thrust this sly satyr from behind, for that was surely what she should have done so rude he was so brash the way he seemed to so deftly be somehow brushing now her vulva with his moist warm fingertips, that she had to go down on her knees, onto the floor, then onto her hands, until she collapsed onto her face, still on her knees. Her hair tumbled down around her face and on the rug beside her. She lay like that. She closed her eyes against the glare of the light. She felt her ballgown, the skirts of her Balenciaga, way up around her shoulders. She heard the metal clink sound his belt made as his trousers struck the floor at his knees and at the same time she stretched up her hindquarters as high and widely spread as possible to feel him basting the hot bulb of his sex on the smelly juices of her vagina, for he wasn't evidently taking any chances, and soon enough this huge thing slid so way up inside her that she had to sing with laughter and joy, surprise, and had to sob with laughter while he was up there and continuing to do some very expensive, provoking light body pinching all over the surface of her jugs and nipples and her belly, pawing, also, with those same free fingertips all around the area of her crotch, which woke her up, made her get onto her hands, pull her knees forward a little, so he could dip up with a quick little squiggle of his groin, then pull down, slip it up. These things, she wanted his body over hers, wanted him to hold her love, those hands her breasts, bite fuck her nape, she could spear her underlap with his crazy golf ball right tug-up in her belly, butted her back then up, splaying big back thighs, so onto him she could rise and fall and feel the grinning surface of his so-white teeth on the kidskin of her neck riding the horse in the saddle warmly tucked butt fast where he could lean forward behind her. Together they rode like this at a clip. She no longer cried. That was earlier. She was proud to be a woman. Exultant. Chin high. He grinned there right beside her as they rode. Bruce Fox. He had a little mustache. He had those eyes that narrowed in the wind. There was something sort of marvelously clear and free, now she'd got her back straight and could move her torso on the saddle without much more than moving buttocks to the rhythm of the horse, threw her hair back, held breasts up for Bruce to hold with her nipples between his gummed fingers for balance so they could gallop. Her dress was on fire. She had to scream. Such a rude man, he put the whole palm of his moist hand like a damp cloth over her nose and mouth so roughly to clog her scream even though really screaming she burned so hard right up her scorching back and also the other thing was she forced it into the fire as far as it would go by lifting knees up and tipping naked body on horseback into the fire and pulled way up on the long thin burning gear, which was there as rather a shock. Important then to get away from it this way: to crouch down on it, bend forward, forget it that way, no, get away back up on it, no get down go forward, no get backward, knock forward, heart can't get time, get forward, can't get out, push, yes, push my head down boy don't you ever stop. On hands and knees once more. Now so prosaic. Oh this was the thing: simplicity, numbness, she recalled, recalling God, looked up with sudden exultant cry and then two things: One, God. The other hard to keep them apart: God up there, and the hot deep, deep pull, head caving in. Then: something she would just have to endure, she guessed, like a bad plane ride, so exciting, so much fun, such chaos, so much imminent death, all jostled around inside the jet, such mad laughter, such sudden pounding, such air pockets of swoon, such a flash of gleaming eggs, black eggs on either wall lit up in one white brilliant wash of light, that's what it was she didn't want, couldn't stop, all at once remembered now too late that awful reawakened ache inside that now she'd have to hose down. She crouched and winced and held herself in such a sudden ball of contained ecstasy, hot and cold. Oh, how she didn't need this. It wasn't his fault. He was only fucking. He was doing his part. He was only fucking. He was only fucking, which was his job. He was just manfully fucking. He was fucking regular. He was fucking at a certain regular pace. She was holding, shaking. She was holding, shaking. He was only fucking with his legs spread way out now so his thighs were clamping hard on hers and his whole belly was shooting over her bowed hips and his chest she could feel on her spine and his wet mouth sobbed on her shoulder so she was ready when he jetted. Caught it. Got it on the tiny diamond dot. Let it flood along the inside of her belly, pumped him out.

She wouldn't let him go, kept him with her all night long, canceled her dinner date at Ambassadeurs with the earl of Dunraven, canceled the maid, couldn't believe he could maintain an erection like that off and on the whole night, yet he did; very, very long erection, too, which she had to suck for fun such wanton lust had overcome her chaste and paralyzed soul, much longer than she ever would have guessed for a young man who looked like that, so boyish and skinny in appearance with his comical angelic facial expression, his grinning cherub lips, and innocent blue eyes, too blissfully the piping Pan for her taste: his Adam's apple protruded too nakedly, his jug ears burned, his cheeks glowed like bright little apples when he grinned. Yet he possessed a penis, when she actually saw the thing in full erection, that looked like a throbbing, puce-headed python or some such thick and life-eager thing with a fierce will that could not be denied and seemed to lead its master like a divining rod, no no he couldn't leave her bed until she'd had that thing inside her twenty or thirty times, that was all she wanted, he quite surprised, he caught up so short that when she insisted he climb athwart her and enter while she held her thighs with both hands. He was suited, moreover, to her petite dimensions; they were perfectly matched miniatures. She adored him, needed him, loved him, would not turn off the light and said so, would not turn off the light again ever, for now she found that this would take up the rest of her life, this thing, cost all the money she had ever amassed just to keep it mainly up inside her, keep it fed and nourished and properly clothed and adored and bejeweled and working like a stallion or a good Lear jet or a nice viscount, had to assuage those awakened inner banks of black, gleaming eggs that ached and needed constant washing down.

She'd marry him, probably. This was something she couldn't *not* have. They'd have to somehow announce the death of Henry Albrecht. Or she could keep Bruce Fox somewhere, but not in the eyes of the Lord. She was so giddy. He propped himself up on an elbow beside her, ran his liquid fingers through her hair, licked her neck, rolled his tongue in her mouth, butted his long member up until it nudged the undersides of her breasts, she climbed aboard. Each time she got it in her was a new surprise. All those years. Now this. Now love at last. How long did they remain together in that bed? Another day. And then she had to see him all the time, work her life around this extraordinary new development.

So began the odyssey of Bruce Fox. He began a life dedicated to following the instructions of Gretchen Albrecht. At first he managed to carry out the dictates of the love affair and pursue the demands of his career as court photographer at the same time. From the outset, however, the excitement of the love affair made it all but impossible to concentrate on his assignments. In Paris, at the Georges Cinq, he found a message from Gretchen on Roissy stationery, thick pale green notepaper with the deep green embossed Roissy crest; her handwriting was lavish, slapdash, ink-splotched; the envelope perfumed. "Darling B. I do I do I *do* love you, come to me in Rome." She instructed him to fly to Rome, to wait for her at the Hassler, where she promised to meet him in two days. He waited for her nervously in Rome. She sent for him to meet her at the Palazzo Albrecht near the Cancelleria. Too many phone calls. She was in love, however. That much was established. She had to attend a dinner, and he agreed to be at his hotel, where he drank, read a book, did not dare go out because he couldn't miss seeing her when she showed up, which she did very late, he could hear the rustle of her skirts as she flew down the hallway to his room.

"These goddamned papal dinners at the Curia," she declared in her rich contralto voice, and unlatched a gold bracelet set with square emeralds the size of cough drops, dropped it on the dressing table with a clunk. She was very egotistical, self-involved, he realized with some admiration, like a lioness. In the privacy of his room he could feel the raw power of her ego, which, in public, on the occasions of her rare appearances, was felt not as toughness but as glamour.

"Okay, kid," she told him. "Whatever you want."

He wanted to massage her back and feel her soft, loose

flesh beneath his hands while she lay, facedown, on the bed. He liked rich, older women: liked their clothes, their perfumes, toilet waters, liked their powders and their jewelry, their hair and their shoes, he liked their soft flesh, the old smell of their soft flesh under the perfume, the slight stink of stagnant oils, and their soft, pouchy, fallen breasts. The light was on. They always kept it on. He liked to look at Gretchen. Her face, turned sideways on the pillow, shadowed anxiety, the anxiety she felt after a tense evening, and a certain concentration. She had no resistance to Bruce Fox once he got going, but this night, in Rome, after he had made love to her four times, she sobbed: for what? For her lost world, her lost dominion?

In the morning she put on her light green chiffon opera dress, looked a little messy, smoked a cigarette, which she placed on the mantel. He wore a gray suit. They went below together and departed, she for the Palazzo Albrecht, where her entourage, the Draytons and the Stoddards, awaited her, he to New York.

"When will I see you again?" he wanted to know.

"I'll call."

The best thing, given her life, they decided, because his life, his career, were flexible, was for him when he returned to New York to go directly to the Albrecht apartment at the Waldorf Towers and wait there for her call. He did as they had agreed he would and sat in the impersonal opulence of the Waldorf Towers apartment: heavy satin curtains drawn against the night, pale blue silk lamp shades, satin chair covers, everything comfortable and deeply relaxing.

He couldn't go out. She didn't come. Finally, around nine o'clock he descended to the street. It was an alien city. He went to the Bull and Bear, ordered a couple of Scotch and sodas, a beer, a sirloin steak, paid for it. The tab was enormous, but he was using money Gretchen had given him, and he carried in his wallet enough money for ten meals like this one. He paid up and quickly returned, self-consciously, to the comforting dead silence of the apartment. She came in the following morning, burst in with tremendous gusto, red hair swept up in her duchess coiffeur, all corseted, bound up in a blue silk dress, white gloves, while he was drinking his second pot of coffee in the living room. He'd thought about it, he told her. He'd decided he couldn't go on, do this. He couldn't bear the waiting.

"Come on," she said. "Let's talk about it on the way uptown."

In the car she held his hand in a vise. They got out on Park Avenue in front of a building in the eighties. Upstairs, in a lavish apartment, she gave herself to him with all her pent-up desire. They made love in a huge, round bed beneath a mirror ceiling, so that he could watch himself make love to her while she rode him. They spent all morning together in bed.

"I want you there, I want you there," she told him afterward. She meant that she wanted him to be on call at the Waldorf Towers. She could not always be there, but when she was she wanted to know he was there, close to her, because she loved him so much she couldn't be without him, although to make love they would have to come here or to one or another of Mrs. Stoddard's other clients' apartments when they were not in use, until they had figured out what to do. "I want you nearby. I'll bring you out to Cavemoor when the coast is clear. We'll work it out. Do you? Do you really love me?"

"Oh, God," he said, and the curious thing was that he

could hear himself say it, as though he were listening to another person speak, even though he meant it. He meant it with a force of feeling and a sense of abandonment such as he had never imagined himself capable, and with it the unavoidable sense of damnation.

"I want to bury my body inside you," he said.

The discovery by Saint Francis of Drayton of a photo-graph clearly showing his daughter, Amber, striding down a back street on Corfu hand in hand with Ivan Albrecht, repro-duced in *Oggi*, the Italian photo magazine, came as a revela-tion to the Draytons, which they were not at once disposed to share with anyone else at the Albrecht court. At first the Draytons actually tried to hide the magazine, something they knew was impossible to do successfully anywhere within the Albrecht precincts for very long. They did not want to jeop-ardize their living arrangement, which they had come to feel was permanent. To be cast out now would have created in their lives an abyss of meaning deeper by far than they had suffered when Amber ran away. To lose the good offices to which they had become so accustomed seemed suddenly very possible and yet not to be borne, if the tormented Teddy Beresford was any proof of the effect this had on the excommunicated.

That man Frankie Drayton had taken the occasion to dwell upon at some length among the mass of guests who thronged the glassed-over Roman atrium at Craig Court on the night of Gretchen Albrecht's New Year's ball. He was a square-shouldered man of some six feet and more in height who carried himself even at the age of almost sixty years like a Hussar. My God, she had thought at the time, he must be hard on the ponies! His face was clearly handsome, teddy-bearish; blue eyes gazed out from under a glowering brow and the foliage of blond, tufted eyebrows; he possessed flared nostrils, which to Frankie Drayton always indicated a keen zest for life, and an aristocratic upper lip and the overall expression at first glance of an impatient man but one who clearly, once you studied him more closely, was burdened with nearly intolerable anguish, whose steady eyes gazed forth in something like inconsolable grief. His dour mood pulled his mouth down at the corners. Surely here was a man whose soul now trudged laboriously through life. He was tolerated. You could not entertain the South African upper crust, the financiers and mining executives, without inviting Teddy Beresford, any more than he could refuse to be among the chosen few, but where once he had ruled the House of Albrecht as the proud partner of Henry Albrecht, now he was peripheral, a satellite, someone dimly there among the others, glimmering with a dull luster at Gretchen Albrecht's Arabian Nights ball. This fate was not the one envisioned by Frankie Drayton for either herself or her husband. They had come to believe that their supreme good luck would last forever.

Five years had passed since the dark spring evening in April when they had crossed the frontier of the secluded private empire of the Albrechts, and never once had they departed from its influence. For five whole years they had lived at the very heart of great wealth as guests of Gretchen Albrecht. Never in their most intense daydreams could they have conjured the ongoing thrill of power and anticipation that their life provided, an ever-growing sexual overture, which they experienced in an uninterrupted state of comfort and ease. In those five years they had not once experienced physical discomfort. They had been airlifted continuously within the custom-furnished interiors of the Albrecht jetcraft from one place of earthly beauty to another and removed, upon arrival, by chauffeur-driven motor car, to private quarters that appeared never to vary in temperature or in the standard of decorated splendor supplied by Mrs. Stoddard with a view, always, that arrested and soothed the ruffles of dislocation. They had coursed the stratosphere that encompasses the globe. They had come to alight at the most exquisite moment at always what seemed exactly the right place, so that in the presence of Gretchen Albrecht their faces always appeared to be transfixed with wonder, like well-dressed people at a zoo. She took them to a _bal masqué_ at Balmoral Castle. She flew them over the Pamir mountains to show them the Takla Makan desert at dawn in the company of the maharajah of Screech Mysore, and flew them to Bali for breakfast and a swim en route to do some sport fishing off the Great Barrier Reef with the Australian prime minister. She flew them down to the Gazelle d'Or from Paris with the vicomtesse de Roissy, and from there they flew up to Marakesh for dinner with the king. She rushed them to South Carolina to shoot quail with the king of Belgium, and just when the somnolent air of a southern plantation might have begun to depress their spirits, she flew them to Rio en route to South Africa and then out to the Seychelles, all in a matter of weeks. Then she whisked them off to Rome, where for a good solid ten days they could recuperate in that city's glorious Maytime in the Palazzo Albrecht, where Saint Francis found the telltale copy of *Oggi*.

When they thought of Amber at all—and they did, occasionally, recall the cause of their present circumstances—the Draytons experienced an almost pleasurable vague grief suffused with the sweet knowledge of their own continued good life. That's why the photograph in *Oggi* gave them such a start. They had buried Amber. They thought of her as dead. Now here she was alive. She was calling them back to parental obligation from the pages of *Oggi*. Hiding the magazine, of course, would not put her safely back in the grave, where they secretly rather felt she belonged, especially if her continued existence meant that they would have to move back to Gracie Square, which would not have been possible in any case because they no longer possessed the means to buy or even to rent an apartment in a fancy part of town like that. They'd have to move into a rented house somewhere in Connecticut.

Horrified, they carried the copy of *Oggi* all the way back to Cavemoor in Saint Francis of Drayton's briefcase and finally took it to Mrs. Keith. Together they took it to Mrs. Keith. Had Mrs. Albrecht, they wanted to know, had a chance to look at the latest issue of *Oggi*? Mrs. Keith rather thought she hadn't. She was circumspect. She took possession of the now well-used journal, which the Draytons had examined so many times that the pages were limp to the touch, like vellum, and the print slightly smeared in places with the sticky impression made by the contact of Saint Francis of Drayton's moist thumb on the printer's ink of the cheaply processed glossy.

Frankie Drayton immediately wondered why she hadn't taken the magazine to Mrs. Stoddard instead. The brigadier was far more favorably disposed toward the Draytons, although, as both of them had long been able to sense, once the taint of disfavor was on you at the court of Albrecht, you could claim no allies there. Still, Frankie Drayton had never felt entirely at home with Mrs. Keith, who wore green oval lenses in pink plastic frames and tended to favor, as daytime apparel, green tweed suits. She was a sharp-faced woman who was preceded by a nose that was constructed in the shape of a flying buttress and the classic witch's chin, cast in the same mold, that chin, as the one possessed by the vicomtesse de Roissy, another witch of another, altogether more exalted order, a French witch, which in Frankie Drayton's opinion was the sort of witch to be, not, like Mrs. Keith, an English —a Cornish—witch, and a rather vicious, narrow-minded one at that. She was a sorceress, the vicomtesse. Mrs. Keith was just a hag. Mrs. Stoddard was a sister. She, Frankie Drayton, was a mere novice and idolatress. There was a future for her here even so, and this was not the time to lose it. In the moment of urgency she understood all.

The Draytons endured the ensuing days in a state of heightened tension, unable to do anything more than peck at the food they devoured with such barely restrained gusto at any other time _à table Albrecht._ They need not have worried. Gretchen Albrecht sent word through Mrs. Keith from London, where she had been uncharacteristically delayed by events beyond her control, that the _Oggi_ photograph was indeed known to her. "Tell them to relax," she said to Mrs. Keith, who, unbeknownst to the Draytons, had gone at once to her upstairs office to telephone Gretchen Albrecht. "Make them sweat it out for a few days; then tell them to relax. Tell them something cryptic—what's the word I want?—*proba-tionary*," she said. "Say, 'Oh, she knows all about the photographs in'—what is it?"

"*Oggi*," said Mrs. Keith.

"Oh, good. *Oggi*. Say, 'She knows everything about the *Oggi* story and has just been too busy to call but that we have to talk.' That'll put the—that ought to keep them guessing," she said, and laughed.

Mrs. Keith waited until the following Tuesday. She was fully capable of grimly biding her time. Then she met privately, confidentially, in her office with Frankie Drayton. She was sitting up straight behind her desk like a school headmistress, hair in a bun, and wearing, as always, her prescription sunglasses.

Frankie Drayton got the message. The time, she understood, was very nearly at hand when either she, or her husband, or perhaps both of them together, would be called upon to make the necessary sacrifice to earn the next stage of their privileged keep in the House of Albrecht. The apprenticeship was over. A chill wind blew through Frankie Drayton from Mrs. Keith's lips, and she felt it. She stiffened slightly where she sat, chastened. She understood. Their welcome, she realized suddenly, had been wearing thin for quite some time. Saint Francis repeated those stories too many times about Big Bill Tilden and playing doubles with the king of Sweden. He was getting to be a bore. Furthermore, they were there all the time. Even her work arranging flowers had come to seem like a rather repetitive contribution to the good times. Worse yet, they were getting on in years. They were nearly sixty.

Even so, she was battle ready. Frankie Drayton was strong. She was up for the fight that would have to be waged for survival in the House of Albrecht, even if she did not know exactly what sort of fight it would be or with whom, and she was quite prepared to stick it out. She was a trained killer of big game, and these Albrecht years had given her superb opportunities to hone her skill as a marksman. She'd even bagged a dancing polar bear on the Arctic Circle from an Albrecht-chartered chopper, which was the keenest fun. She'd lassoed wild horses in La Camargue from a helicopter. She was fit. She really did not know about her husband. Perhaps he, too, was fit. He hardly ever even drank champagne anymore. He swam every day. He was never seen to exert himself in a manner that might strain him unduly, either on his own behalf or that of anybody else. Even so, his ability to protect himself was an open question. He'd never successfully shot anything that walked, ever, which of course was how he'd come to be called Saint Francis. He'd never hooked a fish. He'd never gone to war. Allergies had kept him out of World War Two. He read spy novels, that was all. But who knows, thought Frankie Drayton, what strange skills may help a man survive?

Crisis was already upon Gretchen Albrecht, although no one would have known it except for Monsignor Cathcart, her confessor, and at the moment she was not quite prepared to tell him everything there was to say. He was a gossip. She did not plan to tell her confessor anything that did not bear repeating. Uppermost of all was her unexpected love affair with Bruce Fox. This was what had held her up uncharacteristically in London. Nothing any longer quite made sense to her in the old way, now that she had fallen madly in love with someone for the first time in her life. Nothing else mattered. It had come at a time when events already had moved somewhat beyond her control; she could feel as she slipped along the steep slope of her now uncontrollable infatuation that she no longer had any power to hold on to. In love she relinquished power, a kind of divine anguish enveloped her like some overwhelming fragrance, she lost the ability to order priorities.

Of course she knew about that wretched child Amber! She was furious when Mrs. Keith got to her in London. Outraged that those stupid people the Draytons didn't realize that she'd known about the runaway lovers for over a year, had finally, using Bruce Fox, tracked the lovers to their Corfu redoubt, knew that her son, Ivan, whom she should have strangled at birth, was menacing the world from an armored vessel. She knew it and did not want to be bothered about it. Not when she was dashing off to Bruce Fox. That love affair was all she could think about. Her heart, unlocked, now absolutely ruled her destiny, or at least it ruled her destination. She couldn't wait to see Bruce in Paris, couldn't afford to make him wait while she dashed back to reassure the Draytons. Even contemplating the distance between London and Paris that separated her from Bruce Fox was an agony for her. She couldn't wait, she couldn't really concentrate, couldn't order everything that must be done.

She'd just come down from Scotland. The lover for whom she yearned, in her mind glowing softly and opalescently as he awaited her in the shadows of the Ritz drawing room, was he as much in love with her as she was with him? Certain things she'd have to jettison to meet him. Her eleven o'clock confession was the first to go. The Monday meetings at Grosvenor House with the International Diamond Exchange people she would put in Adrian Gilbert's hands. Happily, even as she felt her power leak away, much as blood from the wounded silently seeps away into the battlefield, she knew she'd planned well in advance for some crisis of just this sort. She had her resources. Her housekeeper, Mrs. Keith, was one; her decorator, the brigadier, was yet another. These women were steadfast loyalists who long after things began to fall apart would maintain a strict semblance of life as usual. Meanwhile she just had to see Bruce. His lips upon her own, the touch of his moist thick tongue on hers, were sweet elixir, immortal joy that eclipsed all the masses of worldly empire she had built with such enthusiastic vigor with her husband, Henry.

She loved to lie beside the young man and softly run her hand along his reclining nude body, better yet drink it in with her eyes, his form to her more comely than any slender Florentine nude, was somehow the Holy Spirit made manifest. His assurance! The very ecstasy she experienced, the way her body felt when he turned to her on the bed and took possession of her shoulders, kissed the hollow of her collarbone, and then drawing her legs apart with his hand, spreading her secret, yearning, burning coral underlips with such rude sophistication, and so gracefully adjusting his hips to thrust with such thick serpentine impudence, butting and swiveling his astonishing slick wand to split her deep sweet universe into blossom! They could never have enough. She had to keep this secret to herself. She had to hide her spy. He understood. She couldn't believe it! He loved her, truly loved her, said he did. Her mad life was now a song. Her life was now a mad song.

Yet she needed help. This, she suddenly understood in Paris, was what the Draytons were all about. She could use Frankie Drayton to help her out. How? She wasn't sure, but she felt that they had been sent to her in fair exchange for Amber. But how, how? This was what she struggled to understand as she hurried back to Cavemoor, sending Bruce Fox ahead of her to New York by Concorde from Paris, where she'd managed to get word to him via the vicomtesse de Roissy once again. How to use Frankie Drayton? Now _there_ was a woman, she thought, who could by now at any rate be entrusted with the privilege of power and who, she felt in her bones, belonged to this new era in her life that had just begun.

After being in the arms of Bruce Fox, her heart sang, skipped with joy, and what in London had felt like disaster in New York felt like life reborn. In New York she saw Bruce right away again. That was the fun of this thing, and then right away she felt the necessary verve to sally forth to Cavemoor, where she sailed through the living room and plucked forth Frankie Drayton to come with her to Mexico _à deux_. Lucky Frankie Drayton! Little did she realize the precision timing that had saved her and by association Saint Francis, her husband, from ineluctable exile—for she had, Gretchen, most definitely arrived at a crossroads concerning these people, although what to do about them she'd been prepared to leave up to Mrs. Keith. They were in Mrs. Keith's purlieu, had been, that is, until now. For Gretchen Albrecht whisked Frankie Drayton off to the airport with her now: she simply did not stay at Cavemoor for more than fifteen minutes. She had to keep on the move. Briefly she called out, "Fa la la," to Mrs. Keith as she and Frankie Drayton, uncustomarily somewhat flustered, unprepared, and blushing in the vibrant warmth of spring, tripped in high-heeled giddiness arm in arm out the door and down the steps and ducked into her waiting custom-built Daimler to catch the plane that awaited their flight to Mexico.

On the jet they drank champagne. Gretchen was almost

unendurably in love. Did Frankie Drayton see the difference? Not really. She was quietly slightly amazed by
Gretchen, always, by her somewhat riotous effervescence at
all times; for her life was such an ongoing festival, and the
difference in degree of Gretchen's ecstasy was beyond her
powers of discernment. They toasted everything on the
flight. They toasted the upholstery, the fuselage, the pilot,
the springtime. They toasted Saint Francis of Drayton.

"I'm just so sorry we couldn't bring that man, that divine
sweet man, along," she said to Frankie. "Honestly, what a
love he is and such a raconteur. I've never had a chance in all
this time to tell you what a marvelous good-natured man I
think he is. I love him. I love you, too, very much, very very
much, darling Frankie, and I've always wanted you to know
it, and I've just been waiting for a chance to tell you. If I
were a man, I'd want to marry you. True. It's just that you're
not. But we can be more than friends, and in a way we are
perforce related, but we can be *copains*. You know: that's
what I want, you see. It's what I need. I *need* a *copain*, and
you're the one I want. You and of course, as always, the
vicomtesse. We three. We'll be the three graces. That's the
investment I want to make, and if I possibly could, I'd bring
along Saint Francis, but *he* can't be a *copain*, can he? I mean,
he's a saint."

"You mean, I won't be able to see him at all again?" Frankie Drayton asked.

"Probably not. I don't know. I really don't want you to
think about Saint Francis anymore. Be mine," she said to
Frankie Drayton when they arrived at El Parador. "You know
the way the vicomtesse and I are such good friends," she
said. "I'm not going to share you with anybody. I just want
to be with you and lie near you under the hot sun. I want us

to talk and be so close we're almost the same person." She allowed herself a drunken, guttural laugh.

She was capable of a surprising vulgarity that Frankie Drayton never in a million years would have permitted herself, so she was impressed to hear Gretchen say, "We don't have to lap pussy to be *copains*, you know that?" To which Frankie Drayton blushed in reply, nodded assent. She'd never ask this goddess for anything but the chance to glow like this in her intimate presence, with Gretchen, on a sun terrace, just the two of them alone.

"I'll tell you everything," she said to Frankie Drayton. "Everything there is to know. I will have no secrets from you, darling."

They were lying on a mattress in the sun on their backs in the nude so close that Frankie Drayton could feel the heat of Gretchen's diminutive, powerful body reflected on her own ascetic flesh, which felt white now under the sun. So strict she was. She listened to the goddess at her side.

"I am the goddess of greed," Gretchen told her. "You knew that. You've guessed it, haven't you? You are so clever and perceptive, even if you didn't think you knew it, you did, and I adore you for it. And you also know—and if you don't, I'm telling you right now—I'm profligate. Greed is wasteful, uses all the resources it can get its grubby little hands on and then some, needs as much as it can find for all the things it has to do to survive, and things it evidently doesn't have to have but wants. I want, I crave money and simply will not stop at anything to get it, I have to have everything, I guess, and I'm such a willful, wasteful, stupid person, darling, I struck a deal I never should have made with Henry Albrecht. I gave up my little babies." Beside Frankie Drayton on the terrace Gretchen was heaving with sorrow, but Frankie Drayton said nothing, knowing that it wasn't what she was called upon to do. "Madly in love, madly in love." Gretchen blew her nose with some Kleenex she'd snatched from a box beside her. "Anyway, I did *not* love Henry, even though I could have if I'd been a different person. A roly-poly little hausfrau. He was a troll, you know, but he had the Midas touch, so you see I needed Henry, but I never should have done it."

She told Frankie Drayton about the birth of her twins, Ann and Ivan, about knowing while she carried them that they were more than she could manage.

"I wasn't big enough to bear twins. The birth almost killed me. Ivan I should have smothered immediately. Ann's a ghost. They feed on golden souls," she told Francesca Drayton. "Without their golden souls they wither and writhe."

She'd never told anyone these things before. She took Francesca Drayton deep into the forest of her own soul, housed in its prison behind windows that were pressed upon from without by wild trees, so that there was no escape, or so it seemed at last to Frankie Drayton, who felt that she could never, now, return to the world she'd once known, which she'd once upon a time inhabited with her husband, Francis Drayton, and her lovely daughter, Amber, and she sobbed at night, alone, in bed, for she'd given her soul to Gretchen Albrecht. She'd given up Amber.

"You can have Amber," she told Gretchen finally. "We've discussed it, Saint Francis and I, and that's what we've decided."

"Oh, darling," said Gretchen. "You can't mean it."

"No, really," said Frankie. "It's settled."

"You're my little soldier," Gretchen told her in the night as they sat together after dinner in the warm gulf air beside the lighted pool. It was the thrill of having a crack at a big Hollywood role that tipped the scales, prompted Frankie Drayton to renounce everything that had gone before. The thrill of stardom. They flew out of Mexico in the morning back to New York, whence they'd come, but when they reentered the world it was new to Frankie Drayton.

T he person who did not like Frankie Drayton was Ann Albrecht. She disliked having Frankie Drayton present every time she wanted to see her mother. Alone, she had the power to manipulate her mother. In the company of Frankie Drayton, at Claridges, her mother was like a seraphic child. Frankie Drayton's sudden ascendancy sent off an alarm bell within Ann Albrecht. It raised the level of her panic. Whenever she needed cash to tide over Ivan, she went to Gretchen Albrecht, from whom it was always easy for her to extort guilt money in large sums. This, in her opinion, was her mother's primary function. Otherwise she felt vehement contempt for Gretchen Albrecht, which she expressed in no uncertain terms when they dined together alone, _à deux_. Now, however, it was lunch _à trois_, with Frankie Drayton. She could not get her mother to herself. She hated Frankie Drayton, the white-boned demon. The presence, at lunch, of Frankie Drayton drove her to throw a nasty public scene like someone inhabited by the devil and in need of exorcism.

"Who is this woman? What's she doing here? Don't you realize what an insult this is to us? Can't you see it? No, of course you can't, you're too stupid. You scum," she said to the smiling Frankie Drayton, who was seated beside Gretchen on a banquette, dressed in a white suit of tailored linen with décolletage and wide lapels but no blouse. She also wore a matching wide-brimmed bonnet with a black silk band, and the wraparound sunglasses she now wore in place of the cat's-eye ones of yore.

Ann hated the implacable Frankie Drayton because at last she had come up against her mother's perfect checkmate: Amber's mother. She hated the perfect teeth, the tanned, taut skin of Frankie's face, her perfect nose and chin. It was, to Ann, like looking at a death's head, and she hated it. She was uneasy because Amber's mother so clearly had become one of them. How had she done it? She did not understand the meaning of it. She did not understand why her mother referred her to Frankie Drayton when she told her mother that she wanted to see her alone. Was her mother under this woman's spell?

"Who are you?" she sneered to Frankie Drayton. "Who do you think you are that you can tell me when I can, or cannot, see my mother? You and your stupid social-climbing husband. Don't you realize they only tolerate that idiot because everybody feels so sorry about what happened to Amber? I really hate people like you. You move in like barracuda. No wonder Amber hates you. The only decent thing you ever did was have Amber, and now she's left you and never wants to see your face again, you evil woman."

She'd gone well beyond the point of no return, had crossed the line of tempered insult.

"How often do you get a chance to see Amber?" Frankie Drayton asked her.

"You'd like to know, wouldn't you," Ann taunted her.

"We'd all like to know how Amber's getting along," her mother said.

What Ann especially disliked, what made her truly uneasy, was her mother's newly docile manner. She was like someone on a drug. Ann said with almost childlike truculence to Frankie Drayton: "We're going to sue you." That was what she said to Frankie Drayton.

She tried to reach Ivan on Corfu to warn him about this new development, but he was on the boat. She telephoned her husband in Bangkok. He was unperturbed by what she tried to tell him about Mrs. Drayton. He'd known the Draytons in the past as not very close friends of his parents, minor parasites. He told Ann not to worry. "They're kind of bland people," he told her. "I'm not going to bother Ivan or anybody else about them, about people like them."

Ann resented her husband's arrogance, his sheer refusal to take her seriously. The indifference to the danger that she sensed in the presence of Frankie Drayton was extremely frustrating. She could not seem to get anyone to listen to her. Yet she knew that the woman posed a threat, for she now appeared to control Gretchen and surely had access to certain key pieces of family information no outsider ought ever to possess. She could conceivably get control over the House of Albrecht.

Now that her mother had put her life in the hands of Amber's mother, things, in the opinion of Ann Albrecht, had taken an unexpected turn, and she decided to seek out Bruce Fox. He was the one person she knew who could find out for her what was going on. The vicomtesse de Roissy had put her up to this trick. The vicomtesse had her own reasons, which she did not divulge to her godchild, to wit: to find out whether Gretchen Albrecht was having an affair with Monsieur le Renard, as she liked to call Bruce Fox. She wanted to get in on things herself. She'd never quite trusted Monsieur le Renard, because he was a Jew. She had nothing against Frankie Drayton, however. She said to Ann, "Actually she's really a very stabilizing influence on your mother because she's completely even-tempered." Ann did not think so.

"She is the enemy of my mother," Ann said. "She is the enemy of us all. She's waiting to get her hands on our money. She's pretending to get along with the duchess, but she's going to ruin all of us. She's going to destroy Ivan. I don't know how, but she's going to kill Ivan. She wants to do that. She's a killer."

Ann was right. She had put her finger exactly on the truth. All along it had been Frankie Drayton's intention to kill Ivan Albrecht. She'd set her sights on him at the outset, on Fishers Island. Beyond this, Ann had not been able to imagine what Frankie Drayton was capable of doing. She had always thought that it had been a mistake to snatch Amber from the Draytons. It had been unnecessary. Ivan could have waited. He could have found the child of some dumb English working-class people, real servants, not sycophants like these people. She thought perhaps there might still be time to get Amber to go back to them. She did not quite realize that Mrs.

Drayton could not be bought off with the return of her child, nor could her daughter ever dissuade her from her goal to put Ivan out of business and take over the House of Albrecht. She was too deeply committed, one of them.

Bruce Fox had continued to see Ann Albrecht here and there. He was her mother's benign spy. That was okay with her. She never knew where he might show up. He was in New York sometimes when she dropped in on the Waldorf Towers. She always took him out to lunch. She saw him in Paris sometimes at the Ritz. She'd seen him also out in Hong Kong. He'd weaseled in on the Nepal trek.

"You're about the worst spy I've ever known," she told him on the occasion of their meeting in New York, when she'd called him from Paris at the suggestion of the vicomtesse and booked him for lunch the following day. They went to Le Cirque. She'd actually grown somewhat fond of him in the year during which he'd been on her mother's payroll. "You must know what a lousy spy you are," she told him. "It's because you don't have enough money to get the training you need."

Bruce said, "I get on-the-job training. Besides, every once in a while somebody nice comes along to take me out to lunch."

He did look good, Ann reflected. He was very tan. He wore an Italian shirt open at the neck, a gold necklace. His hair was cut so that it looked light on his head, was glossy with hair conditioner, and he wore men's eau de cologne, which was new. Maybe he's gay, she thought uneasily, because on some level she was attracted to him, and he sensed it, which made him bolder.

"What do you know about Mrs. Drayton?" she asked him.

"Weyell," he said. He ordered Perrier. He no longer

drinks at lunch, she observed to herself, the way he used to, which is maybe why he looks a little sharper. "Her husband once played doubles with the king of Sweden," he said.

"I asked you to tell me about *Mrs.* Drayton," Ann said, "what she's up to. My mother never goes anywhere without her anymore."

Bruce laughed. This was too much, as only he knew, because often Mrs. Drayton sat in the room while he and Ann's mother made love. She was not, however, a *voyeuse*. She sat in her armchair and read or knitted. "You can say that again," he told Ann.

The thing about Bruce Fox was that he was free. He had no moral scruples. He'd cast out whatever sense of guilt he still possessed at the time he began his affair with Gretchen. He was a sexual hedonist. He had no reason not to sleep with whomever he wanted. He was flying over in the morning to meet Gretchen in Paris, and in the meantime he was lounging around the Albrecht apartment at the Waldorf. He decided that he was going to take Ann up to the master suite at the Albrecht apartment and make love to her that afternoon. Knew he was going to do it. Why? Because at last she wanted something from him, and that was the price she'd have to pay. He put it to her pretty straight.

"I don't know, Annie Pannie." He grinned.

She wondered, with a start, if his body was oiled all over.

"What," he asked her, "are you doing after lunch?"

"What do you mean?"

He gazed at her candidly. "I don't want to talk about it here. I'll talk about it with you where we can be private, though, like in a room with a big double bed."

"You shit, Bruce," said Ann. She burst with sudden laughter. "You fucker," she said.

"Listen." He squinted at her in the manner of one who is taking aim. He wagged his finger at her. "I am a fucker. I have always wanted to fuck you so much that I have devoted my whole life to it for the last seven years while you've been out there fucking Willy Beresford, and I ain't gonna let you get away now. You get the drift?"

Never had he seemed more obnoxious. She found she had not a great deal to say. "That's why you've been Mother's spy?"

"Yup." He put a fork roll of linguine into his mouth.

"How do I know it's going to be worth it?" she asked him. His mouth was full of linguine, but he said anyway, "It will be." He swallowed his linguine. "It will be worth it."

So they did not linger over coffee. The automobile that awaited their pleasure out in front of the restaurant was a rented stretch limousine, the car and Balkan driver she always hired to take her around town. In the back of this car with its smoked windows he wanted to neck with her all the way to the Waldorf but she pushed him away.

"Come on," she told him. "No kissy face, okay?"

He grinned. He had a huge hard-on. In the elevator, too. He did not care, Bruce, whether he had a hard-on or not, he took her hand and pressed it there. She looked away.

She was both reluctant—frightened, really, by his unexpectedly razor-edge personality, his streak of grinning lechery —and she was attracted to him, also, but couldn't figure out why. He'd always been such a wimp. Now he was a rapacious, uninhibited smoothie, like some greaser or something, and before she knew it, whether or not she liked it, she was stripping off her stockings in the darkened bedroom like someone being forced to do it at gunpoint except she couldn't wait. She kept thinking: Frankly, this isn't what I had in mind.

The Porthault sheets were cold. The maid had already pulled back the coverlet and turned down the top sheet. She was on the bed, climbing into it, when he took her from behind. Such a cheater. His cock was oiled. He kept it coated with an unguent, evidently. She propped herself on her elbows on the cool sheet, leaned forward on the pillow, while he screwed his member up into her and held her body still to do it, like somebody mounting a horse. It was a horse's dick. Thick, slick, long. Frankly, this is not what I expected. Have you ever felt _anything_ that long in your life? It cannot be. They were doing it in silence. He was pulling at her nipples as he might pull cherries off a tree and pulling hard at some plugged-up place inside her. Fox had finally figured out how to get it where he wanted it to be. No one had ever wanted to fuck her so badly in her life, and she was dizzy, slightly nauseated, with the blood pounding in her head and the speed of his whirring organ thick inside her. After a time she could not restrain herself and sobbed, once. It's obscene. Yet she couldn't help collapsing with the feel of his long movement between her, inside her, as he oiled his way so deeply down to her core, humping.

He was crouching over her. He pulled out, onto his haunches. Then he reached over and switched on the bedside light. "Turn over." She saw him as she turned, grinning like a jackal. Turning like this made her feel a little sick again. The light hurt her eyes. She didn't want to see him. She lay, arms at her sides, one leg pulled up, head turned to one side, in pain or sorrow, heart thumping. She could not bear to look at him. Yet once again she yielded to desire. She pulled him down. She opened her legs wide to receive his still greased member. He wanted to watch her while he loved her, in the glow of the bedside lamp. He reached out his tongue and drew the stiffened tip of the organ up the side of

_221_

her jugular as he drew her into another long fuck with the supple, slow, tight positioning of his hips. He licked his tongue flatly across her cheek to shove it in the corner of her mouth, which was turned from him, and held the base of her skull in the vise of his fingers so she wouldn't move her head and prevent his tongue from feasting on the insides of her mouth as his lips closed over it and the length of his body relaxed against hers to press his belly flat on hers, her breasts trapped beneath the naughty preen of his chest, and the whole length of his dick sucked tight by the walls of her vagina. Her inner thighs grazed his flanks as she raised them high to give him all the space he needed to dig up to the hilt, so their pubic hair was matched, heard the suction gasp of her own love-glutted cunt. His oiled belly suctioned. "Please," she whined. She trembled. His tongue lapping up her face. The scratching surface of his face as she turned her head to evade his sucking mouth. She was water. She held the tensed muscles of his buttocks in the palms of her hands to pull him even farther up inside her arching body. It was a funny sound, the tiny whine, a plea on the threshold of sexual surrender. She had never wanted anything but this. The pounding. It came now as a steadfast, noiseless, rhythmic, constant tamping on the membrane of her inner hollow drum. His jockey's jackal grin. A constant knocking she wanted to crush. Just that huge smooth round drumhead to somehow fit her whole tight inner-core self around and ride the plunging drumbeat. She did it, slipped her whole body over it, exploded.

Everything was shot to smithereens. A contingency force had taken the Turin factory at night, disarmed security, quietly bound and gagged a few disarmed guards, slipped into the building that housed the main works, planted explosives at six key points throughout the complex, set the timers, and vanished before the dawn explosion. No one had seen them come or go. It was a faultless operation. Gretchen in Paris left at once for London by jet. Frankie Drayton, who was with her at the Ritz, remained behind to meet with Bruce Fox. It was her idea that Gretchen should go and make a pretense of being with her husband. There was no way of knowing what would happen next. Ivan appeared to have taken everyone by surprise. It was typical of him to have acted thus. He clearly trusted no one, not even Ann or Lansing Noble.

Bruce Fox was still in bed with Ann Albrecht at the Waldorf Towers when he received a call from Frankie Drayton. They conferred at some length and agreed that he should stay in New York with Ann. The idea was that if Ann Albrecht tried to travel on any commercial airline at this point, she could very possibly find herself in danger of being apprehended as the accomplice of Ivan Albrecht. She'd confessed this much to Bruce Fox.

He was jubilant. He was standing in the living room, naked, idly fondling his demierection as they talked, at four in the morning New York time, over the transatlantic line. Ann was still asleep. Nothing would ever be the same for him.

"Stay exactly where you are," Frankie Drayton told him. "Keep Ann Albrecht covered. You're a darling."

"You betcha," Bruce Fox replied.

Meanwhile Frankie Drayton called Mrs. Keith to close the Cavemoor gates, lock them, keep everybody out, except the people who were already on the premises. "Delivery men especially are very likely to be armed," she told Mrs. Keith. She ordered Mrs. Keith to put the brigadier in charge of Cavemoor defense and referred her to the rifles in the gun room. She told her not, under any circumstances, to let Saint Francis use a gun. Her orders were crisp and very to the point, and Mrs. Keith assumed that they came directly via Frankie Drayton from Gretchen Albrecht. She liked clear, crisp commands. She liked an attention to detail, a command of the facts, a good grasp of layout. "The Albrechts are *both* doing very well," Frankie Drayton pointedly said to Mrs.

Keith. However, she warned Mrs. Keith not to anticipate any communication from _either_ of them directly until the Turin thing had been settled.

Nightrider II, at Frankie Drayton's command, had been sent to Gatwick airfield. Ivan Albrecht's next move, it was clear, would very possibly be to take his mother hostage. She took the step, therefore, of ordering Gretchen to leave England by plane, at night, for the safety of El Parador, to remain in hiding there until Ivan had been brought to heel. Gretchen realized that she must do exactly what Frankie Drayton ordered her to do not only for her own safety, but for that of the entire House of Albrecht, which was under attack. "There are too many reasons why we have to stop this thing from happening," Frankie Drayton told Gretchen also by telephone, from Paris, where she had turned the apartment at the Ritz into her command headquarters.

"We have to handle Ivan without the help of the international _gendarmerie_. I have no intention of seeing either Ivan or Amber in one of those ghastly Italian courtroom spectacles. I mean it."

"Darling, I love you," Gretchen replied, and kissed the receiver mouthpiece. "I'm so glad someone else at last is going to take responsibility for Ivan."

She was almost giddy with happiness. She would go to Mexico and prepare there to meet with Bruce Fox when he could finally get away to join her. All she cared about was hanging on to her huge fortune so that she could spend the rest of her life with Bruce Fox, in command once again of her vast domain. She'd sell the company but hang on to the mines. The mines were everything. She could not let her children have the mines. She'd already figured out what to do. They'd trump up a charge of murder against Ivan belatedly for killing his father and have him summarily brought to justice in Mexico and executed very quickly there. She'd talked it out with Frankie Drayton, who'd agreed it must be done. Gretchen was at peace. She'd done her best. She'd arrange it with the president of Mexico, her pal, and after a suitable period of mourning Monsignor Cathcart would marry her and Bruce Fox at El Parador. Cathcart came with her on board *Nightrider II* for the flight to Mexico. The time had come at last for her confession.

Frankie Drayton by the end of a year in the company of Gretchen Albrecht had visited every room in the House of Albrecht. She had seen just about everything there was to see. Gretchen Albrecht had no secrets from Frankie Drayton, and Frankie Drayton had heard things of which Gretchen Albrecht remained ignorant. She had flown on errands to far-flung Albrecht domiciles for Gretchen Albrecht and had come back to tell the tale. She had been privy to the disintegration in Gretchen Albrecht's life of all semblance of order. The very madness of her tempo had been a sign to Frankie Drayton that although Gretchen Albrecht had not altogether lost her truly remarkable, her *divine*—let's admit it—sense of global choreography, the frenzy of her inner music was making her sloppy. She had a tendency anyway to be a little sloppy. She was in the habit of leaving little deposits of cigarette ash on the carpets of her domain, small piles that Lorenzo went about sweeping up with the pocket whiskbroom and dustpan he used to sweep the crumbs off the dining room table between courses. Gretchen Albrecht also had a way of leaving loose cash lying around on tables and on the tops of dressers. In her haste to meet the demands of her love affair, she made appointments that she could not keep and grew careless about her alibis, often leaving word with Mrs. Keith that she could be reached at the Palazzo Albrecht when she'd suddenly decided to change plans and meet her lover on the island of Jerba without bothering to inform anyone who might then be in a position to cover for her. What happened was that she dropped out of sight often for twenty-four hours at a time, even longer, to surrender body and soul to her lover, whom she moved around the world as it were by remote control so that when the urgent need arose she could meet him for a tryst.

Frankie Drayton had been witness to her enslavement. It was a revelation to the _petit soldat,_ as the vicomtesse called Frankie Drayton behind her back. As the only person in a position to know what was going on, she was the most powerful deputy in the House of Albrecht. She was privileged to be present in the bedchamber while the lovers were coupling. Her vow of chastity had conferred upon her this right. She also held controls on the access to Gretchen Albrecht, who relied on Frankie Drayton for her protection. Frankie Drayton took the calls. She was in the altogether agreeable position of being able to keep Mrs. Keith marking time often for days. She had the ear of Gretchen Albrecht. She could make Gretchen Albrecht blush by what she whispered in her ear. She had the power. She understood how to use the power she now possessed, how to harness the chaos of what was happening all around her to her own, personal advantage. She was perfectly equipped to handle this power. She was not overwhelmed by ambition. What she liked was the sport of power; being a sportswoman, the play of power was what gave her such a keen sense of life on the threshold, and her age further worked to her advantage because age gave her a sense of the finite. She did not expect too much. She kept things in perspective. She ruled with her head, not with her heart. Her ego was under control, and she understood, having given the matter a certain amount of serious thought, that Teddy Beresford's egregious flaw was the egomania that drove him to exceed his reach, to blunder when something else, a respect for *timing*, for Tao, might have saved him.

Frankie Drayton had been primed to rule. The House of Albrecht needed a new ruler, this much had been clear to Frankie Drayton for quite some time. She had assessed this on her extensive travels. In every corner of the empire things were in disarray. The leadership of a vast enterprise had lapsed, and she, Frankie Drayton, was the only person in it who knew that and was also equipped to take the matter in hand. It was not something she had taken in hand all at once, but as she'd begun to field phone calls and chair meetings for the absent Gretchen Albrecht and to make decisions that once might have been the province of Gretchen Albrecht or Henry Albrecht, she got a handle on what the Albrecht resources were, how much money was flowing in, how much of it was being spent, how much invested, and so forth. She'd come to understand soon enough the enormous waste of money the Albrechts were causing by pouring good money after bad into losing companies they owned. The Compagnie Belgique was an albatross. Albrecht stock was stagnant. She began to realize that Gretchen Albrecht was a woman of scant business sense when it came to keeping accounts, a matter that Frankie Drayton resolved to do something about once she'd taken over the House of Albrecht. Thus, gradually, with a burgeoning sense of wonder, Frankie Drayton came to understand that she was running the business. Her position at the side of Gretchen Albrecht had been duly recognized. Her position of importance could not be denied.

Frankie Drayton had sealed tight all the entrances and

exits to the House of Albrecht. She was the one person in it who could move freely now wherever she wanted to go. She was on top. Not much time to spare, even so. Wilhelm would be waiting for her signal. She had at the very outside forty-eight hours to act. She knew that if she did not act now, Ivan, with the help of Teddy Beresford, would quickly move to take control by some means. Teddy Beresford would be the one to act. He'd see the game was up if he didn't, and then it would be too late, because Ivan would be gone. Surprise was everything. The timing was close. She left word with Mrs. Keith that she was leaving command central on a brief reconnaissance and to await further word. She packed a wet suit in a Louis Vuitton overnight bag, combed her hair, which she now wore close-cropped, like a cap, and white blond. She wore black tights under her Burberry. She flew at once, alone, to Athens.

Doreen handled all the arrangements with her usual frightening efficiency. She got them both on a plane to Athens out of Jan Smuts the next morning. She booked a suite at the Grande Bretagne through a local travel agent, assured herself that passage could be secured on an Olympia Airways flight two days hence to Corfu. She hired a girl to come in to care for the boys while she was away, packed, and even managed to arrange a car rental on Corfu.

Teddy Beresford left word at the office that he'd been called abroad on sudden business. He made the usual apologies to Wilhelmina. He prayed to God he wouldn't actually encounter any of his numerous international business acquaintances on board the flight, and God heard him, evidently, because no one he knew seemed to be flying off to Athens that day. Doreen made him wear his British army beret as a sort of disguise. Then on the plane he felt the ineluctable speed of it all as he hurtled over Africa toward his all-too-sudden destiny.

In Athens his luck held. In the lobby of the Grande Bretagne he thought for a moment he saw someone he might have known in some resort he'd frequented, but he couldn't recall which one, and it was of no importance because to his relief, whoever it was (an eccentric female almost as incognito as he was in a hooded cape, dark glasses, black tights) did not recognize him. He hated Athens, hated the dust and the wretched exhaust fumes from the buses. He stayed upstairs until they were ready to leave again for the Athens airport on the final leg. On Corfu a rented Renault awaited their arrival. It all happened so swiftly that for Teddy Beresford the expedition had the inevitability of a nightmare.

When they stepped off the plane on Corfu he realized there was no going back. He was cornered. He realized it too late. Now here he was, forcing down a lukewarm repast of baked lamb and potatoes that had been heated up for them in the hotel kitchen. The weather threatened rain: a brooding, overcast sky was visible above the choppy sea out beyond the picture windows of the immense, empty dining room. He dreaded meeting Ivan, the man. He wanted to speak about it to Doreen, beside him at the table, but he didn't have the heart, so they ate in silence. He thought: I should have murdered Ivan. I should have killed him there and then.

He'd tried never to think back on that day, or on the boy, or on the circumstances of their encounter. He'd never successfully been able to drive out the picture that was embedded in his memory of the tsarevitch behind the glass doors at Cavemoor, where he'd been watching all the time. He'd have to face him now again, that ghostly visage out of Edvard Munch: blue-white face, eyes wide, black hole of open mouth, a soundless scream. Instinctively he'd turned to see Ivan there. Still gripping the silver handle of the kukri with both hands, he'd wheeled around, and there was Ivan, ghost child, standing behind the glass. What to do? He'd turned back to see the scarlet geyser of Henry Albrecht's blood pump up and splash over his yellow pullover, onto the paving stones, as the obese body kept trying to rise in protest, and when he'd glanced back, it was too late. The boy was gone.

"We can handle Ivan," Gretchen had assured him. Her cherished, secret Ivan. She'd whisked him off to Switzerland, Teddy Beresford assumed, to keep him out of harm's way. Now there was no escape for either of them. He ordered a double Metaxa for the road.

Doreen drove. He sat in the gunner's seat. He felt foreboding assume a deeper hue now as they drove north along the twisting corniche. She'd made him wear his bugle and kukri lapel pin to reassure the men, and he wore his beret. She'd given him Wilhelm's regulation pistol in a holster, which he wore under his windbreaker. It had been years since he'd shot at anything that moved, and even then marksmanship had never been his strong point. He was better with a kukri. He thought: You talked me into it, Bruce Fox. I let you play upon my vainglory. You knew too much. You knew about the money, you knew about Doreen, you knew about the killing. You saw me lose the game.

As he sallied forth to play this final hand, Teddy Beresford had no illusion that this move would come to anything. He knew Gretchen Albrecht too well. She'd only strike a bargain at gunpoint. Nothing else could faze her. God had granted him no final warmth at all, but he'd come through with the gift of clarity at last. Teddy saw where he'd gone wrong. He hadn't needed it. He hadn't needed any of it. He hadn't needed Doreen. He hadn't needed the money. Yet once Bruce Fox had met with him in London to tell him that Ann and Ivan needed him to help them overthrow the duchess, the game was up for him. He'd let Bruce Fox spin for him an irresistible fantasy of power. He'd let Bruce Fox talk him into meeting with Ann. That was his mistake.

"That's it up there," Doreen said all at once.

He saw it, too: a pink house in the trees of a pine grove down below the road up ahead. Doreen pulled off to the side to let him out. She patted him on the cheek.

"Go to it, Teddy," she said.

He stood in among the trees to watch her drive on up the road around the curve and out of sight of the house. A few minutes passed, and the car returned. Doreen waved, and then he waited until he could no longer hear the car engine. He didn't have to do it. He had options. One did not have to blindly act out one's destiny. He could, without any difficulty, walk away from everything. In his present British military disguise it wouldn't be likely that anyone who knew him would recognize who he was. He thought of that. It gave him a rush of hope. But he wasn't a bounder. He didn't run away from things because the challenge dismayed him. He thought about that. He'd never bolt. The idea was distasteful. He'd known, always, how to play the man. He was someone who had the natural authority of a commander. How had this sense of himself become eroded? He still had something left of his self-esteem. He had bluff. He was Major Teddy Beresford, a man to reckon with. His approach, then: he'd amble into it. He'd amble up the road and see for himself what was going on. He'd be a retired major on patrol.

He was tense as he walked through the trees to the house. It appeared to be shuttered, closed up; the sound of the wind in the trees made an eerie accompaniment to the surrounding quiet. He heard the rap of his knuckles on the door echo in the trees. When he twisted the handle, the door opened easily. He entered. Immediately he could see the house had not been used. This struck him as strange, to say the least, for it had been his understanding that this was where they'd bring the recruits, to train them, and it was where he'd expected to meet them after the attack on the Turin factory. Yet there was no sign that the contingency force had ever been here. He pricked his nostrils to scent the stale air. No cooking smells. He moved stealthily around the house, glancing into darkened rooms, in the manner of someone playing hide-and-seek. Surely this was a joke. Or a trap. He suspected the latter. No sounds betrayed a concealed threat, however. He went back into the living room, crossed over to the door onto the terrace, and moved aside the curtain to look out upon the melancholy, silent afternoon. Of course. It came to him at once. They were out on Ivan's boat. They'd gone out there to wait. Bruce Fox had explained it to him. They kept Ivan on a boat out beyond the mouth of the bay, and now, as he looked down to the serene and isolated bay, he understood. He'd have to go down to the boathouse, the little abandoned chapel, where they kept a dinghy.

It was more than ever like a dream, although he felt calmer now that he'd figured out where they had gone. It was like a dream because he felt that he had already done this on some other occasion, in some other dimension, in another life. It was coming back. It gave him heart to realize that he was not afraid. He breathed deeply the pine-scented air. The scene was one he felt he knew well: the hillside, covered with pine needles and bark; the tall spindly bare pine trunks with their upper reaches massed together and above them, through the branches of evergreen, the troubled sky. The hill sloped steeply down to the water's edge. He made his way in the direction of the causeway out to the chapel, down through the ancient grove, stopping only to catch his breath and listen to the soughing of the wind. It was most fortuitous for him to arrive like this, he thought, as a lone gun. He felt the strength rise in him; the zest of adventure began to return. He'd already considered how he'd do this (at nightfall, so he wouldn't be seen coming across the silent water in the dinghy). He came down to the edge of the pines and was about to walk onto the causeway when he saw her once again, the woman from the lobby of the Grande Bretagne.

"Oh, good Christ," he muttered to himself.

She was standing against the whitewashed chapel wall. She wore the black cape; she stood with her arms folded underneath the cape; she wore huge sunglasses; she wore black rubber tights. She was right there, really, within calling distance.

"I say," he said. It was all part of the dream, but now he felt an unpleasant excitement surge through him. His voice rang shortly on the air. He didn't like the grip of tension in his belly. You see, I should have known this when I saw her then, he said to himself. He stopped where he was and looked directly at her, as if to say, Shall I come over, or were you planning to join me here? She wasn't playing.

"You make a stark contrast," he said in a normal tone of voice. He knew now who she was. She was Dame Fate. He couldn't shake that conviction. What he had to do was to somehow get that gun out of its holster under his jacket. She sauntered forward from the chapel. Wretched creature wouldn't speak. Where had he seen this woman? Should he turn and make a run for it? This dream experience was preventing him from moving. It was like being underwater. Keep calm. Go forward. Don't slip. Be the charming brigadier you never were.

"Just one moment," said he, waved, stumbled on the causeway. Why so slow? He dreaded all of this. He dreaded Ivan. He dreaded the awful acting that he had to do, the performance. All a wretched business.

Then, when next he looked, only one yard from where she stood at the end of the walkway, he saw her with the gun. She held it up with both hands in front of her face, big bloody thing it was, must have a silencer on it, nasty long barrel pointing at him: sexiest feeling in his life, naked like this, rubbery knees, it made him go hard in the crotch out here with no cover to protect him while she aimed that big black blaster at him. And that was when he had the final flash, just when she plugged it in: it's not so bad, it's free at last. That and having his head blasted off his neck at full fathom five.

She kept in check a powerful impulse to go out to see her child on the *Zephyr Ehco* and hold her in her arms again and tell her everything would be all right. It's what the mother in her yearned to do. She was no longer strictly speaking a mother, however, and in her professional capacity she understood that Ivan must remain ignorant for at least another seventy-two hours if their plan was to succeed. After that, whatever maternal instinct remained could finally express itself, financially. She had no time for Amber now. There was work to do.

Dragging the trunk of Teddy Beresford along the causeway and into the dark cave of the abandoned chapel took an hour

of her precious time. She had to pull his massive, inert body
inch by inch. She felt giddy afterward from the effort, as
though, like a paper origami bird, she might rise up into the
air and flutter away on the late-afternoon breeze across the
Mediterranean to the castle on Lake Como where Wilhelm
was awaiting her instructions with the Gurkha security force.
How she wished indeed that she could just be wafted there
in such a manner.

Actually, the plan called for her to go to Athens and then
to Milan, where an Albrecht jet was waiting in the shadows
with Lansing Noble on board. He'd been waiting all his life
for someone to ask him to do something useful, for a change.
She'd found him, in company with Damian, at the Beach of
Passionate Love, still guarding those poor tribesmen. He was
so relieved to turn them over to Wilhelm so he could resume
his night life in Bangkok. What a good-natured boy he'd
always been. He was the despair of Catsy Noble, who only
wanted him to settle down in Upper Brookville and propa-
gate, when it turned out that all he really wanted was to be
able to watch himself turn to stone in front of a mirror while
his lover—but it was too silly. That's what Gretchen had said
when Frankie disclosed how she had accidentally opened the
wrong door one day in Udaipur to see him posing nude while
some young goat-footed Dionysiac Rajasthani lover was but-
tering him all over with clay. Posing nude before a mirror.
She'd broken the spell, of course; he'd grinned at her reflec-
tion in the mirror. She'd been drawn to investigate certain
grunts she'd heard as she'd come along the corridor of the
Water Palace Hotel in Udaipur after their shikar, and that's
what she'd beheld. He liked her.

"What on earth," she begged to know, "were you doing
with that satyr?" She'd seen the grinning satyr's face over

Lansing Noble's shoulder in the mirror as he'd applied the thick brown-red modeling clay; he was standing on a coffee table.

"Doing frozen statue," Lansing told her with a grin.

They were hunters together, she and Lansing Noble. They shared an aptitude for killing anything that moved, although for Lansing Noble it was merely something he'd been brought up knowing how to do, while Frankie Drayton had talked her way into a weekend at the ducal estate of one of her father's English patients when she was a bored young post-debutante on the Grand Tour. She'd done it in order to learn how to shoot, and she'd had to work very hard at shooting ever since, maintaining memberships in gun clubs and subscribing to the _Shooter's Bible_ and all that, and she'd put in two mornings a week every winter of her married life at an Upper East Side armory doing target practice in order to shoot big game with the pros. Whatever his distinct peculiarities ("and everybody has at least one," Saint Francis always used to tell her), she could only admire someone who hunted with the effortless grace of Lansing Noble.

He'd gone off to Bangkok with "the Monkey." Ann was in Europe. Wilhelm stayed at the Beach of Passionate Love for three weeks with the Gurkhas until they were properly trained to use the arms Lansing Noble had procured for them from Ivan's Turkish sources. They used Uzi machine guns. Wilhelm had done a marvelous job, given the limitations with which he'd had to work. She'd kept in touch. Lansing Noble had agreed to be the "point" man, whatever that was, and was more than eager to help them in this new version of the plot. "You're only finishing up what Ann started," Lansing pointed out, and it was true, that was exactly what she was doing, but she put a finger to his pretty lips. "No one has to know that, love," she told him over drinks at the Oriental, beside the pool, with Damian in attendance, dressed in Lansing Noble's kimono. He turned out, Lansing, to be every inch the "point" man. He chartered the plane that flew them into Switzerland, and he got them down to Turin in an unmarked van, out of there before dawn, and back up to his uncle Spaulding's castle on Lake Como.

She wasted no time. She returned to the airport to await the morning flight to Athens. She was edgy about getting to the mainland pronto. She did not want anything to go awry. She could have gone back to the Corfu palace and undertaken a strange, misguided chat with Doreen, who was waiting there impatiently for word from Teddy Beresford, but she was too disciplined for anything so foolish. Instead, impatient to get out, she chartered a twin-engine plane for an astronomical sum—five thousand dollars cash up front—to fly her immediately to Athens so she could get an early-morning flight to Milan. Speed was of the essence. What Saint Francis called her "puritan instinct," and what was nothing other than a Scottish bred-in-the-bone thrift, constantly chafed at the huge hunks of cash she was called upon to lay out in order to cut corners. She had not overcome her resistance to this. She wasn't, like Gretchen Albrecht, a free spender, one of those people who believed that the more you paid out, the more you got back. The world is chock-a-block with millionaires of all different kinds, and though she was not, yet, a millionaire in her own right, Frankie Drayton would prove to be a shrewd spender once she was. She'd buy her sloop in bankruptcy auction and staff it with Gurkha recruits.

There was nothing that Gretchen Albrecht could do. She was in Mexico when Frankie Drayton came to her on board the Albrecht jet that Lansing Noble had been holding for her in Milan. The Albrecht jet flew Frankie Drayton to the Yucatán peninsula with her personal security force of six Gurkhas, armed with Uzis, trained by Wilhelm Beresford. Lansing Noble had overseen the manufacture of their battle dress in Bangkok. They wore black boots, black breeches, black cotton tunics, and black berets. Three of them took up a vigil on the roof from which they could monitor the low surrounding jungle and all the entrances to the main building. The other guards accompanied Frankie Drayton when she presented her proposal to Gretchen Albrecht in the loggia overlooking the pool terrace. They stood against the wall behind her, frozen at alert, ready to open fire with their machine guns at the slightest provocation, expressionless though they were and bland to look at, as Gurkhas tend to be.

Monsignor Cathcart and the vicomtesse de Roissy were also present. They both urged Gretchen Albrecht to sign, but the negotiations dragged on well into the Mexican night. It was so very painful. It was a declaration abdicating executive control over the House of Albrecht. In addition she was being asked to turn over preferred shares of her own Albrecht stock worth over five hundred million dollars. Frankie Drayton had opened a Zurich bank account in Amber's name. "It's what you owe us in damages," Frankie Drayton told Gretchen Albrecht.

Gretchen Albrecht knew better than to protest too vehemently. She, too, wanted to come out of it with something, and she was grateful to Frankie Drayton for never saying a word to anyone about her passionate love affair with Bruce Fox. The family holding company, Sylvania, she fought for and held on to intact. The Albrecht family still had a say on every important Albrecht issue, even though they now held only thirty-nine percent of Albrecht shares. Gretchen Albrecht's impulse was to call up people she knew of great political and military might in countries where the Albrechts had purchasing power, but this might have unleashed forces under the command of Wilhelm Beresford, who, she was given to understand, was prepared to go to work on other Albrecht manufacturing subsidiaries besides the one in Turin that he'd already put out of commission.

"This Gurkha business," Gretchen said. "I hate it."

Frankie Drayton waited it out in the loggia. Nobody talked much. Time went on. Gretchen Albrecht kept going over the papers that Frankie Drayton had prepared for her to sign. She grimaced. Every now and then she brushed away a tear with the back of her long, pale hand. The vicomtesse sat stiffly at an angle to Frankie Drayton, across from Gretchen, and looked at Frankie Drayton with a tight, fed-up expression on her face, and every so often she'd say, "I mean, *really*."

The monsignor was sunk in gloom beside Gretchen on the couch.

"I guess I'll go ahead and sign it," Gretchen declared. "Oh, Teddy Beresford, where are you now that I need you?"

"He's dead," said Frankie Drayton crisply. "I shot him."

"You *what?*" shrieked Gretchen Albrecht. She stared at Frankie Drayton. She beheld *le petit soldat* as though for the first time she was seeing her truly, and her face expressed the stunning discovery. She wore a half smile poised on the edge of disbelief. Never had her flared nostrils signaled such restrained fury. "You shot Teddy Beresford?"

"Someone had to do it," Frankie Drayton said. "He was a rogue. He murdered Henry Albrecht."

"I never," Gretchen Albrecht wanted to say something but stopped herself. "How do you know that?"

"My husband," Frankie Drayton said, "figured the whole

thing out. Don't ask me how. He's an armchair spy. He's had a great deal of time on his hands. He's something of a hero, in my book. I'd always thought that Ivan was the killer. I was all set to put a bullet in his poor, adorable head, but it wasn't Ivan at all. So Saint Francis really saved his life."

Gretchen Albrecht looked at Frankie Drayton with an expression of desolation on her face. She was a Fairy Queen, sitting on her sofa, with a suddenly angry face.

"You killer," she said. "I knew it. I knew she was a killer. You killed him with that gun. The one in your drawer. You dirty, rotten, sniping little killer."

"Which is exactly what Ann told me when I saw her in Paris last week," the vicomtesse de Roissy chimed in. "I mean, _really_."

"I am an extremely good shot, if that's what you mean," Frankie Drayton said to Gretchen, ignoring for the moment the vicomtesse, who had resumed her fixed gaze of indignation. "As you yourself are very well aware. As for Teddy, darling, I make no great claims on my behalf there. He was a standing target."

She had nerves, evidently, of steel. She never moved from her chair, an Empire armchair that had arms carved to resemble the downward plunging graceful necks of swans, painted with gold leaf where their beaks had come to rest on the frame. She wore a dark blue suit by Balmain, a Hermès scarf stuck with a pin, a florette of emeralds and diamonds that matched the green silk upholstery of the chair on which she sat. The scarf and pin had been among the many little surprise trinkets that Frankie Drayton had received from Gretchen Albrecht during the early days of Amber's captivity. She wore a new pair of wraparound sunglasses. She did not move. She did not smoke. Gretchen and the vicomtesse

smoked constantly the long gold-tipped cigarettes that the
monsignor was continually jumping up to light with the platinum gas lighter he kept for just that purpose in the deep
pocket of his cassock of brown wool, so heavy in the Mexican
heat that his brow ran with sweat.

Finally, Gretchen Albrecht raised her hand in a manner
instantly recognized by her steward, who kept a row of pens
clipped to the outer breast pocket of his white jacket. The
old Italian, Lorenzo. He leaned down to offer one to his
mistress, who took it and signed the document with a dashing
stroke and handed the pen back to old Lorenzo, who clipped
it in his pocket once again. She was now retired. The precise
meaning of that would only strike her several weeks hence,
at Versailles. There, after a birthday fireworks display arranged for her by the vicomtesse, Bruce Fox and Ann Albrecht Noble intended to have their engagement announced
to the assembled guests over a public address system by the
French minister of foreign affairs, who was a close friend of
the vicomtesse. Gretchen would retire to El Parador, attended by nuns from a nearby convent. Wilhelm Beresford
was now the CEO of the House of Albrecht, with a fixed
salary of five million dollars per annum plus overtime and
bonus payments of Albrecht stock. Frankie Drayton took no
official title for herself. She had what she called the Amber
money. In their lifetime she and Saint Francis would live off
the dividends of their preferred stock. A monthly allowance
payable to Amber would be deposited for her in the Zurich
account. Frankie Drayton wanted nothing more. Finance
bored her. She really mostly liked to hunt big game.